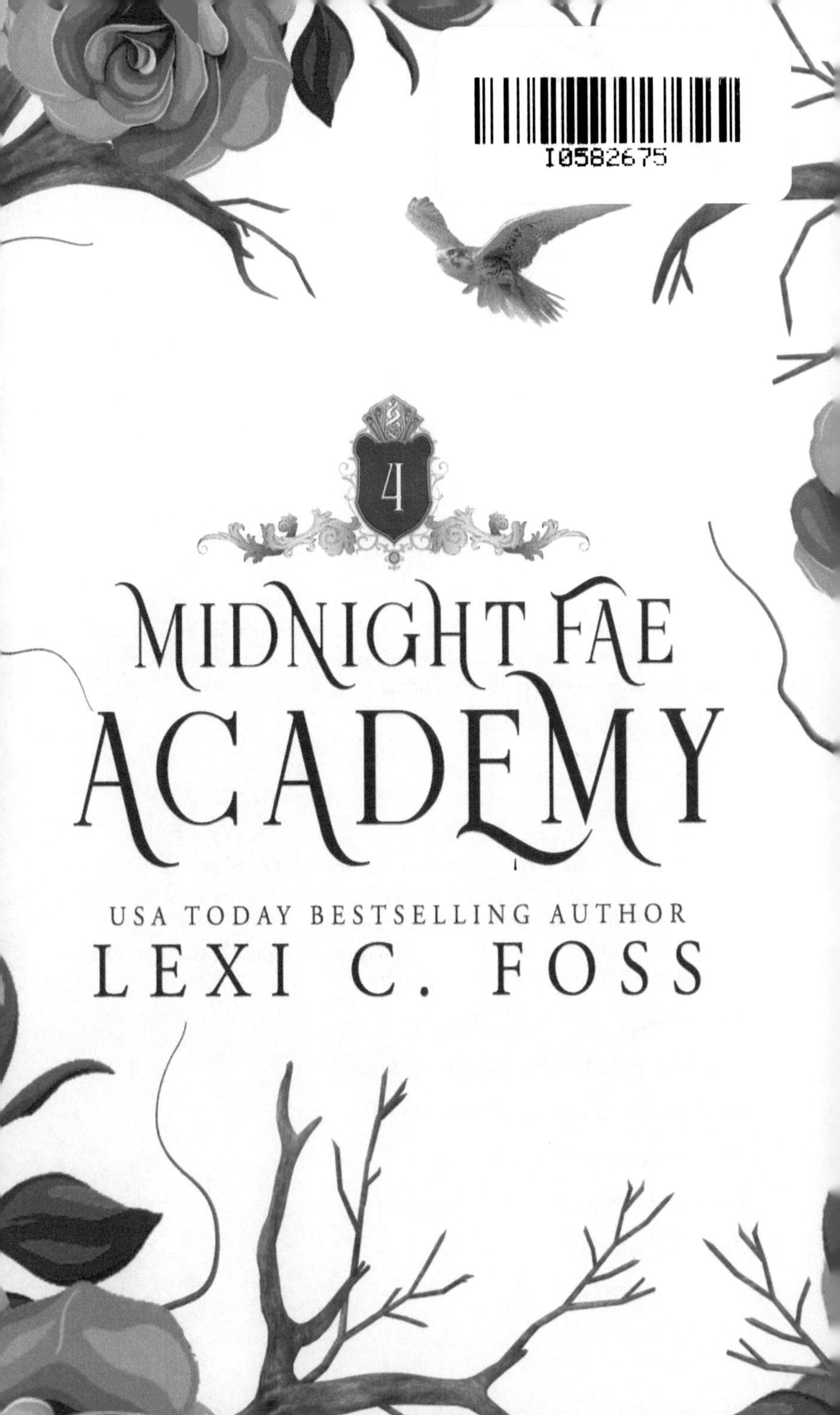

4

MIDNIGHT FAE
ACADEMY

USA TODAY BESTSELLING AUTHOR
LEXI C. FOSS

Midnight Fae Academy: Book Four

Editing by: Outthink Editing, LLC

Proofreading by: Jean Bachen & Katie Schmahl

Cover Design: Lori Grundy, Cover Reveal Designs

Character Designs: Arnild Aldepolla

Published by: Ninja Newt Publishing, LLC

Paperback Edition

ISBN: 978-1-68530-163-7

To Matt, for encouraging me to dream. To my readers, for making those dreams come true. And to the stars, for inspiring my dreams.

MIDNIGHT FAE ACADEMY

BOOK FOUR

Welcome to the Midnight Fae world.
It's bloody.
Dark.
And led by an ancient vampire who needs to die.

My days as a pawn in this war are over. I'm taking over as queen on this board, and in my version of the game, everyone bows to the queen. Even Constantine Nacht.

He thinks he's clever by roping me into these ascension trials, all meant to kill me and my mates.

But I'm going to prove him wrong.
We're stronger than he thinks.
And we're going to make him bleed.

Earth Fae are all about life.
Midnight Fae prefer death.
I'm a mixture of both.
So let's see what happens when life marries death, shall we?

Hand over my crown, Constantine.
It's time for you to kneel for your queen.

Prologue

Do you know what it's like to leave a dream and tumble face-first into a nightmare? Because I do. One moment, everything is warm and happy, and the next, it's stark, frigid, and daunting.

Just like Constantine Nacht's golden irises. They remind me of icy, hard metal. Whirling with power. Sucking me deeper into his web. And grounding me in a reality that isn't mine.

He smiles. Callous. Cruel. Cold.

And then he begins to chant.

An ancient rhyme. A hum I don't understand. Magic swirls through the air, calling to my Quandary Blood heart. I memorize the words. I study the patterns. I hold on for dear life. I drown beneath the wave of foreign energy engulfing me from head to toe.

He said he wanted to talk.

He lied.

No shocker there. He's a wicked old Midnight Fae with a black soul, and it's swallowing me whole, dragging me down, down, down…

I shiver.

I scream.

I freeze.

Then I *burn*. So intense. So bright. So insanely *dark*. Earth weeps inside me, my spirit fracturing beneath the onslaught of energy threatening to consume me.

And on he chants.

Chants. Chants. Chants.

My name is a whisper on the wind. An ascension is brewing. *Consuming.* Lighting me on fire from within.

Wrong, I think. *This is wrong.*

My roots are dying.

My flowers cease to bloom.

The sun turns to night.

Darkness. Death. Blood.

It's overwhelming and bleak and ripping me in two. Inky lines crawl up my arms like poisoned ivy, slithering and purring and captivating my focus. They remind me of snake-vines, hissing and daring me to play.

This isn't real, I tell myself. *This is a nightmare. I'll wake up soon. I have to wake up soon!*

"You're ascending," a deep voice says.

Constantine Nacht.

"Soon they'll see you for what you are, Queen Aflora. An abomination in the truest form. A monster. A being consumed by power, both Elemental Fae and Midnight Fae in nature. And I can't wait to watch you burn."

He cackles.

I scream.

Then silence engulfs us both, his final words a threat on the breeze, swathing my being in a kiss of obsidian. "Welcome to your first ascension trial, future dead one. May it forever destroy your soul."

POWER ROLLED THROUGH THE PARADIGM, electrifying my senses as the Source Architect.

One moment, I'd been indulging my mate in a flirtatious mental promise. And the next, I took off at a dead sprint toward where Aflora slept.

Constantine was *here*. I felt him in every breath, his Elite Blood aura tainting the paradigm with his malevolent presence.

I dove into the source, searching for his magical core. It throbbed brightly at the center, his powers fully engaged and suffocating everyone and everything around him.

What is he doing? I wondered, stopping cold in my tracks as I watched a volt of magic enter another soul. *Oh, shit! Aflora!*

I took off again, her aura screaming in agony at the unexpected intrusion of the dark enchantment.

Too much power, I thought. *That's too much power.*

I tried to grab hold of it in my mind, to rip it away from my mate, but the source had already anchored itself inside her, pouring wave after wave of energy into the core of her being.

"*Fuck!*" I shouted, bursting into the cabin covered in wilting flowers.

Her earth magic was weeping at the intrusion, her soul fracturing beneath the wrongness of Constantine's actions.

"He's forcing her ascension," I said, talking to no one and everyone at the same time. "He's redirecting the source *into her.*" It came out on a growl, my fury palpable and violent.

I fell to my knees beside her, the inky lines spreading from her heart to her limbs decorating her as the source's choice.

"That's impossible," Kolstov breathed. "That's not how this works."

I shook my head. Because he was wrong. "It's entirely possible," I replied, furious at myself for not seeing it before. "She's mated to two royal lines and the Source Architect." That provided Constantine with the access he'd needed to the core of her essence. It had allowed him to breathe the enchantment used to call upon new rulers, and redirect it to the rightful heir.

The fallen Midnight Fae Prince's mate.

The Source Architect's chosen other half.

The Death Blood Prince's soul mate.

An Elemental Fae Royal.

All markers that would note her as a potential candidate.

"*Shit.*" I cradled Aflora's face between my hands and attempted to redirect the heart of our power away from her, to rewrite the path and send it back to Constantine, but the source had already chosen.

Worthy, it whispered darkly. *Fresh. Young. Honorable conduit.*

The words weren't real, just sensations that prickled my spirit and told me there wasn't a damn thing I could do to stop this.

Instead, I reached for Aflora and tried to guide her, to ease her pain, to shift her into the ascension with a softness the source lacked.

Her screams echoed in my head, her confusion piercing my heart. She didn't understand what was happening, had lost herself to the fog of the obsidian essence mounting inside her.

"Zakkai!" someone snapped. A deep voice. Harsh. *Furious.*

I lifted my eyelids to meet a pair of fuming green irises. "What?" I demanded, irritated by the interruption.

The Warrior Blood—*Zephyrus*—appeared ready to kill me. "Tell us what you're doing."

"Helping her ascend," I replied shortly.

"Do we need to bite her? That's what we did last time she exploded with power."

I shook my head, gritting my teeth. "No. That was from my ascension." The night I became the Source Architect. There hadn't been an outlet for my power exchange, so everyone had felt it. Including the Nacht family. It had caused Kolstov to unleash his power in a rampage that had destroyed Aflora's room. And then she'd come undone in the LethaForest.

I hadn't witnessed it. But I'd sensed it. And I'd later learned about it from Shade.

"Biting won't help her this time. Constantine is overloading her essence with dark magic and forcing an unwilling royal to ascend." I locked gazes with the Warrior

Blood. "I know how to help her, but I need to be able to focus." And I couldn't do that with him interrupting, something I told him with my expression.

"Do it," he demanded.

I didn't acknowledge his *permission*—because I refused to call it a command. Instead, I closed my eyes to return to my task.

Silence followed as I continued down my original path, only this time Zephyrus's protective energy trailed after me. It served as a foreign taunt to my senses. I wasn't used to feeling the warmth of a Warrior Blood. Of course, it wasn't for me but for Aflora. Regardless, it created the aura of safety that I needed to dive further into Aflora's psyche. Because I didn't have to focus on my surroundings. Zephyrus had that part covered.

I dug deep into the core of her, flinching as her agony pierced through my mental shields.

Ascending *hurt*.

Like molten fire flooding the inner spirit. I'd experienced it when I'd accepted the Source Architect position. However, I'd gone into the situation knowing what to expect.

Aflora was neither willing nor expectant.

I should have seen this coming, but I would never have anticipated this from Constantine. He was handing her the source. Only because he intended for it to kill her. Still, she could survive—*would* survive—making it a huge risk, one I never thought he would take.

"I don't understand how this is possible," I heard Kolstov saying. "The ascension trial requires blood."

"Nacht blood," Shade replied.

"Yes," I agreed, my voice slightly strained from trying to maintain a connection to Aflora while also talking to her mates. "Her connection to the Nacht family line—via Kolstov, and I suppose through Zephyrus's Guardian bond—

would have granted him initial access to perform the enchantment. Then the source accepted the link because she's mated to a Nacht and a Morte."

Morte being Shade's bloodline. Though he rarely used the surname.

"She's also the Earth Fae Queen," I added, swallowing as a volt of energy slammed into me from the source. It served as an order to mentally step away from Aflora and allow her to fully ascend. I responded by crafting an intangible wall around her and then made myself a proverbial door. The energy pushed against me, forcing its way through and turning me into a siphon of sorts.

It burned.

But I accepted the burden.

Because it was the only way to ease her into this… to give her a fighting chance.

"A royal by nature and blood," Shade said, his voice oddly distant. "So all Constantine needed to do was recite the ritual—"

"And the dark source went right for her," Kolstov finished for him. "Shit."

"Precisely," I tried to say, my lungs squeezing with the effort.

A hand met my shoulder, the palm large and unwelcome. Then Zephyrus's power rolled over me, his protective enchantment providing a foreign balm of sorts.

I shuddered, the tranquility of his touch… unexpected.

It granted me space to breathe and somehow shifted my burden to him temporarily. I studied his charm, curious as to what spell he'd cast. *An absorption spell*, I translated faintly. Not what I'd expected, nor anything I'd ever experienced before.

Zephyrus pushed more into me, forcing me to take it.

I almost shoved it back at him in retaliation. This group

dynamic was going to annihilate my patience. I didn't work as a unit. I preferred to lead and be followed, not collaborate.

But for Aflora… I'd try.

And as this helped me relax, I accepted his assistance.

"She needs to pass her first trial," Kolstov said, answering some question I'd missed. Or maybe he was just thinking out loud. "*Trust.*"

I nodded in confirmation. She would have to rely on those closest to her to guide her. "But it hasn't started yet. The source is still settling." I could feel it filling every inch of her soul, blackening out her access to the elements. Or trying to, anyway. Her roots were fighting the intrusion, denying the dark source a proper home.

She gasped, still unconscious and yet fully awake at the same time.

The inky lines writhed in annoyance.

Her roots held.

"Fae," I whispered, awed and terrified by the convoluted mix of magic dancing inside her. It was hypnotic and beautiful and so damn wrong. Cerulean sparks bonded to black lines, green flares, purple smoke, and deep red contours. But at the center of it all was a thriving tree, the branches a swirl of color and magic, as the dark source tried to penetrate her elemental home with a variety of cruel twists. "She's fighting it."

Perhaps not intentionally, but instinctively.

"Her earth source is refusing to release her," I continued, lost to the stunning array of enchantments unfolding inside Aflora.

I'd closed my eyes again, the lightning display absorbing every ounce of my attention.

I was lost to it. To *her.* To the beauty of the sources dueling and marrying and dueling again. Every time the darkness found a new entrance, a strand of cerulean met the ends and untangled them, my darling little star learning and memorizing spells faster than I'd ever seen.

I felt her tugging on my mind, my power, my energy, and using it to craft and mold her reactions appropriately. So quick and nimble and alluring.

"She's *teaching*," I whispered, still utterly engrossed in the sight before me. "She's teaching the sources how to join inside her." That was why it looked like they were fighting, then connecting, and then fighting again. She was finding a way for both powers to exist inside her, to ground herself in earth and hold on to the dark magic as well.

Temporarily, I thought. *This is your temporary solution.*

"She's giving us time," I told the others, then frowned. "But we can't stop the ascension." I voiced that statement out loud and through the bond to Aflora. She didn't comment, her mind lost to the power engulfing her spirit. I wasn't even sure if she could hear me. However, she definitely felt me. Just as I felt her tugging on my essence to help ground her.

"No, we can only ensure she survives it," Kolstov replied. "By passing the initial test." He paused, and I sensed him looking at Zephyrus even though my eyes were still closed. It was a weird sensation, one that confirmed we were truly *bonded.* At least on the first level. Because I'd saved him, using my blood to bring him back to life. Thereby tying our fates together for eternity.

Perhaps that was why Zephyrus could help me as he did —my ties to Aflora and Kolstov, two of his fully bonded mates.

Blood worked in tricky ways, especially for Midnight Fae.

"It'll evaluate her relationships, just like it did to me and mine," he said.

"Which means it'll involve all of us," the Warrior Blood inferred aloud.

I'd undergone a similar trial as the Source Architect. My

trials were different from those of a royal ascension—more convoluted and in the form of puzzles and riddles. Aflora's would likely be a mix because of her ties to me.

"You had to rely on Tray's instincts and my sight," Zephyrus continued. "To make it through the blinding light."

Kolstov's responding shiver was palpable—something I again felt more than saw. "Yes." It came out soft, the memory lurking in his voice. "The source will put her in a situation that won't allow her to escape on her own."

That sounded about right. Except my task had been completed alone. Because there hadn't been anyone for me to rely on—my mating link had been cut off, and my father had insisted I master my source ascension by myself.

It hadn't been easy.

But nothing with the source ever was.

Kolstov blew out a breath and repositioned himself beside me on the bed, causing my eyes to flicker open. He'd pulled on a pair of boxers and nothing else. Zephyrus and Shade remained naked on the other side of Aflora, their concern evident.

"Any second now," Kolstov said after evaluating the obsidian lines crawling down Aflora's arms.

I agreed with a nod, the energy seeming to settle around her, preparing for the next phase. It had all passed through me now, leaving her to battle the remainder on her own.

Silence fell as we all held our breaths.

A scratch at the door disturbed the momentary peace. All three men took up defensive positions, their wands seeming to appear out of thin air.

"Relax," I said, aware of who had made the sound.

Zimney.

My arctic wolf familiar nudged open the door with his big white muzzle, then shoved it wider to allow Clove to fly through. The falcon's wings nearly clipped Zephyrus and

Shade as she soared between them to land right beside Aflora.

It was a familiar's job to protect the fae who had conjured it. And Clove clearly sensed Aflora's unease, just as Zimney had likely sensed mine. Or perhaps he'd followed Clove. The two were bonded in a unique manner since it'd technically been my magic that Aflora had tapped into to create her familiar. It meant Clove responded to me, too. Which she would have anyway as Aflora's mate.

I eyed the two creatures and frowned. "They sense something." I couldn't quite hear it, but I felt the knowledge of it traversing through my connection to Zimney. "They're here for the first trial."

A bat entered next, settling on Shade's shoulder.

Followed by the hiss of a three-headed snake that magically manifested around Zephyrus's neck. Three sets of creepy eyes went to my wolf, the slithering creature clearly agitated by my much larger familiar. Zephyrus muttered something to the reptile, ending with the name *Raph*.

I glanced at Kolstov, curious to see what animal would appear for him. But none did.

Because Kolstov had died.

Which meant his familiar had perished as well.

Shit.

"That's the test," I realized out loud, my heart skipping a beat. "Something with your familiar." Would Aflora have to bring the being back from the dead? Conjure a new one? Work through a puzzle involving his fallen familiar? There were so many options. *Too many* options.

I ran my fingers through my hair, the ash-blond strands falling into my face for just a moment and hiding my reaction from the males around me. A reaction underlined in momentary uncertainty.

Had we all bonded enough for Aflora to successfully pass this test?

Because I didn't trust any of them. Not really. Only my little star.

However, what if the test wasn't just for her but for all her mates as well?

Would I be forced to rely on the others? To put my faith in those who had mated Aflora? Saving Kolstov from death had been trial enough. Except that I hadn't even hesitated in helping him. Once I'd seen what it would have done to Aflora to lose him, I'd known he'd had to live. Would this be all that different? How much was I prepared to sacrifice to ensure Aflora's survival?

I wasn't given a moment to consider the answer to that because in the next breath, Aflora started to shake.

I pressed my palm to her breastbone in an attempt to hold her down, only to have my skin burned by the power radiating off her.

Zephyrus cursed.

Shade winced.

And Kolstov collapsed beside her on a violent shudder.

Clove released an agonized caw, making Zimney growl. Then magic spilled in through the room, fracturing the paradigm around us. Shade jumped to his feet, spells spewing from his lips as he tried to hold the enchantment in place. I immediately bolstered the edges, giving him the leverage he needed to repair the breaks, and Zephyrus underlined it all with his Warrior magic.

A natural team effort.

One being threatened with every passing second.

The trial had begun. Aflora's first task was to wake up.

And the only one who could help guide her through the test was the fallen royal beside her.

If they failed... she'd die.

Another thunderous hit against the paradigm sent a shiver through my being. "Constantine knows where we are." Because he'd used all of this as a distraction to locate us, knowing we'd be weakened while Aflora attempted to pass her first trial.

Clever bastard, I seethed, sending up a massive wave of power to rewrite all the spells surrounding the exterior of the makeshift dome. It wasn't visible, just an alternate use of space that Constantine had clearly located by using Aflora as a beacon of sorts.

That was what I'd felt last night, why I hadn't been able to rest.

He'd been close by, his power a fiery blade against my senses that had alerted me to his nefarious whims without providing the finite details.

And then he'd distracted me by forcing Aflora's ascension.

Zephyrus cast a defensive spell that captured my awareness, the Warrior Blood proving incredibly capable in the moment. I memorized his enchantment and echoed it throughout the paradigm, bolstering it with a little Quandary Blood twist that would make it a bit more difficult to undo.

Shade added his own flavor of Death magic, allowing the three of us to craft a unique shield that would hopefully buy us a little more time.

"I need to find somewhere for us to jump to," Shade said quickly.

"Go," I replied, power deepening my voice to a rumble.

Zephyrus sent up another enchantment that I immediately copied as Shade disappeared into a cloud of black smoke.

"He'd better come back," Zephyrus said under his breath.

"He will." If there was one thing I could count on Shade

for, it was his protection of Aflora. "Keep bolstering the paradigm."

Zephyrus grunted in response but did exactly what I'd told him to.

Although, I doubted it had anything to do with my demand and everything to do with the unconscious pair on the bed.

They were the owners of his heart.

And so he did what a Warrior Blood was trained to do—*guard*.

A maze.

Everywhere I turned was a dead end, the riddle sprawling out before me in an impossible mess of obsidian vines. Not snakes, but midnight roots intertwining and binding and holding me hostage.

I spun around in a circle, lost to the foreign darkness.

It consumed me, threatening to destroy my earth. But I fought back. I forced it to behave, to blend, to bind with my current existence and allow me the chance to breathe. It'd been a natural response, one grounded in Zakkai's power. His essence had washed over me, followed by a kiss of protection underlined in Zeph's ability. Both of my mates had helped me ascend into this garden of dead roses.

Then the vines began to whirl and build, locking me inside.

And Constantine's final words repeated on the wind. *"Welcome to your first ascension trial, future dead one. May it forever destroy your soul."*

I shivered. This was a test of sorts, some type of trial designed for me to fail. I didn't know the rules or what it all meant. I didn't know how to survive. However, I had no choice. Constantine couldn't win. Not like this. He'd forced this power into me, ensuring my abomination status, and I would find a way to undo it.

I'd memorized the chants and the magical creation. I just had to figure out how to unwind those binds and release the source once more.

After I escaped this maze.

Kols? I whispered, trying to connect to the one who I knew could help me most. As an Elite Blood and the true Midnight Fae Prince, he'd know what to do.

But silence met my words.

Shade? I tried next.

Silence.

I bit my lip, uncertain. Was this even real? Or was I still lost in a nightmare within my mind?

The power pulsing inside me felt real. As did the forbidden weave of magic marrying the dark source to my earth source.

Claire, I thought, trembling slightly. *Can the Elemental Fae feel what I've done? Am I hurting them right now?*

Chancellor Elana had darkened the elements with her connection to Midnight Fae magic. But that'd been an active, conscious decision on her part to absorb more power.

I didn't want more; I wanted less.

I tried to push it to my mates, to relieve some of the fiery ache blistering inside me, but the block between us remained.

I don't accept that, I decided, pushing against the barrier and searching for the source of the obstruction. It had to be a spell—one Constantine had woven—and I'd just have to undo it.

Ignoring the maze, I closed my eyes and focused. This was all inside my mind, a mental gymnasium of writhing energy and foreign connections.

A tree had sprouted at the core of my being, the branches all whirling with an array of colors.

Red for the Elite Bloods.

Navy for the Sangré Bloods.

Green for the Warrior Bloods.

Purple for the Death Bloods.

Black for the Malefic Bloods.

And cerulean at the heart, dancing along the veins of the trunk for the Quandary Bloods.

I mentally stroked the beautiful creation, marveling at the multicolored leaves that sprouted along the twigs. So strong and full of life. Yet tipped with ash.

It'd been my compromise—the way I'd coaxed my earth source into coexisting with the dark source.

Such an unnatural formation, and yet, it felt as though it belonged.

I allowed myself a final glimmer of admiration, then focused on my mates and our obstructed bonds. Zakkai had helped me ascend, as had Zeph. I'd sensed Kols as well, his bloodline thriving through my veins. And Shade, my forever dark shadow, had gifted me with his assurance that everything would be fine.

All of them were with me and yet not.

Because of Constantine.

You will not win, I told him. He couldn't hear me. Or maybe he could. Or maybe all of this was just some sort of wicked nightmare.

Regardless, the sentiment remained.

He'd tried to kill my mate. And now he'd forced me into this ascension.

I'll undo it. Then I'll ensure you can never hurt anyone else ever again.

I had no idea how I'd achieve that, but I felt the assurance of my task deep within my roots. He would pay for his sins.

Inhaling slowly, I delved deeper into my bonds, searching for the magic that didn't belong. I sensed it circling Kols, my link to his bloodline seeming to have provided Constantine with the access he'd needed to weave his nefarious enchantments.

Zeph, too, I realized, tugging on that cord and finding an anchor in my Warrior Blood mate as well.

The strands linked back to Shade and Zakkai—from Kols. Because of their initial mate-bonds that were established last night.

Constantine's spell presented itself in intricate waves, the fiery ends fizzling with embers that made touching it dangerous. I peeled apart the layers with my mind, seeking the enchantment's pattern, but he'd woven too many together to undo without risk.

I needed Zakkai.

Which meant I needed to figure out how to pass this trial.

I opened my eyes, the darkness around me having grown while I'd poked at my mate-bonds. It was almost pitch black now, the weaving vines having formed a canopy of sorts over my head.

A chill swept down my spine. This definitely wasn't a nightmare. But it wasn't real either. I could sense the magical binds lining the horizon, the dark source serving as the designer of this course.

I knelt to touch the charcoal blades, my earth magic

flickering to life as I absorbed the genetic makeup of the landscape and tried to manipulate it to my will. Flowers sprouted along the vines, dotting the world with color. Then the petals turned to ash in the next instant as the black magic killed my new life.

My heart ached at the loss, my breath catching in my throat.

I tried again, demanding the world shift to accept the core of my being. But it responded by strangling my energy, denying me any form of light.

"Aflora." Constantine's familiar voice floated to me on the wind, causing my teeth to grind together in frustration.

He'd returned to watch my trial. *Tulip-burning willow stump*, I thought, standing to face him. I couldn't see him, just heard him, his shadowed figure about ten feet away.

"Thank fuck," he breathed, his dark form stepping closer. "Are you all right?"

I arched a brow. "Is that your version of a joke? Because you'll have to try harder to provoke a laugh from me."

The being stilled. "A joke? Why the bloody hell would I joke about this?"

"I'm not sure why you do a lot of things," I admitted. "Like forcing an ascension on an Earth Fae Royal, for example."

"You think I did this to you?"

"I know you did," I retorted, placing my hands on my hips. "But I'm going to find a way to undo it. And I'm going to survive this trial, marking you as the *future dead one*." Not that I would kill him. That would make me no better than him.

Earth Fae craved life.

And I would be an Earth Fae until my dying breath.

"Who do you think I am?" Constantine asked slowly.

I ignored him and focused on my surroundings. He was

clearly here to distract me from my task, and I'd already wasted enough breath on him.

My flowers had all turned to ash again while talking to him, and the remaining light overhead glimmered like little stars between the dark vines. I tried to tap into their magic to unweave them, but the dark source hissed in response.

"All right," I said to it. "Then how about this?" I took hold of the roots and called on a burning thwomp. It sprouted high and proud, fire billowing from its limbs and blasting right through the roof of my canopy.

I grinned, proud.

And then the thwomp cried out in pain as it incinerated into dust.

My heart skipped a beat, the sudden blow knocking me to my knees.

Constantine rushed forward, his hand grabbing my arm as he shouted my name.

I shoved him back with a bolt of power, Zeph's Warrior Blood thriving inside me and alighting me from within. The spell left my lips on instinct, the enchantment one Zeph had taught me during one of our sparring matches. And it shoved Constantine to the ground.

"What the fuck?" he demanded on a wheeze.

"Touch me again, and I'll paralyze you." Then I cocked my head to the side. "A spell courtesy of your prickly little thorn, Dakota." It would be fitting to use the enchantment on him since he'd sent that lying fae to infiltrate Zakkai's camp.

"What are you talking about?" he asked, sounding shocked and dismayed. "Aflora, who do you think I am?"

"Is this the part where you remind me that you're a former king and demand I bow? Because I don't think I'm in the mood for that. If anyone is going to bow, it'll be you." And I would thoroughly enjoy making him do it. Assuming I could. The fact that he bent beneath Zeph's spell was an interesting development. Constantine should have been powerful enough to block it.

"A prince," he hissed. "And no, *princess*, I'm not going to demand you bow. But hit me with another spell and we're going to exchange some words."

"Sounds like an empty threat since you're already talking," I told him.

And again he'd distracted me from my task.

Sprinkle dust, I need to focus.

He was just a—

A volt of electricity hit me in the side, knocking me to the ground on an "Oomph."

In the next beat, the shadowy figure had me pinned to the ground with a knee between my thighs. "What's wrong with you?" he demanded.

"Get off of me!" I shouted, a spell lining up on my lips.

But his mouth captured mine, silencing me in an instant.

Technically, I could still utter the spell in my thoughts. However, I wasn't as well versed in the art of mental enchantments. And my brain also failed to function properly.

Because Constantine is kissing me.

What in the lily cookie?

Why is he…?

His tongue parted my lips, the familiarity of the taste hitting my taste buds and cascading me beneath a wave of confusion.

Kols.

He tastes like Kols.

How?

Because they're related?

Ugh, gross. Gross, gross, gross! I tried to shove him off me, but the male remained heavy on top of me, his hands on my hips.

Something jolted inside my head, my mate-bonds screaming in fury.

I tried to latch onto them, to unlock the spell, but those blistering ends threatened to singe my mind—and the minds of my mates—in the process.

A tremble worked down my spine, my mouth responding to the familiar kiss while my body rebelled.

Why is he kissing me? I wondered, my brow furrowing. Constantine had no reason to do this. Sure, he could evoke confusion in this manner… but he'd already been succeeding in that before touching me.

He also hadn't fought back when he could have easily blocked my spell. *No.* Constantine *would* have blocked my spell.

So why let me hit him? Why kiss me afterward?

Unless…

Unless this wasn't Constantine at all, but Kols.

I blinked.

No.

He sounds like Constantine.

But I couldn't *see* him.

Who do you think I am? he'd asked twice. And he'd called me *princess.* Constantine referred to me as an *abomination* and *future dead one.*

Kols often called me *princess.*

Which Constantine would know if he'd somehow tapped into the history of our bond. Was that possible? I had no idea. But I didn't know anything about Midnight Fae or how the ascension and bloodlines worked.

However, Kols did.

I bit his tongue, drawing a low rumble from his chest. "Aflora," he growled.

"Stop," I demanded.

"Try to blast me with another spell and I'll kiss you

again," he warned. "I know we don't have time for it, but that fucking hurt, Aflora. And I can't exactly hit you back."

Constantine would be able to retaliate. Unless he was playing another trick on me.

I tried to make out the features of his face, but they were masked behind a curtain of black.

"Can you see me?" I wondered out loud.

"Can I see you?" he repeated. "Of course I can fucking see you."

I tried to find his mouth, then his eyes. I knew where they should be but couldn't make out the details. "You're shadowy and dark."

"What?"

"I can't *see* you," I explained, reaching up to touch his face. He still sounded like Constantine. However… he didn't feel like Constantine. Not that I really knew what the Elder felt like, but I didn't sense him in this shadow figure.

It could be a ploy.

Or the ploy could be making me think this was Constantine.

"Kols?" It came out on a whisper, mostly because I felt foolish even asking. But everything was… a mess.

"Yeah, sweetheart?"

"You sound like Constantine," I admitted quietly, biting my lip.

He fell silent for a moment, then cursed. "It's the trial. It's about trust. So you're seeing me as someone you absolutely shouldn't and wouldn't trust at all."

"Trust?" I repeated.

"Yes. There are seven ascension trials, each one designed to test different aspects of royalty and leadership. And the first one is about trusting those who support you." He cupped my cheek. "The dark source is testing your ability to trust your mates, Aflora."

"By making you sound like Constantine," I said, leaning into his palm. Constantine wouldn't waste his breath explaining the trial to me. He'd just wait for it to kill me.

Which confirmed that this wasn't Constantine at all, but my Kols.

My earth bond pulsed in agreement, the link to him a thick root that connected our souls. That wasn't something the Elder Midnight Fae could manipulate. He had no control or manipulative power over my earth magic.

I brushed my lips against Kols's mouth, telling him without words that I knew it was him. Then I drew back to look up at him. "What now?"

"Now we find our way out of this maze and wake up," he replied softly. "And to do that, you need to follow your instincts."

"My instincts say to burn the vines to the ground and allow the light to illuminate my path." I always preferred the light over the night. But Midnight Fae were all about the dark.

He gently went back to his knees, then stood and held a hand out for me to help me up. I accepted, realizing as I stood that I could see his shadow clearly despite the blackness settling around us.

Actually, he was the only figure I could make out now that the twinkling lights above had been fully covered by the vines.

That had to be related to this trial—my ability to see the one I trusted through the obsidian fog.

"Where are the others?" I wondered out loud. "Why can I only sense you?"

"I don't know," Kols replied, a frown in his tone—a tone that still sounded like Constantine. "Zakkai thought your test would have something to do with Night."

"Your familiar?"

"Yes. All the others appeared during your ascension, except for my Night." A hint of sadness tinged his deep voice, further confirming this was Kols and not Constantine.

"Maybe we need to find him?" I suggested.

"I felt him die," Kols whispered. "When… when I died."

I winced, recalling what it had felt like when I'd lost Clove all those months ago. I hadn't known I could bring my familiar back. But Kols had been the one to teach me. "Have you tried calling for him?"

The silence that followed indicated his hesitation.

He hadn't tried.

And I understood why.

"You're afraid he won't reply," I said, reaching for his hand and squeezing it. "You once told me familiars are tied to our lives, that they only die if we do, and you didn't die, Kols. Shade held on to your life strand long enough for me to give it roots."

Which meant Night was still here.

He had to be.

Because Kols was very much alive.

"Try calling for him," I encouraged, my voice low yet underlined in confidence. "Bring Night back to you."

My Elite Blood mate remained quiet for another moment, making me wonder if I'd been wrong, if this had all been a trick, but that pulse inside me throbbed with knowledge. *Earth mate. Midnight Fae mate. My Kolstov. My prince.*

Kols wasn't known for his hesitation. He thought through his options and acted.

But this was a surreal situation.

He'd almost died.

He'd felt his familiar's death.

It was on him to trust his own soul.

My eyes widened. "That's it," I breathed. "Trust."

"What?"

"You need to call for Night." Because it would prove he trusted in himself… because I trusted in him. "You need to *trust* him to find you." I pressed my palm to his chest, my opposite hand still holding his. "He's here. I know he's here. Call for him so he can help us find our way out of here."

I felt the rightness of this path to my very soul.

Kols had said this was about trusting my instincts and trusting my mates.

And now I just needed my Elite Blood mate to trust me.

The full circle.

A complete trial.

With only one path forward.

It was Kols's turn to choose.

THE ASCENSION TRIALS were never straightforward. They tested more than just the source heir; they tested everyone *linked* to the heir as well.

Which made Aflora's statement true.

I needed to trust Night to find me. I needed to trust that he'd survived. And I needed to trust that what Aflora and the others had done was enough to bring not only me back from death, but my familiar, too.

Her dark hair framed her beautiful face and fierce expression as she waited for my agreement. She knew this was the right path, and I needed to *trust* her instincts.

These trials were devised to trick us all. Only the strongest were meant to survive. I'd been more than strong enough, but I'd been tricked by the Elders—my own grandfather—and betrayed by my Council.

I would seek vengeance in my own way, starting by helping my mate ascend.

Constantine Nacht wanted Aflora to fail, to make a mockery of her ascension.

I'd ensure the opposite happened.

I'd help her become queen.

"*Ahaminee*," I breathed, invoking the incantation for calling a familiar. "*Ahaminee, Night.*"

Aflora's fingers curled into my chest, her blue eyes glistening with approval.

She had said I resembled a shadowy creature to her. How very odd. I had no trouble seeing her. But everything else was dark and covered by the power vines. It made me wonder if I'd even be able to see Night.

Assuming he was still alive.

I swallowed, the echo of his dying caw infiltrating my senses and eliciting a wince from deep within. He'd been a part of me, a being of my own creation. And I'd failed him.

Not by choice.

Not even on purpose.

But because of my grandfather's greed for power.

I'd never anticipated him going to the extent of killing me to take back the throne. It had all happened so quickly, so unexpectedly, that I'd never even considered the potential outcome.

And now this—forcing the ascension onto Aflora. It made no sense.

What are you trying to prove? I wondered as a wave of power swirled around us.

An echo of cawing began, the darkness moving in flaps of wings as the vines melted into a series of crows. Aflora gasped, her grip on my hand tightening. I wrapped my arm around her lower back, holding her to me as the feathers beat over our heads.

It reminded me of the transportation yard back at the Academy with all the crows forming a vessel for students to travel to and from within.

But no keypad appeared here.

This whirlwind of energy wasn't meant to help teleport Midnight Fae; it was meant to serve as a test. Another layer of trust. "We have to follow our instincts," I realized out loud.

More than that—I had to follow mine, and Aflora had to trust me to choose. To pick a crow I thought might be Night and follow him to our freedom or our doom.

I explained the realization to Aflora, felt her stiffen against me, and understood how difficult this task would be for us both.

She had to trust me.

And I had to trust myself.

I wasn't in a position to rely on my instincts. I'd nearly died yesterday. All my powers were convoluted and messy, strands of various magic helping to bolster my soul and keep me alive.

I was no longer an Elite Blood, but something significantly other.

An abomination.

Just like my mate.

I could feel Shade, Zakkai, and Zeph inside me. Aflora, too. A collection of strength that shouldn't be possible, yet existed nonetheless.

"Kols?" Aflora whispered, the feathers closing in around us. "What are your instincts telling you? Because mine are saying to run."

"Hold on," I replied, closing my eyes to focus on the beating wings. *Where are you, Night?*

Rather than focus on the sounds around me, I searched for the familiar strand of life—*my* life. Both new and old. Former and current. But the essences swarming through the air all blended together, masking the one I sought.

Minutes passed as I chanted the spell under my breath, demanding my familiar find me.

Yet nothing happened beyond the whirl of feathers, some of them slicing my cheek and arms like charcoal blades. Not feathers, but metallic stone. Dangerous. Lethal. Cruel.

Come on…

Night had to be here somewhere. Aflora's certainty washed over me, giving me the strength I needed to keep searching. She trusted me to find him. Which meant he was here somewhere, cloaked behind the mass of power created by the dark source.

Aflora's palm wrapped around the back of my neck, her lips capturing mine.

It took me so off guard that I didn't immediately return her embrace.

But as her tongue parted my lips, I realized her plan —*blood*. Her essence hit my senses, lighting my veins on fire with her power. I swallowed her heated kiss, her energy swarming inside me and grounding me in a field of existence beyond comprehension.

Mine, I thought. *Aflora's mine.*

Some sort of barrier fizzled into ash between us, our connection smoldering to life. And in the next breath, she released me, my mind suddenly clear and focused on my task.

There! I yanked my mouth away from Aflora's, my gaze locking on a crow just a few feet above my head. "Come here." The bird cawed in response, clearly agitated over being called away from the swarming array of feathers, but as he dove down, I felt the rightness in our connection. *Night.*

Aflora hummed in agreement, a spell warming her breath as she weaved some sort of Quandary magic through the air. An invisible dagger sliced through my heart, stealing the air from my lungs, and on my next inhale, I felt rejuvenated with life.

Finally, she said into my mind. *Constantine did something to our bonds. I figured out how to unfasten his hold on you, but the others are still quiet.*

I frowned, attempting my link to Zeph and finding it closed off. I'd been so focused on Aflora before that I hadn't thought to reach out to him. Having a mental link to him was still new, but so was my link to her. And yet, all my attention had been on finding her.

Odd.

A year ago, my first instinct would have been to reach out to him.

That didn't necessarily mean I loved her more or him less, just that my priorities had changed. I supposed I'd also been consumed with the need to find her because of the ascension and my desire to help her.

Kols, Aflora said, drawing me back to the present. She looked up with her pretty blue eyes, a smile tugging at the edges of her mouth. I followed her gaze to find Night hovering above us, his wings spread wide as he soared in a circle around our heads.

I dropped my arm away from her back and grabbed her hand once more. "Lead the way," I told him, confident in his ability to guide us out.

Night took off through the mess of feathers, creating a path for us to follow, and we sprinted after him into the sea of darkness.

A resounding hiss trailed behind us, the power vines sizzling and reforming into something new and dangerous.

But I kept my gaze on Night, my hand firmly holding Aflora's, as we ran… and ran… and ran.

Not once did she glance backward, no matter how much noise and chaos echoed through the air. Aflora was resolute in her choice, her faith in me a tangible kiss to my senses.

I'd known from our first meeting that she was an ideal mate. Royal. Beautiful. Strong. Feisty as hell. And now she was truly mine. For eternity.

She'd brought me back from certain death, claimed me with her power, and rooted herself so deep inside me that I would forever belong to her, and her to me.

I love you, I whispered, the words a stroke against my heart. I hadn't said that to her before. I hadn't really considered it entirely. But I knew with every fiber of my being that Aflora was always meant to be mine.

I love you, too, Aflora replied, her blue eyes momentarily meeting mine. *But we're escaping this place.*

I know we are, I assured her. *And when we do, I'll confess my feelings out loud.* Because I hadn't said the words to her now out of fear; I knew we would make it out of here alive. The moment had just felt right.

I pushed those emotions to her now, the certainty of our fate underlined in the love I felt.

She didn't outwardly smile, but I sensed her responding joy.

Just as I sensed her tingle of uncertainty as Night led us to a bright white light. It blanketed the world in white, chasing away the darkness and leaving nothing behind.

"Kols?" she asked.

"We jump," I told her as Night disappeared into the horizon.

"Okay." She didn't falter. She merely kept running, our hands still linked.

And we leapt into the core of the dark source's power,

the light blinding us both. Her palm disappeared from mine, but we woke up in the bed beside one another in the next breath. I inhaled sharply, looking at her and meeting her gaze.

Then the mattress shook beneath us as power ripped through the air.

Zakkai and Zeph were both on their feet, their wands in their hands as they fought an attack from outside. *Fuck*, I thought, trying to sit up and join them. But my body refused the movement. Aflora appeared to be having the same struggle beside me, both of us weakened by her first ascension trial.

You passed, I assured her. *Six more to go.*

She groaned in response. Then she closed her eyes and began murmuring enchantments that had my eyes widening. They were advanced incantations, ones I hadn't taught her.

But a glance at Zakkai told me where she'd learned them —through their mating link. His silver-blue gaze fell to her, pride momentarily lightening his expression before he growled at the incoming attack from the outside.

The foundation rocked around us, knocking me into Aflora. Power blasted out of her, hitting the sides of the paradigm with a fortification charm that had my heart stopping in unadulterated awe.

Energy rippled down her arms, the dark source's mark marring her pale skin with inky lines.

She finished the incantation on an exhale, and the world fell silent.

Zakkai and Zeph immediately fell to the bed, their exhaustion evident.

Then Zakkai bit into his wrist and held it to Aflora's mouth. "Drink," he demanded.

Zeph followed suit, putting his wrist to my lips. "You, too, little prince."

I tried to snort at the nickname, but I could barely form the sound. So I latched onto his vein instead, sinking my incisors deep into his skin and taking my fill of his blood.

It only took a few pulls for life to thrive through my being, reinvigorating my reserves and drawing me firmly back into the present. The dreamlike filter over my eyes dissolved, allowing me to truly see the damage around the room.

Although, I wouldn't exactly call it a room anymore.

Because there was no roof.

And the bed?

It was a mound of dirt overlaid with dead flower petals.

"What the fuck happened?" I asked as I released Zeph's wrist.

"War," Zakkai replied flatly. "A damn war."

"Constantine attacked shortly after you fell unconscious," I added. "Shade fucked off to who knows where, leaving Zakkai and me to uphold the paradigm alone for… I'm not actually sure how long."

"Two hours and seventeen minutes," Shade announced as he appeared. "I've been trying to get back inside, but Constantine had a mass of energy blocking all entries and exits." He looked at Aflora. "I have no idea how you did that, little rose, but it's mighty impressive."

I was torn between punching him in the face for leaving and agreeing with him.

Considering he returned, and it probably was Constantine's fault that he hadn't been able to enter, I opted for the latter. "Very impressive," I echoed, brushing my knuckles across her cheek.

Then I frowned. "Now why can't I hear you?" I couldn't hear Kols, either.

"Constantine did something to our bonds," she said, her attention going to Zakkai.

A question formed over her lips, but the Quandary Blood said, "Take what you need," before she had a chance to voice it.

He leaned down to press his forehead to hers, their mouths grazing in a light kiss that had me narrowing my eyes.

Kolstov and Shadow I could accept.

Zakkai was going to take time.

He'd taken my mate. Kept her from me—from *us*. Hidden her. But he'd also protected her. Which was the only reason I allowed him to remain in such an intimate position with Aflora.

She closed her eyes as energy pooled around her. Clove flew in from above to settle beside her in the destroyed remains of the bed, her wing brushing Aflora's shoulder.

Zakkai's wolf lingered in the former doorway while Raph slithered around my neck.

Then Kols's familiar soared in to land beside Clove. I blinked at the crow's ash-tipped black wings, the color rivaling the ends of the Elite Blood's auburn hair. He glanced at Night and noticed the same thing, his fingers reaching out to stroke the discolored feathers.

They'd both been marked by death.

Shade's icy gaze traced over Kols and Night as well, his expression holding a touch of wonderment. Then he flinched as magic swarmed around him. The same happened to me half a second later, my mind suddenly paralyzed by Aflora's enchantment.

Something snapped.

Prickled.

Crumbled.

My heart ached for a solitary beat before emotion and thoughts came rushing through my mind and soul, Aflora's affection and frustration and fear and relief a torrent of sensations that stole my breath.

I reached for her in the next breath, pulling her mouth away from Zakkai and up to mine, my gratitude at having her inside me again an oppressing wave that I couldn't release. She returned my embrace with equal fervor.

"Good thing she was done," Zakkai muttered.

I ignored him, my focus on my beautiful mate and the power rippling through her. *My queen,* I thought reverently.

Not yet, she returned, her fingers threading through my hair. *I... I don't know if...* She trailed off, her uncertainty winning over her other reactions.

"It's all right," I whispered against her mouth. "We're going to figure this out."

"I want to undo it," she admitted just as softly. "There has to be a way to undo it."

Kols's opinions on that graced my psyche, but he didn't voice them out loud. *Not possible,* he said first. *And even if it is, is it the right recourse?* I followed his analytical reveal, reveling in the ability to be so utterly close to him and his beliefs.

"Voice that out loud," I suggested to him. "Tell Aflora."

"Tell me what?" she asked, her focus on me and then the others. "I assume you're talking to Kols?"

"He is," Kols replied, flashing an irritated glance my way. "You being in my head is problematic."

"And very useful," I countered. "Tell her."

He sighed, his fingers combing through his thick reddish-brown hair as he shook his head. "My grandfather forced your ascension in an effort to kill you. However, you passed your first trial. Not only that, but the source also embraced you. I was just thinking through what that means and wondering if fate might have a point. If perhaps you should be the Midnight Fae Queen."

I righted my spine, my palm still around the back of Aflora's nape. Zakkai stood nearby with Shade on his other side. But my pixie flower's eyes were on Kols, who still rested beside her on the petal-adorned bed. "How could I be the queen? I'm an Earth Fae."

"An Earth Fae who is mated to four Midnight Fae," he said softly. "An Earth Fae who found a way for the two sources to talk to each other. An Earth Fae who should be thrumming with an overabundance of power right now, seeking to destroy—at least according to all the rumors about abominations—and yet I can hear you still putting your people first. You're not thinking about yourself or what it'll mean for you, but for everyone else. And that is the mark of true royalty, Aflora. That is the mindset of a queen."

I released Aflora, aware of Kols's intention.

His palm found her cheek as he rolled into her. "You were always destined for this," he whispered, his mouth brushing hers. "I think Shade's known that all along, too."

The Death Blood merely smiled, but the look certainly confirmed Kols's statement.

"As touching as this is, we need to move," Zakkai interjected, his tone lined with authority, but I caught the flicker of regret in his silvery gaze. He didn't want to interrupt. However, the brush of energy to the exterior of the paradigm told me exactly why he'd felt the need to.

"He's right," I agreed, my defensive energy already flaring to life. "Constantine is still here." Or nearby, anyway.

"Midnight Fae Academy?" Zakkai asked, arching a brow at Shade.

"Yes," the Death Blood agreed. "My grandmother

gained the appropriate permissions, but he's demanded a meeting with you."

Zakkai snorted in response. "Of course he has. He's been trying to meet me for years."

Shade just lifted a shoulder. "You know how he feels about making deals."

I frowned at them. "Who are you talking about? And why would we go to the Academy? That's the first place they'll look for us."

"Your Academy, yes. This Academy, no." Zakkai redirected his attention to Shade. "And I accept the deal."

"That's not the only one they made," Shade replied. "He also wants a boon at his point of choosing."

"From me or Zenaida?"

"You know my grandmother prefers to be called Zen." Shade gave him an indecipherable look. "And *he* didn't clarify."

"I see," Zakkai murmured. "Well, I'm prepared to pay whatever price so long as we're hidden. I'll be sure to thank *Zenaida* later for arranging it."

The Death Blood snorted. "It's already done because I agreed to it on your behalf."

"Presumptuous of you."

"I knew you would do anything for Aflora," Shade returned.

"True," Zakkai agreed without missing a beat, looking down at her now. "We need to go, little star."

She nodded. "I can feel him."

"We all can," Kols said. "But what Academy are you talking about? There's only one in existence for Midnight Fae."

"Is there?" Zakkai countered. "Where do you think all the outlawed Midnight Fae go to study? In the Human Realm?" He conjured a flaming dragon in the next breath, sending it up into the sky to attack those beyond the paradigm walls. "Because I doubt they teach this at local universities there."

Shade just shook his head and disappeared again.

I glared after him. "Another damn secret."

Zakkai smirked. "He's full of them."

"As are you," I replied, stepping toward him. His arrogance was starting to grate on my nerves. "If this is going to work, we all need to start communicating."

"If?" His smirk intensified. "You act as though there's a choice in the matter."

"There's a choice if I remove you," I threatened, not at all amused by his tricks and games and riddles. He was just as bad as Shade. No, he was worse. A lone wolf used to doing whatever the hell he wanted, however he wanted. I started to take another step, but Aflora slipped off the bed to stand between us, her palm against my chest.

"Can we all try to focus, please?" she asked, her voice regal in its softness. My gaze immediately dropped to the lines of power writhing over her arms, my heart leaping into my throat.

She was right.

There were more important items to focus on right now.

I cupped her jaw, my Warrior Blood gift flourishing beneath my skin with the dark desire to guard her. "We'll figure this out, pixie flower. I vow it."

She nodded, but her hesitation remained. She wasn't sure she wanted this.

However, I agreed with Kols's statement—she was made for this.

Zakkai moved into her back, his power an irritating wave of warmth that I could feel pulsing around and through Aflora.

Kols slid off the bed then, joining us, our bodies forming

a protective circle around our Aflora. Her shoulders relaxed slightly as she breathed in our scents, her resolve somewhat thickening.

I glanced at Kols, his gaze reflecting what I already knew. There would be more trials, all of them equally dangerous and difficult.

While Kols had had his entire life to prepare for them, Aflora had only spent a few months at the Academy. Her knowledge was inferior, her skills rudimentary. Kols had also benefited from his father being the one to outline the trials.

However, Constantine was in charge now.

And there was no telling what he would do or how he would frame Aflora's future.

Preparing her would be the hardest task of our lives. But I silently vowed in that moment to do whatever was necessary to guard her and help her ascend.

I'd die for her.

Kols echoed the sentiment, both of us promising her eternal loyalty.

She would be our royal.

Our future Midnight Fae Queen.

SHADE RETURNED several minutes later with clothes that rivaled our Academy wardrobe—slacks and button-down shirts for the men. Cloaks, too.

And a skirt with a blouse for Aflora. She pulled on the boots with a sigh, her fingers brushing the fine black material. It was a unique leather made from Midnight Fae magic rather than animal product. She seemed to approve, her Earth Fae side preferring enchantment over unnecessary death.

I finished buttoning up my shirt before wrapping my arm around her slender waist and pulling her to me for another kiss. She seemed to have calmed down now, her acceptance of fate growing with each passing second.

Yet I still sensed her trying to find a way to reverse the

ascension.

She and Zakkai were having some sort of mental discussion about it. I couldn't hear it, just felt the hum of their discussion brushing my psyche.

What will happen if she undoes the ascension? It had nearly killed me, but that was because of the manner in which my father had done it. My heart ached just thinking about it. But it hadn't been him. My grandfather…

I swallowed.

Phoenix fires.

I couldn't even process it.

And Tray. I pulled away from Aflora on a jolt. *Shit, Tray!*

"Tray will be okay," Zeph rushed to say, his hand reaching for my shoulder to give it a squeeze. "Once we're somewhere safe, we'll reach out to him." His green eyes went to Shade. "Which reminds me, where are we going, Shadow? You never actually said."

I tried to allow his distraction to pull me from my dark thoughts and concerns, but I felt to my soul that something was very wrong. Tray wasn't okay at all. None of us were.

Aflora leaned into me, her head on my chest. She didn't say anything, just offered me her emotional strength and support by cuddling me in a moment of intense need.

Zeph was at my back as well, his intensity a protective cape that billowed around me.

"To a place Constantine can't go," Shade said softly. "To the Academy he knows exists but can't breach."

I frowned. "He knows about this other Academy?" It'd never been mentioned to me. Of course, it seemed the Council and the Elders had hidden several key items from me. So I supposed this wasn't new information.

"Your grandfather knows everything," Zakkai replied before Shade could speak. "I'm guessing your father does, too. But I find it fascinating that they kept you in the dark. Did they do the same for your twin?"

"Kai," Aflora interjected, her tone quiet yet stern. She still had her head against my chest, but her focus was on the Quandary Blood.

His silver-blue eyes went to her, and his features softened marginally. "I know, little star." He looked at Shade. "Does Lucifer want to meet me now or after we arrive?"

"He didn't say," Shade said before I could react to the infamous name of the Hell Fae King. "So I believe we have safe passage to the paradigm, at least until he decides otherwise."

"We're going to the Hell Fae realm?" It came out as a question, but I meant it as more of a statement. Because that was the only explanation for what they were saying. "The other Midnight Fae Academy is hidden… in the Hell Fae realm?"

Zakkai and Shade both looked at me with expressions that said, *Obviously*. But only Zakkai actually said the word out loud.

"How long has this paradigm existed?" I wondered out loud.

"Zenaida arranged it with Lucifer about seven hundred years ago, right?" Zakkai casually asked the question, like this wasn't a big reveal or life-altering information.

"Roughly," Shade replied.

"That's where you disappear to," Zeph said. "You shadow off to the other Academy."

Shade lifted a shoulder. "On occasion. But not for classes."

"And my grandfather knew." The words came out slowly, my mind failing to believe them even as I voiced them.

"Yes. My grandmother lives nearby." His icy eyes went to Aflora. "It's where Aflora's meadow is, too."

"In the Hell Fae realm?" she whispered, her head leaving my chest so she could look at the Death Blood. "That's where the paradigms are for the Quandary Bloods who prefer reformation over retribution?"

Shade dipped his chin. "Yes. Lucifer already gave you entry as a marked abomination. As you're probably aware, he has a soft spot for them." His gaze lifted to mine. "Which is how I negotiated your entry as well. Zeph was the primary issue."

"Well, in that case, I refuse my meeting with Lucifer and Zeph can stay here," Zakkai replied.

Aflora bristled in my arms, her attention shifting from Shade to the Quandary Blood. "*Kai.*"

"I'm joking, little star."

"Hilarious," Zeph deadpanned. "Can we go now? The defenses are beginning to fail again."

Aflora nodded. "Yes, I feel them crumbling."

"Shade?" Zakkai prompted.

"Already working on it." The Death Blood's voice sounded strained, his eyes closing on a grimace.

Frowning, I locked into my link with him and noted his waning energy reserves. *You need more power.*

He grunted in reply, our mental connection firmly intact even at the first-level mate-bonding.

Take some vitality from me, I told him.

You're not the one I need to tap into, he replied, shutting me out with a click of a door.

I scowled. "Don't be a stubborn dolt," I told him out loud since I couldn't voice it in his mind. I didn't know how he'd blocked me out, but it was a trick I wanted to learn.

"Fuck off, Kols," he gritted out.

"Shade," Aflora said, slipping away from me to reach for him. "What do you need?"

"Power," I answered for him. "His reserves are depleted from whatever he's been doing for the paradigm."

"I'm fine," he snapped.

"You're not fucking fine. You're on the verge of passing out." This whole solitary operation needed to stop. We were a unit now—*all of us*—and it was time we all accepted it. "Let us help you, Shade. We're your mates."

"He's right," Zakkai said, surprising me. "You're hurting all of us by saying you're fine when you're not. Do you need Aflora's blood?" He studied the other man. "Yeah, that's what you need. Not much, just enough to push forward." He nodded to Aflora. "Don't let him refuse."

She grabbed Shade before he could even try to argue, her lips finding his on a demanding kiss. A hint of metallic blood tinted the air, suggesting she'd bitten her tongue prior to embracing him. His responding groan confirmed it, his arm circling her waist as he indulged in the essence she fed him. Zeph's arm came around my upper body in a partial hug, his chest meeting my back. I relaxed into his familiar embrace as Zakkai moved forward.

A black cloak whirled around us all half a beat later as Shade engaged his ability to shadow.

My stomach rolled with the sensation of moving through space and time beneath his enchantment.

Then goose bumps prickled my arms as we landed on a dusted path of embers and charcoal fibers.

Hell Fae realm, I thought, wincing at the heat blazing around us. My grandfather certainly wouldn't track us here, not with the blistering magic and underlying cruelty in the air. He also wouldn't be welcome.

However, it was rather fascinating that Lucifer had allowed Zen to build a paradigm here.

Hell Fae weren't known for their kindness. She'd either

traded him something extremely valuable, or they had some sort of unique arrangement.

Quandary Bloods were extremely powerful. The Hell Fae King would find that useful.

Shade released Aflora's mouth as we all materialized, a sigh of content coming from his lips. The familiars appeared shortly after, his spell having captured them as well. Or perhaps they'd followed on instinct. Familiar magic was unique in how they could appear and vanish at will.

"The entrance is just over there." Shade gestured with his chin toward an obsidian arch. "A set of gates will exist on the other side. They'll remind you of the other Academy, but once you enter, you'll immediately sense the difference. All the excommunicated Midnight Fae—at least the ones who chose not to follow Laki—and creatures reside in there. It's sacred and deadly and very well protected. So any ill will won't be taken lightly."

"You act as though we plan to burn it down," Zakkai drawled. "I've visited your grandmother before, Shade. Just recently, if you recall."

"My warning wasn't for you," Shade replied, his gaze finding mine and Zeph's. "Don't overreact. With everything going on, we can't afford to be ousted, because there is literally nowhere else for us to go. The Midnight Fae are searching for us in droves right now, furious over Aflora's ascension."

I frowned. "They already know?"

Shade's expression took on a sardonic twist. "Yeah. Constantine told them all that she stole the throne and she's a power-hungry fae who is out of control. He's notified the other fae as well."

"How do you know all that?" Zeph demanded, suspicion underlying his tone. He still had his arm around my upper body, his tension palpable at my back.

"Because my grandmother told me," Shade bit back. "We've entered the proverbial endgame now, so I have no more tricks up my sleeve. I'm telling you everything I learn as I learn it. But I just spent several hours trying to return to you, so forgive me for the delay."

"Thank you for being forthright," I interjected before Zeph could speak. I felt his ire and annoyance boiling through his thoughts, and I didn't want to instigate any more fighting. We needed to work as a unit, and if that meant leading by example, I would. "Do we know how the Elemental Fae are reacting to the news?"

Shade's lips curled down, then he gave a subtle shake of his head.

"They'll excommunicate me," Aflora said softly. "Especially after what Elana did to them."

I hated to agree with that statement, but knowing Exos and Cyrus as well as I did, I found myself nodding. "They'll fear what they don't know."

"Which is why I need to revert the ascension," she pressed. "I can't be an Earth Royal and queen to the Midnight Fae kingdom. All of the fae realms will hunt me and try to kill me."

"They're going to do that anyway," Zakkai inserted. "Which means we need you to be the most powerful being to ever exist so you can protect yourself."

I nodded. "Yes."

"No," Aflora replied. "I don't want all this power."

"Which is why you're the perfect fae to embrace it," I argued. "You won't use it for nefarious purposes. You'll provoke change."

"Much-needed change," Zeph echoed.

"Precisely," I murmured.

Aflora sighed and shook her head. "Let's just… go inside.

And then we can keep talking about it. I could really go for a sandwich."

"Shroom loaf?" Zeph offered. "Mustard berries?"

"Mouseberries," she corrected with a smile.

"Mussleberries," he said softly, a grin in his tone. "Of course. Coming right up."

Aflora rolled her eyes, but some of the tension in her stance melted at the playfulness of his words. "Spritemead, too. And a dragon steak."

"Someone's hungry. Did we not feed you properly last night?" He released me with a kiss to my neck, then walked around me to press his lips to her cheek. "Because I seem to recall feeding you quite well."

Her cheeks turned a beautiful pink shade as she tried to glare up at him. "*Zeph.*"

The Warrior Blood brushed his mouth over hers, his palm wrapping around the back of her neck. "Come on, pixie flower. Let's go explore this new Academy. Then I'll ensure you're *properly* fed. Again."

She swallowed. "Then I want a salad patty."

"I'll give you everything and anything you want, Aflora," he replied softly, his forehead resting against hers for a brief moment. "Including *mouseberries.*"

Her expression brightened. "Yes, please."

"I thought he was a Guardian turned headmaster," Zakkai said conversationally. "Is he a chef, too?"

"He's good with a wand," Shade explained.

"Ah. The food spells make up for other weaker areas." Zakkai nodded. "I understand."

Zeph ignored him.

Aflora just shook her head.

Shade smirked.

And I started taking mental bets on how long Zakkai and Zeph would last in a room together before one of them tried to kill the other. Both men were alphas to their cores, neither inclined to bend.

I'd have to keep an eye on them.

Especially when alone with Aflora.

She might not survive a duel between them.

A concern for later, as we had much more pressing items to deal with—such as the issue with my grandfather telling all of fae kind that Aflora had manipulated her own ascension. Given the trial requirements, this would be a problem. Because one of those levels required her to gain approval from Midnight Fae kind.

And that wasn't likely to happen if they all believed her to be a power-hungry abomination with the ability to ascend illegally.

I rubbed a hand over my face, exhausted just thinking about it.

Hopefully, venturing into the Hell Fae realm would give us a little more time to prepare. Or a lot more time. I'd been gifted twenty-plus years to ready myself for the trials.

Aflora… had had all of a few minutes to accept it.

No wonder she wanted to revert the ascension.

Shade stopped by the obsidian arch and pressed his hand to the right side of it to pull up a keypad. Then he demonstrated how to enter by giving us the codes to activate the swirl of power beneath the arch and the subsequent passcode meant to prove our allowance to proceed through the enchantment.

It felt like a show of faith from him—a way of confirming that we'd finally breached his inner circle.

About fucking time, I heard Zeph think.

I snorted in agreement.

While I understood Shade's penchant for secrets all these months, it was nice to finally be on the other side.

However, as we stepped through the gate onto the

Academy grounds, I realized there was a myriad of secrets yet to be revealed. Because holy fuck, the exterior resembled Midnight Fae Academy.

The stone walls were all covered in hissing snake-vines. A pair of gargoyles stood by the gates, their swords already drawn.

My brow furrowed. "You said we were welcome."

"We are," Shade replied, confusion evident in his tone as the snake-vines began to writhe angrily.

A series of charcoal crows cawed in fury above.

Burning thwomps shot fire into the sky.

Gargoyles inside all took up arms, rushing the gates.

Stonepeckers snarled.

A phoenix landed a few feet away to expand his feathers in a furious show of color.

Fire gnats began to swarm.

And a sinking sensation churned in my stomach.

"Shit," I breathed, locking gazes with Zeph. His expression told me he'd figured it out as well.

"What?" Aflora demanded. "What's happening?"

"It's your next ascension trial." With Constantine running the show, he hadn't bothered to give her a break. And of course he chose to engage this one next. "You remember how I told you all Midnight Fae creatures were mine to command?" I asked softly, stepping up beside her.

"Yes," she whispered, her fear palpable.

"Well, you're the incoming monarch now. The second ascension is about taming the Midnight Fae creatures to your will. Show them you're their queen and they'll kneel at your feet."

Fail... and they'll eat you alive.

YOU AND I are going to have a very serious discussion about these trials and what to expect, I snapped at Kols through our mental link. *Assuming I survive.*

You will, he replied immediately. *I'll ensure it.*

Those snake-vines say otherwise. I'd never been a fan of the hissing, writhing vines that surrounded Midnight Fae Academy. And they'd never been a fan of me.

But Kols had always commanded them before, which meant they'd mostly left me alone.

The way they were circling and acting now told me that would not be the case today.

Tell me what to do, I thought at Kols. *Quickly.*

You need to win them over by proving you're their superior. I recommend picking the biggest and baddest of the creatures to tame first. Some of the smaller, less volatile ones will bow on instinct.

I took in all the beings surrounding us—including the fiery birds soaring above. They were smaller than the phoenix but still deadly in appearance. Mostly because their feathers were flames, not soft bristles.

"Clove," I whispered, calling my falcon to my shoulder.

She landed with a ruffle of wings, her beady black gaze on the sky and the approaching creatures.

A dome of magic appeared from Zeph in the next instant, his defensive skill manifesting just as two of the fiery birds dove toward us.

They hit the green-glowing shield with a sizzling spark that reverberated through the air, their agonizing cries splintering my heart.

Death isn't necessary, I thought to myself. *But death is the Midnight Fae way.*

Did that mean the creatures would only understand if I reacted violently?

There had to be another way, a more peaceful manner to tame them. To prove my worth. To be their queen. It didn't matter that I wanted to undo the ascension later. I needed to master them now, to survive this trial, then find a way to fix everything.

However, I refused to do it through dark methods.

Zeph's shield zapped another approaching creature, making me wince.

That's not the way.

Two more fell from the sky, their beautiful lights fizzling out as the birds perished from whatever enchantment he'd woven. I understood that he was just trying to protect us, that all Midnight Fae had been taught to fight savagery with responding barbarity, but Earth Fae believed in *life*. We desired light and sunshine and fresh air and flourishing flowers and happy animals.

I knelt, my fingers digging into the dark rocks of the path, my eyes falling closed as I sought out the plants and trees around me.

The burning thwomps.

The black flowers.

The charcoal blades.

All the foreign Midnight Fae *life*, and showed them the source inside me. Not the dark one, but the one filled with sunshine and elements—my connection to *earth*. Then I manipulated their strength and bolstered their vitality, renewing their purpose and providing enhanced growth.

Roots settled deeper. The charcoal blades stood a little taller. The flowers bloomed.

Around them, the fire gnats buzzed in curiosity, temporarily distracted by the thriving plant life.

My power stretched and grew to the snake-vines, the organism more plant than reptile. They resisted me at first, displeased by my manipulation. But a few gentle strokes of vivacity had them purring instead of hissing, their vines thickening to a more robust shape that slithered with a strength resembling the rocks behind them.

Which was what I stroked next—the gargoyles.

They were made of stone, beings of the earth, and I surrounded them with my element, marrying the darkness to the light and providing them with a freshness and vigor unlike any they'd ever felt before. I felt their confusion and surprise, two emotions that bled into respect and adoration.

It all happened so fast, so naturally, so *kindly*, that the other creatures began to swarm in curiosity rather than anger. They'd expected retaliation—a fight. But I showed them affection instead. I introduced them to the Elemental

Fae way of existence while also proving my dominance by being the one in charge of their restoration.

You're all mine to groom, I was telling them. *Mine to strengthen. Mine to empower.*

What wasn't said—what they all *knew*—was that they were also mine to destroy.

Yet deep down they could sense my unwillingness to hurt them.

Which I proved by pushing life to the fiery birds that had fallen, demanding their wings flap once again.

That came from the dark source, the ability to resurrect and revive life a Death Blood trait that I naturally understood with a spell from Shade's mind. Or maybe it came from Zakkai. All my mates were so much a part of me that I could pick and choose enchantments at will, my Quandary Blood connection allowing me to write and rewrite incantations without much thought.

So perhaps it had been a combination of effort, coming from Shade and Zakkai both.

Regardless, it worked, the firebirds flapping their glowing wings as they took off for the sky once more. Zeph had dropped his shield, ensuring that the beings weren't harmed again. The other creature had been a stonepecker—the rare birdlike rodent known for absorbing and dismantling spells.

He took my enchantment now to bring himself back to full health, then scurried off to hide among the snake-vines.

The phoenix was last, the large bird standing so tall that I looked directly into his multicolored eyes as I slowly returned to my feet. He cocked his head, intrigue flourishing in his intelligent gaze.

We didn't speak so much as communicate with our spirits, mine brushing his in astute praise of his beauty and prestige.

He responded by fluttering his stunning plumes, showing

off in a masculine way that reminded me a bit of my mates. *I bet you do that for all the pretty girls, hmm?* I thought at him.

He preened in response, strutting along the ground and showing off his long, elegant stride.

Yeah, you know you're pretty, I told him, lifting my hand. He stepped forward without fear, his assuredness born of being a profound predator known for dismantling his prey.

His feathery head met my palm, his stunning plumes soft and welcoming beneath my fingers. "Very beautiful," I praised.

Clove clicked on my shoulder in agreement.

The phoenix bowed in response, his beak brushing my stomach before he took a step back.

"Cocky fucking bird," I heard Zeph mutter to Kols.

"If you're envious of a phoenix, then I suspect you and I are going to have issues later," Zakkai drawled.

Zeph snorted in response.

Shade smothered a chuckle.

I merely smiled, tilting my head in a bow back to the phoenix to show equal appreciation. He released a loud caw in response, drawing the attention of several creatures as he expanded his wings to take off into the sky.

A series of chitters followed, the charcoal crows following in his breezy wake.

And then an echo of stones moving followed.

I turned to see the gargoyles stepping through the gates with their weapons drawn in a battle stance. I frowned, confused for a moment until they all took a saluted position along the path, their arms rising high to create a wall of stone and sharp swords, all their edges pointed directly up to the sky.

"How long did it take you to pass that trial?" Zeph asked conversationally. "A week?"

"Nine days," Kols replied. "Nine very long fucking days."

"Hmm." Zeph sounded amused.

"She had the earth advantage," Kols said, his tone light and his expression full of pride. "Using life to court life." He nodded in approval. "Very effective, princess."

Shade grinned. "Constantine is going to be pissed." He glanced at Zakkai. "I hope Tadmir records his reaction."

Zakkai didn't seem to share his amusement, his expression serious as he analyzed the gargoyles and surrounding creatures. "We should go inside while we can. If Constantine realizes she passed this quickly, he'll just engage the next trial."

"Which is?" I prompted.

"A topic for once we're through those gates," Zakkai replied, pointing at the entry. "After you, my queen."

My grandmother stood just inside the gates with a platter of cookies, her smile welcoming and knowing.

Because she'd probably foreseen that trial outside the gates.

A heads-up would have been appreciated, but that wasn't her way. Fortune Fae never wanted to alter fate, just project potential paths. And I'd made it my life's work to alter my own—hence Kols standing beside me.

My grandmother cast a cursory glance over him, her blue eyes taking on an appreciative gleam as she studied his hair.

I arched a brow, daring her to say something.
She didn't.
Instead, she held out the treats for everyone to enjoy

while formally introducing herself to Zeph and Kols. I didn't partake in the cookies, because I knew what they meant—more bad news.

"Take them on a tour," she advised. "Then come see me afterward."

I dipped my chin in agreement, knowing she meant for me to visit her, not the others. But a glance at Zakkai told me he saw right through the act and he would be attending that meeting with me.

I'd hidden a lot from him over the years. However, he always seemed to know, as though he could remember the timelines just like I could. I knew he couldn't actually recall them because that was impossible—his memory had been altered with all the others.

Although, his Quandary Blood ability probably allowed him to sense those alternate timelines. Or perhaps the manipulation of the power was what he felt.

Regardless, he'd suspected my interference and questionable allegiances our entire relationship. Which meant he would either follow me to the meeting or attend at my side.

The latter was preferred, especially as we both were tied to Aflora now.

She walked along beside me as I provided the tour my grandmother suggested. "It's similar to the other Academy, at least in terms of architecture. But this campus doesn't have a Death Blood dorm or building, or an Elite Blood, or anything categorized. All the classes are combined because the majority of the fae are Quandary Bloods. However, there are a few from every type. There are also a handful of other fae, like Hell Fae, who attend. It's part of Lucifer's arrangement with my grandmother."

Among other things.

I didn't understand everything they'd worked out, as their

deal predated my existence by several centuries, but I'd gathered educational opportunities had been involved.

"These are the dorms," I said, gesturing to a series of gothic-style buildings. They were reminiscent of the other Academy grounds, framed with darkness and a high moon, but they weren't exclusive to a single Midnight Fae type. And they didn't require spells for entry.

Gargoyles moved around more here, walking or flying to different locations, rather than residing behind doors.

They bowed to Aflora as she passed, their reverence palpable. But she was too busy studying the campus to notice.

"You don't have charcoal blades," she noted, gazing out over an obsidian courtyard of sharp rocks and dangerous grooves.

I caught her elbow as she bent to touch the ground. "Don't."

She frowned at me, then gasped as a swirl of fire erupted from the center into a geyser of furious flames. "Mother Earth…"

A few passing fae tossed sparks into the pit, their cerulean embers dancing with the red and yellow flickers. Then it all whirled together into a tornado of heat and sucked the air around it right back down into the hole, disappearing.

"It's like… like a burning thwomp?" she guessed.

"Only worse," I replied. "There are certain aspects of the Hell Fae realm that couldn't be erased, so my grandmother altered the paradigm to accept the nuances."

"That's fascinating." Kols had gone to his haunches on the cobblestone path, his burnt-gold gaze on the black rocks. "I can feel the merging of magic."

I nodded. "Yeah, certain areas of the paradigm are stronger than others."

"The meadow?" Aflora wondered.

"Is in a neutral area. Not all of the Hell Fae realm is fire and heat. It's… sporadic." And why other fae refused to visit.

Well, that and the Hell Fae didn't take kindly to visitors. They were all shunned abominations, with Constantine Nacht being enemy number one among them.

"Where will we be staying?" Zeph asked, his arms folded over his chest as he analyzed the field with a speculative expression.

"In one of the dorms near the back of the campus grounds," I told him.

Aflora appeared disappointed. "Not in your cabin?"

"Our cabin," I corrected her with a squeeze of her hand. "And no. It's too far from the Academy grounds. We need room to practice and learn, and we can't do that in our meadow. These buildings are meant for training and mastering magic. So it's best for us to stay here."

"Oh." Her lips pinched to the side, then she slowly tilted her head in agreement.

I urged us along, showing them a few of the academic areas and recommended enclosures for practicing offensive and defensive arts. Zakkai and Zeph took interest in those, their calculative natures taking over. Kols just seemed to take it all in stride, observing all the Midnight Fae we passed and studying the general makeup of the paradigm.

It was all very real—as paradigms should be—but the underlying presence of Hell Fae lurked in the area around campus. Mostly because of the protection charms. Since some of Lucifer's most powerful fae attended the Academy, he helped bolster the natural defenses around us.

The village where my grandmother resided didn't have the same feel because it was on neutral ground.

I used a spell to bring up a map for Aflora, explaining where the different sections of the paradigm resided and how each one interacted with the Hell Fae realm. She gaped at it, fascinated.

Zeph appeared to be memorizing it.

Zakkai merely gave an appreciative grin. "Zenaida's clever." He admired the sky and the buildings, his approval evident. "I never considered mingling elements the way she has. It bolsters the structure while helping it blend."

"Going to pass notes to your dad?" I wondered out loud.

Zakkai snorted. "I doubt he'll want to talk to me anytime soon. I saved a Nacht, after all."

True. It didn't matter that Kols was innocent in the war; his grandfather had started it. And the Quandary Blood wanted the Nacht line exterminated.

"Am I still considered a Nacht?" Kols called a cloud of magic to his hand, the colors a swirling mix of purple, red, cerulean, and green. "I don't really feel like an Elite Blood anymore." The flames extinguished in a flip of his palm, his burnt-bronze gaze flickering with curiosity and a hint of something else. Not sadness—I felt his comfort with being part of our mate-circle thriving via our connection. Yet there was a sense of loss in him.

For Tray, I realized.

Yes, Kols replied, our link open and allowing him freedom in my thoughts. I considered pushing him out like I had earlier but didn't. Instinct told me he needed the bonds right now. Because the one he'd established at birth was suffering.

He couldn't exactly feel Tray, but their souls were joined in a unique manner—one that would never truly be severed. "You're still a Nacht," I said. "But a good one. Like Tray."

Kols blinked at me.

However, it was Zeph who spoke. "Was that a compliment?" Shock underlined his words. "Like an honest-to-fae compliment?"

"I think so," Kols replied, humor in his tone.

"How odd." Zeph's green eyes found mine, a grin lurking in their depths. Probably a joke at my own expense. Or maybe I'd pleased him. It was hard to say with the Warrior Blood.

"Shade has many layers," Aflora said, dissolving my map spell as she stepped through it to wrap her arms around me. I kissed the top of her head, her embrace immediately putting me at ease.

Thank you, little rose, I whispered.

She responded with a rumble in her stomach, her hunger evident.

Zeph smirked. "Someone wants some mustard berries."

Aflora shook her head against me, mumbling the appropriate term back to him like she always did.

The Warrior Blood's gaze sparkled with delight, loving their banter.

Zakkai ignored them all, his focus on me, his eyes telling me that he was impatient to meet with my grandmother. He'd wanted a full briefing on security and everything else that went with the paradigm, too.

"The dorm we're staying in is just over there," I said, gesturing with my chin over Aflora's head.

The others followed as I led the way, Aflora's hand in mine once more. A week ago, this would have felt surreal—like a dream. Seven timelines had ended in destruction and near death.

And number eight had led to this.

To a union between five Midnight Fae.

I knew better than to rejoice in the victory. We were nowhere near done. Focusing on unity became all the more imperative with Constantine engaging us in this new dangerous game.

Zakkai and Zeph were the two who posed the biggest threat.

Two alpha males vying for dominance.

Aflora was the key to keeping them in line, and I wasn't entirely convinced she had Zakkai under control.

He moved behind me with silent steps, his presence a threat and a comfort. Power radiated off him, his connection to the source rivaling Aflora's ascension.

I moved up the stone steps to the double doors of the dorm where two gargoyles waited, their eyes cast down in a sign of respect.

A third stood just inside with Kols's crow perched on his stone head. "Sir Kristoff," I greeted with false cheer. The little creature loathed me for all my dates with time. He didn't know all the details but possessed certain memories of Kyros and me twisting fate on numerous occasions.

"Death Blood," he muttered. Then he inclined his head. "Mistress Aflora."

She paused midstep, her blue eyes falling to the short stone being. His head didn't even reach her knees. "Mistress Aflora?" she repeated.

Kols moved to her other side. "You're the ascending royal, sweetheart," he explained against her ear. "And you passed your second trial. The creatures all respond to you now."

"I transferred your box to your new quarters, Master Kolstov," the gargoyle informed him after standing up straight. "Nothing is remiss."

"Good to know your loyalty is unwavering," Kols replied, grinning.

"I've never liked Constantine," Sir Kristoff muttered. His tone displayed a hint of emotion—a rare trait for a gargoyle. "Power-hungry and cruel."

He stomped off toward the stairs, taking over the job of host. My grandmother had only told me we would be staying somewhere in this building, mentioning something about the gardens behind it. Fortunately, it seemed Sir Kristoff knew where to take us.

"Do all Midnight Fae creatures know how to find this paradigm?" Aflora asked as we trailed after the gargoyle.

"They know how to locate Midnight Fae," I replied, my hand releasing hers and going to her lower back as I moved upward beside her.

"Does that mean they're all allowed here?" Her mind added a follow-up inquiry soon after, telling me why she'd voiced the first question. *If Kristoff can enter, is it possible for Constantine to send in a less loyal gargoyle or something worse?* she asked herself.

"No," I answered, addressing both of her queries. "There are numerous protective spells and layers that will prevent anyone and anything with ill intentions from crossing the boundary into the paradigm."

"Can't they just use a stonepecker? Like that day on campus?" she pressed.

"Hell Fae wards are not something stonepeckers can absorb and regurgitate," I assured her. "Which means it wouldn't even be able to reach the paradigm boundary to try to learn the spells."

"Because the ill-intentioned creature would be destroyed upon entering Lucifer's gates," Zakkai added from right behind us. "Extremely useful setup, and also why your grandmother afforded us that meeting the other week. She knew I had good intentions."

I lifted a shoulder. "Caution is what keeps her alive."

"It's more than caution, Shadow. Zenaida's brilliant." The conviction in his tone told me he meant the praise in his words.

I nodded in agreement and continued up until the stairs stopped, indicating our floor. It was nearly impossible to know what level we were on because the steps had just continued up and up and up until they ended on a floor with a single door.

"Concealment charms," Zakkai mused. "As I said, brilliant." He stepped up behind Aflora, his hands finding her hips and trapping my palm between his abdomen and her lower back. "Can you sense the magic, little star? All the secret wires pulsing through the floors and hiding all the rooms except the one intended to be ours?"

She leaned into my side and back into him, allowing us to hold her as she considered the enchantments of the building. "It's… intense."

"It's beautiful," Zakkai whispered. "Like you." He kissed her neck, then relaxed his chin on her shoulder. "But can you see through it? To the electrical energy beneath?"

"I sense it," she admitted. "But I don't understand it."

"Close your eyes," he breathed, his arms slipping around her middle while my palm remained between them. It created an intimate connection between the three of us, Zakkai seeming unbothered by the fact that I stayed close while he engaged their mental link to coach her through the magical lesson.

Her thick black eyelashes splayed across her cheekbones as she did as he'd instructed, her lips parting at whatever he unleashed inside her.

Kols and Zeph shared a look while Sir Kristoff stood stationary in the hallway.

Static hummed through the air as Zakkai and Aflora spoke mentally to one another, and after several minutes of intense silence, Aflora opened her eyes once more.

"What floor are we on, little star?" Zakkai said.

"The fourth one. Room seven."

"Well done," he praised, kissing her neck again. "Very well done." He released her then, his focus falling to the gargoyle. "Continue."

Sir Kristoff gave a subtle bow, acknowledging Zakkai as superior because of his Source Architect role. Or maybe because he was Aflora's mate. Regardless, the gargoyle led us to our room and through the door into a living area surrounded by windows.

My eyebrows lifted at the courtyard beyond it. "Fourth floor?"

"Another impressive illusion," Zakkai said. "That's a roof garden above one of the other rooms."

"Filled with real plants." Aflora practically ran forward, her intrigue clearly replacing her need to eat because she ran right past the kitchen and open dining area to the sliding doors at the side. Zakkai sent a spell ahead of her to open the glass doors, allowing her to dart straight into the garden of flowers and trees.

The four of us chuckled at her excitement, then Zeph wandered after her and leaned against the doorway. "Are you going to strip like last time, pixie flower?"

That piqued Zakkai's interest. "She stripped in a garden?"

"In Central Park." Zeph didn't take his eyes off her while he spoke. "The humans didn't approve."

Aflora muttered something back about only removing her sweater last time before collapsing onto a pile of green grass beneath a tree. "Oh, so pretty!"

My lips twitched at her amusement. Then I glanced up at the high moon. This part of the paradigm never saw the sun, so it was hard to determine the time. However, I suspected my grandmother expected me any minute now.

I glanced around the open living area, spotted a hallway to the side, and wandered down it by four different bedroom doors—all of them open. The biggest bedroom was at the end of the hall, where I found a walk-in closet filled with clothes. Most of them were feminine and appeared to be

Aflora's size. There was also a dresser inside with four wands on top.

Because Aflora still didn't have her own.

Odd that the dark source hadn't gifted her one yet.

With a shake of my head, I grabbed my own and turned to find Zakkai behind me, expectant. "Do you want your wand?" I asked him.

"No. Leave it for Aflora."

A good answer, I decided. He followed me back into the living area, where Zeph and Kols were both watching Aflora in her element. She'd completely lost herself to her Earth Fae nature. Roots were dancing along the ground as she renewed the soil with life, causing the trees to elongate and the flowers to blossom.

"I need to go meet with my grandmother before she sends for me," I told them. "Can you make sure Aflora remembers to eat something?" Because I suspected she had forgotten all about her hunger now.

Zeph nodded without looking at me.

Zakkai didn't bother commenting, just turned to lead the way.

Because we both knew he was going with me, and he didn't feel the need to mention it to the others.

Rather than comment, I followed him out and ensured that my connection to Aflora remained wide open. It was my way of telling her there would be no more secrets.

Whatever my grandmother said, I'd share.

Because Aflora and I were finally on a true path—as fully bonded mates.

No more alternate timelines. No more Paradox Fae. Just a single way forward, with all four of us by her side.

Hurry back, she whispered to me, acknowledging that I'd left.

I won't be far, I promised.

I know, she replied. *Just like I know how to find you now.* She breathed a spell into my mind, telling me she'd not only learned how to use my shadowing ability, but she'd also memorized it.

Good, I murmured. *Eat something.*

Mmm, she hummed, her mind purring with life and earth once more.

I laughed under my breath as we exited the building. "When this is all over, we need to find a place with a real garden for Aflora."

"So we can watch her frolic in the nude?" Zakkai asked.

My lips twitched. "Among other things."

Many other things.

WARMTH. Beauty. Passion.

I reveled in it, rolling around in the grass and soaking up all the magic. "There are so many types of earth," I marveled out loud, speaking to no one in particular. "So much life!"

There were plants from all the fae realms, including some from my own. And the human world, too.

"These are tulips," I said, encouraging one to blossom. "So very different from the orchid." Which was beautiful and white but required much more attention than the tulip.

I returned to the tree again, leaning against the trunk and sighing happily. "Such a mighty oak you are," I praised. "Strong and big, with a stunning girth."

"Is that a euphemism?" Zeph asked as he approached with a plate in his hand. "Should I be jealous?"

I giggled, high on life and drunk on the earthy vitality surrounding me.

Zeph's lips curled as he sat across from me. Kols trailed behind him with another plate and a large mug.

"Spritemead." The word escaped through my lips on a prayer, my mouth suddenly parched. I reached for the frosty glass, practically panting with need.

"That look is giving me so many ideas," Kols said as he lowered the mug for me.

I grabbed it and took a big sip, my heart rejoicing at the splendid flavor. *Yes, yes.*

"Was she like this in Central Park?" Kols inquired as he sat down beside Zeph.

"Yeah, only topless as well," Zeph replied.

"No wonder you fucked her up against a tree." Kols set the plate down on the grass, the salad patty and dragon steak making me squeal in excitement. I handed him back the spritemead and dove right into the feast.

No silverware required.

Just hands.

And food. Delicious, amazing food.

Zeph's plate cradled a loaf stuffed with mouseberries. A red pudding rested beside it, causing my eyebrow to inch upward. "What's that?" I asked around a mouthful of salad patty. I'd forgotten all about my hunger, and now it returned with a vengeance.

"Sweet paste," he replied.

That certainly wasn't something from the Elemental Fae world. "What's in it?"

"Blood." No hesitation. No mincing words. Just a single statement that had my stomach churning. "You need it, pixie flower."

I shook my head, denying him. Because, no, I did not need blood right now. Particularly, not with my food. *Yuck.* Drinking from my mates was one thing. Imbibing with my meals was entirely another.

"You're ascending as a Midnight Fae," Kols said gently. "Blood is how we connect to the dark source, Aflora."

I gagged, the salad patty suddenly losing all flavor in my mouth.

My head moved back and forth in denial. *No.*

"Hmm, I think she needs a little coaxing, Kols."

"I think so, too," the Elite Blood agreed. "She had no problem with blood last night."

"No, she definitely didn't."

"So maybe we need to engage in something similar to inspire her?" Kols suggested, setting the mug of spritemead down in the grass.

"It's like you can read my mind," Zeph drawled, his finger swiping through the red paste. I half expected him to bring it to my lips, but he lifted his hand to Kols's mouth instead.

And proceeded to paint the texture along his lower lip, his gaze on me the whole time.

Then he slowly leaned sideways, his attention shifting to the other man, and licked the paste from Kols's lip before dipping his tongue inside to kiss him thoroughly.

My Elite Blood mate groaned in approval, his eyes falling closed as he lost himself in Zeph's embrace, the two of them indulging in each other as much as the taste of the food.

Fire licked through my veins at the sight of them, my stomach tightening in expectation.

Then Kols took some of the paste with his own finger and drew a line down Zeph's neck that he followed with his mouth, licking his skin clean in the process.

If you were shirtless, I would do this to your breasts, Kols whispered into my mind. *Then I'd bite your rosy nipple and sink my teeth into your flesh to really taste you.*

My thighs clenched in response.

Zeph created a zigzag pattern along Kols's throat and used his opposite hand to begin unfastening my Elite Blood mate's shirt. His mouth followed the path down, the buttons releasing ahead of his tongue until he reached the other man's navel.

"Fuck," Kols breathed, falling to the grass.

"So easy," Zeph murmured, skimming his teeth along Kols's lower abdomen to his hip. "Do you think Aflora would help me lick your cock clean if I decorated it with sweetness?"

Kols groaned, his eyes falling closed. "Don't make promises you won't keep."

"I would never do that," Zeph replied, his palm going to Kols's groin.

"Liar," Kols growled, arching into his Guardian's hand.

Zeph chuckled. Then he popped open the button of Kols's slacks and drew down the zipper.

No boxers.

Just bare skin.

My lips parted, my pulse skipping several beats.

Zeph bent to press a kiss to the growing arousal, then his smoldering green eyes met mine. "What do you want to do, pixie flower? Torture Kols?" He reached for more paste and traced an inviting line down the other man's thickening length. "Or please him?"

He lowered his mouth to demonstrate, eliciting a sensual moan from Kols. Then he created another alluring red trail and invited me with his eyes to join him.

I promise you'll like it, he whispered in my mind. *And I'll reward you for tasting it, too.*

His gaze lowered to the apex between my thighs, his nostrils flaring with enticement.

He meant to reward me by licking me *there*. With the paste.

Dear Fae, I thought, swallowing thickly. *How…devious. And so very Zeph.*

His irises pulsed in response, his expression expectant. He knew I wouldn't decline. Not with an offer like that.

But if I hated the taste, it would certainly spoil the mood.

Only one way to find out. I shivered, taking in Kols's pulsating shaft and the promising gleam in Zeph's green eyes.

Trust me, he murmured to me. *You'll enjoy every minute. And so will he.*

I slid the plates to the side, leaving them near the discarded mug of spritemead. Then I crawled over to Kols.

His pupils dilated as he watched me, his muscles flexing along his torso as he clenched his fists at his sides. "Thank fuck," he said, his tone thick with need.

I lowered my mouth to his abdomen, kissing him just below his belly button. Then I started downward with my tongue, tasting his skin along the way and reveling in his renewed life. A hint of sweetness taunted my nose as I inched closer to his groin, the paste boasting a subtle aroma that reminded me of hot cocoa—a decadent drink Elemental Fae enjoyed making with cinnamon and floral berry infusions.

Blood wasn't a staple in my diet.

But I'd tasted it from my mates before.

And it hadn't been horrible.

Actually, it'd been rather erotic.

Swallowing, I moved the final few centimeters to Kols's pulsing erection and tentatively licked the tip.

He cursed in response, his body strung tight from what

probably felt like the ultimate tease. "Aflora," he murmured, his fingers brushing my jaw.

Zeph caught his wrist and placed his hand by his side once more. "No touching."

"I fucking hate you." It came out on a growl, Kols's desire a hot sensation against my mouth.

"You'll love me again in a second," Zeph promised.

Rather than torment my mate more, I closed my mouth around his head and started a path downward. His hiss encouraged me to go deeper, the food painting his skin an intriguing flavor that had me groaning in response.

Because it was good.

No, it was *delicious*.

I took as much of him as my throat would allow, then released him to lower my mouth to the base and finish licking him clean.

Zeph added more paste in the next second, having retrieved the plate once more. I indulged in another taste, and then another, treating Kols like some sort of decadent treat.

His hands were fisted at his sides again, his arousal hard and throbbing in my mouth. Zeph switched focus to Kols's mouth, kissing him deeply while I licked him to completion.

It was erotic.

Hot.

Perfection.

Zeph reached for me, his fingers threading through my hair as he helped guide my pace, his opposite palm against Kols's throat. "Don't come yet, Kolstov."

My Elite Blood mate growled in response, causing Zeph to chuckle darkly. "Sadist," Kols accused.

"Mmm, but you already knew that," Zeph replied, kissing him again.

His control was resolute, his grip unyielding as he

continued to dictate my movements as well as Kols's pending orgasm.

The display had my thighs straining, my insides burning with an intensity that reminded me of the source.

Heat spilled through my veins, lighting me on fire from within, and I realized I was feeling Kols's growing pleasure. He couldn't contain it, the arousal spilling into his bonds as he pushed his need to me and Zeph.

"Cheater," Zeph stated on a low groan.

"Let me come and I'll share that, too." Kols's tone held a promise and a threat in it, his voice deep with yearning.

Zeph hummed in a considering manner, his grip forcing me to take Kols even deeper. His gaze slowly lowered to mine as he remained beside Kols from above. "Are you ready to swallow, pixie flower?"

Yes.

"Out loud," he encouraged, not allowing me to move upward. "Say it around his cock."

"Yes," I managed, the sound slurred and obstructed by Kols's pulsing heat in my mouth.

"Fuck," Kols panted in reply. "*Fuck.*"

"Is that your preference? Instead of her swallowing?" Zeph asked, his attention returning to the Elite Blood.

Kols made a dark noise, his fingers digging into the ground beside us.

Zeph smirked knowingly, then he slowly lifted my head up to the tip and plunged me back down again. A shocked gasp escaped me, the penetration deep and cutting off my airway.

But the responding growl from Kols made it worth it. He shook beneath me, his abdomen clenching as his release shot into the back of my throat.

I swallowed because there was no other option. Not that I desired one. Tasting Kols was like a reward, his essence one

I craved and needed to survive. He lifted one hand from the ground, his knuckles brushing my cheek as he continued to come undone, that solitary beautiful touch a display of gratitude while he came apart beneath me.

My heart warmed in response.

There was so much love and adoration in that graze against my skin.

I love you, he said into my mind. *So fucking much, Aflora.*

I love you, too, I replied, drinking from him both figuratively and literally.

He shot off one more trickle down my throat, then calmed beneath me, his explosion one I felt warming our bond and igniting a fire within me.

But I sensed he gave more to Zeph, using his orgasm as a way to punishingly taunt the other male. The Warrior Blood palmed himself, a growl mingling with a groan as he squeezed his shaft through his trousers. "I'm going to return that favor later," he threatened.

"Good," Kols replied, his tone lazy and sated. "I look forward to it." He went to his elbows, his bronze gaze finding mine. "But first, I believe you owe our mate a reward. Unless you'd like me to do the honors?"

"You can help," Zeph offered, his green irises smoldering with promise. "Lie down, pixie flower. And lift your skirt." He swiped his finger through the paste again, leaving little to the imagination as to what he wanted.

And I wasn't about to refuse.

So I did what he'd asked, lifting my skirt and showing off my lack of underwear.

Both men groaned in response.

Then I spread my legs and they cursed.

Kols moved to my mouth first, his tongue tracing the seam of my lips to demand entry as his palm went to my breast. I moaned against him, arching into his touch while returning his kiss with reckless abandon.

Alive, I thought. *He's alive.*

I knew this, had been part of his resurrection, but the continued reminder of his existence set my soul on fire for him. Because he was mine. In more than one way—*mine*. And I would have been utterly destroyed without him.

I ensured he knew that by opening my mind to his, pushing him my feelings of gratitude and devotion, wordlessly telling him what he meant to me.

He responded with a broadcast of his own emotions, drowning me in his adoration and worship.

Then Zeph parted my folds with his tongue, demanding my focus.

Ohhh…

His finger followed his mouth, then he traced his touch, licking the paste from the intimate heart of me.

Who knew food could be so exciting?

I shivered as he did it again, then Kols's lips trailed down my neck as his fingers deftly unfastened my blouse.

Goose bumps trailed across my skin, my body primed and ready to explode.

But a nibble to my clit told me I didn't have permission yet.

You really are a sadist, I thought at Zeph.

He hummed in agreement, his mouth wicked and skilled and far too knowing against my sex.

Kols added to the fun, painting my breast with the remainder of the paste and doing exactly what he'd vowed to do earlier—decorating my nipple and taking it into his mouth. Then his teeth sank into my flesh as he drew my blood, his tongue licking the wound in his wake.

An inferno blazed through me, knocking out my senses and reducing me to a writhing mess of insane craving.

My two mates reveled in it, drawing me close to climax only to deny me the end result.

Beg, Zeph told me. *Beg for what you need.*

"Please," I whispered. "I… I need to…" I jolted as Kols bit me again, this time on my other breast. "*Oh!*" I was going to die by the touch of my mates. Blow up in a source of madness and sensation. "Please let me come." The words came out in a jumble—or they sounded distant to my ears, anyway—because I was too lost to their mouths and tongues and hands to think through my words.

Zeph made a noise of approval, his teeth sinking into my delicate flesh and eliciting a guttural scream from my throat.

It hurt.

It burned.

It captivated me entirely.

Fae… It was like he'd turned me inside out, drawing the deepest of pleasure from my soul with his teeth, and yanked the blossoming flames from me with a pull of his mouth.

Blood. My blood.

I felt him swallowing in approval, his yearning for me a searing kiss to my senses.

Now, Aflora, he said, giving me the permission I sought and craved. *Come for us.*

I didn't have to think; I just complied, my body trained to his will and listening to him more than me. Stars blinked into my vision, darkness overtaking my senses, as I fell headfirst into a consuming ocean of ecstasy.

Down, down, down, I went.

Drowning.

Blissfully surviving on pleasure alone.

Shaking and combusting and losing myself to my mates.

They owned me. My heart. My soul. My body.

But I owned them in kind, their strength rooted into my spirit and yanking me back to life in my next breath.

Zeph's mouth captured mine. Then Kols. Then Zeph again. Their hands were everywhere, stroking me with undeniable affection and grace.

Water surrounded me in the next second, my mates having taken me to wash off in a shower.

I barely felt the warmth of the droplets, my focus on Zeph and Kols and their exploring fingers and touch.

They did this to me—took away all my worries and concerns and introduced me to a world of sensation and living unlike any other.

Shade's mind brushed mine, his knowing thoughts driving me onward.

Zakkai was there, too, his protective energy allowing me to completely let go and just *be*.

I collapsed into Zeph and Kols, let them bathe me, love me, cherish me, and indulged in everything they had to give.

My mates.

My loves.

My world.

AFLORA SAT at the table in a robe, her dark hair falling in wet waves around her shoulders. She had a satisfied gleam to her features, her cheeks pink from the exhilaration of the shower.

Zeph had taken her from behind while I knelt and worshipped her clit. Then I'd fucked her up against the wall.

She'd taken it all, her mewls of pleasure a residual sound in my head as I twirled pasta around my fork.

Her blue eyes fell to my plate, her forehead scrunching. *Bloody noodles and brown crap.*

I chuckled, recalling our first meal together. "Spaghetti and meatballs," I corrected her before taking a bite.

She grimaced and picked up her version of a sandwich.

Zeph had one on his plate, too. He seemed to be making

a conscious effort to eat Elemental Fae cuisine with her. But I sensed his distaste for the soggy texture when he bit down.

I smirked. Then I took another mouthful of my favored Italian cuisine.

While the foods were similar to those from our first night together, the feelings around the table couldn't be more different. Trust and content floated between us.

And it only strengthened when Shade and Zakkai returned.

Both of them kissed Aflora on top of her head, then rummaged through the fully stocked fridge for something to eat.

They both opted to join me in spaghetti, making Aflora's nose scrunch upward.

Then Zeph distracted her with a plate of dragon steak, and she no longer seemed to care about anything other than the meat in front of her.

I shook my head, amused by her antics.

Food was clearly the way to her heart.

Zeph waved his wand to add a round of mugs to the table, all of them filled with spritemead. Aflora's eyes sparkled with approval. Then she looked at me. "Now would be a good time for that ascension lesson."

My lips twitched. During our first dinner, we'd discussed Midnight Fae order at a high level. And now she wanted to get to the heart of it by reviewing the trials.

"First, I want to know if Shade's grandmother had anything interesting to say," Zeph interjected, his sharp gaze on the Death Blood. "No more secrets, Shadow."

Shade ran his fingers through his thick, dark hair and relaxed into his chair. "I'm not Kols. I don't do orders."

I snorted. "If you think I accept all his demands, then you don't know me at all." In the bedroom, I indulged in a few of Zeph's commands. But only because I regularly enjoyed the reward of appeasing his sadistic side.

"Shade," Aflora interjected, her voice soft yet underlined with authority. "Please."

His expression warmed at her words. "Anything for you, little rose."

Zeph grunted.

I merely grinned and took a sip of the spritemead.

Shade offered a brief rundown of his discussion with his grandmother, focusing on the important bits. Which were mainly surrounding the trials and her urging for all of us to prepare. Advice we didn't really need, but I understood Zen feeling the need to stress the importance of readying ourselves for the trials.

"We have to work as a unit," Shade concluded. "That's the gist of what she was saying." His focus shifted to a silent Zakkai. "Pretty sure that entire lecture was for your benefit."

"I gathered that after the third sentence," Zakkai replied flatly. His silver-blue eyes met mine. "But I think there was an underlying word of caution regarding certain trials, too."

"Respect and unity," I murmured, having inferred that from Shade's summary of what Zen had said.

"Indeed." Zakkai set his fork down. "Those will be the biggest challenges, as Constantine is claiming that the Source Architect redirected the power from you to Aflora. He also has everyone believing that I possessed Malik, which I did not." He looked pointedly at all of us as he uttered that last bit.

"I know you didn't," I said, my instincts telling me that statement was needed. "I've only met my grandfather a handful of times, but it's become quite apparent that he's an excellent strategist." It was a truth I couldn't deny. "But together, we will outmaneuver him." My attention drifted to Aflora beside me. "Which brings us to the ascension trials."

"Yes," she agreed.

"There are seven," I began. "They can come in any order but have historically followed a specific pattern. Although, with my grandfather at the helm, it's possible that pattern will be altered."

I dove into an explanation on how the current monarch typically organized the trials. With the Midnight Fae King being the closest to the dark source, it made sense for him to foster the tests accordingly.

"However, my father has clearly been possessed." A comment that made me grimace. "Which is why I believe my grandfather will lead the trials, particularly as he's the one who forced the ascension onto you."

"Also a fair assessment since he just orchestrated two in one day," Zakkai inserted.

I nodded. "My father would never do that. Nor would he force Aflora to ascend in this manner." My father valued his connection to the dark source and took his mantle seriously. He would never risk it by forcing the power into a non-Midnight Fae. Nor would he ever force another to become an abomination.

No, this had my grandfather written all over it.

And the fact that he was spouting lies about the ascension to all the others only confirmed his orchestration of the events.

"There are seven trials," I continued. "Trust and creatures are the two you've already passed, the first being to test your connections by proving their worth through a trust trial. The second one being to win over all the creatures in the Midnight Fae world."

"And creatures in general," Zakkai interjected. "At least, as Source Architect, I had to win them all over because of the uniqueness of my abilities."

"I only had to win over those who reside in the Midnight Fae realm," I clarified.

"Interesting." Zakkai picked up his fork again to continue eating, telling me with his eyes to keep talking.

"The other trials revolve around acceptance, unity, sacrifice, respect, and the final source ascension. These tests can be delivered through a variety of means. My acceptance trial was the easiest for me because it was about accepting the dark source's power and understanding what it could do. As the son of the current king, I was born understanding and accepting my place. Unity was my fourth trial, which focused on you."

"Because your father wanted you to bring the factions to a unifying decision on her fate," Zakkai translated. "Clever."

"What was yours?" I wondered out loud.

"Uniting the Quandary Bloods for retribution," he replied. "Which, when you consider it, seems like the opposite of unity, given that it divided the Quandary Bloods into two factions."

"You won the respect of both sides through your leadership," Shade said softly. "My grandmother might not agree with the thoughts of retribution, but she's always honored your ascension and rightful place as Source Architect."

Zakkai dipped his chin in acknowledgment. "It's why our two sides have never warred. Something I fear is about to change after what she said regarding my father's displeasure."

Shade's lips pinched to the side. "We'll cross that bridge when it arrives."

"Do you expect him to come here?" I asked, choosing to literally translate Shade's statement rather than allow the cryptic response to hang in the air undefined.

"Yes." Shade's icy eyes met mine. "Yes, I do."

"He'll want to discuss new terms," Zakkai added. "It might serve as Aflora's unity trial."

"My grandfather would never orchestrate that."

"The source may not provide him with a choice," Zakkai pointed out. "Not all trials can be controlled. And I'm also the architect, so I do have some say in how this progresses."

"Fair," I agreed. "Well, I failed my trial by not bringing the fae together." A fact that would forever haunt me, but not nearly as much as almost being killed by my father's hand.

"No, you didn't," Zeph inserted. "You were still in the middle of your trial, but Constantine took over and destroyed your ability to pass."

"He's right." Zakkai twirled his fork around some noodles while Aflora watched in obvious disgust. "Actually, I imagine the dark source would agree with your choice. Particularly as it accepted Aflora's candidacy for queen. You kept her alive so she could ascend. That's a successful outcome, not a failed one."

I hadn't previously considered that point of view, but it was a fair assessment, one I much preferred to my own.

"You may not have unified the Midnight Fae, but when Aflora does, you'll both pass," Zakkai concluded, the assurance in his tone lacking any note of hesitation.

"Okay, but what if I undo the ascension?" Aflora asked.

We all fell silent.

She'd said this a few times, and while it might be possible, I feared the outcome of that decision.

Zakkai broke the silence by returning his fork to his plate again and inquiring, "Why do you want to undo it?"

"Because it's wrong." She uttered the words as though they were obvious. "I'm an Earth Fae, not a Midnight Fae."

"Yes, you've said that, but you're mated to four Midnight Fae. And as you've witnessed, our magic bleeds into our mates when we bond." He lifted his finger and whispered a spell that created a smoky cerulean structure in the middle of the table. As it grew, I realized he'd crafted a tree of sorts, the magical strands flickering bright with multicolored branches.

Aflora admired it with a hint of a smile.

"I see this inside you," Zakkai murmured. "You crafted a joint source of magic, marrying your Earth Fae heritage to the Midnight Fae blood running through your veins." He looked pointedly at the inky black lines writhing beneath her skin.

"I did that to survive the ascension."

"You did that to become queen," he corrected. "Zenaida's right about certain things—we need reformation. And I believe you are the key to that reformation."

"A millennium of male-led authority," Zeph mused. "Driven out by a woman."

"And an *abomination* at that," Zakkai added. "You have the power to prove to all fae kind that abominations can be good, Aflora. That they don't need to be feared."

"Constantine Nacht is the reason fae hunt and kill abominations." Zeph glanced at me and then at Aflora. "It would be entirely fitting for you to dismantle his throne of power by proving him wrong."

"It would," I admitted. Constantine Nacht might be my grandfather and blood, but that hadn't stopped him from trying to destroy me. And I fully intended to repay that favor.

"You all make this sound so easy," Aflora muttered. "But what if I become the abomination they all fear? Elana—"

"Isn't you," Zeph interrupted, not allowing her to even finish that thought.

"All you think about are others and what's right for your kingdom," I said quietly. "It's what makes you a suitable queen, Aflora. It's why my soul called for yours from the very beginning, why I've considered you a worthy mate all along. You're everything a royal should be, and more."

The others nodded in agreement.

"What if I don't want this?" Aflora asked in a low whisper. "What if I don't want to be the Midnight Fae Queen?"

"You don't," I replied, my voice just as soft. "Which is what makes you perfect for the task. You're going to accept the role because it's what's right, not because you desire it. But because you know you're the best one for the job." I reached over to cup her face, my thumb tracing her cheekbone. "You were born to be a queen, Aflora. You're strong. You're smart. You're a survivor. You're going to make history and change us all."

"And we're going to help you every step of the way," Zeph vowed, taking her hand.

The tree on the table began to throb, a heart pulsing at the center of the trunk. "Trust us to guide and teach you," Zakkai said. "We're your heart for a reason, little star."

"And I didn't go through seven lifetimes just to fail now," Shade added. "We're in this for eternity, Aflora. Not just now. Not just yesterday. But forever."

"We won't let you down," I whispered, drawing her in for a kiss. "To us, you're already our queen."

She shivered and melted against me. "You guys are going to kill me."

"Only in the bedroom," Zeph drawled.

Aflora huffed a laugh and shook her head, tears glistening in her blue eyes. "Thanks for believing in me."

"We'll be the belief you need when you doubt yourself," I promised her. "But you're wrong about one thing."

She stilled. "About what?"

"It absolutely won't be easy," I said seriously. "We might make it sound that way, but we know what's coming."

"Which is why we need to begin training immediately," Zeph replied.

"Indeed," Zakkai agreed, meeting my Guardian's gaze. "I already have a course schedule in mind."

"Good," I interjected before Zeph could demand a full itinerary. "Traditionally, Midnight Fae ascend in their twenty-fifth year, giving them ample time to prepare. But with my grandfather absorbing the dark source and forcing it on Aflora, the rules have clearly changed. We'll need all the structure we can get."

Ascensions were powerful.

And Aflora's would be legendary.

We had to begin preparing now.

"What happens if I fully ascend?" Aflora asked after a beat, her expression hesitant.

"*When*," I corrected. "*When* you fully ascend, you'll become one of the most powerful abominations in existence."

I'D CHOSEN the bedroom closest to the living area, preferring to be the first line of defense. It'd seemed to work well for Kolstov and Zephyrus, who had decided to take the largest room at the end of the hall together. Shade had picked the room beside mine. And Aflora... had bypassed the remaining room to join Kolstov and Zephyrus.

However, I felt her awake now.

Restless.

Pacing.

I sat up to find Zimney curled up at the foot of my bed, his eyelids lifting briefly before closing once more. *Not moving*, he was saying.

I snorted and slipped from the covers to pull on a pair of pajama pants. Shade's grandmother had fully stocked our closets and rooms with everything we needed. Whether she'd done it herself or hired someone, I wasn't sure. But I thanked her silently for it nonetheless. It made life easier.

That she knew which rooms we would pick—evidenced by the correct sizing of our wardrobe—served as a show of power. She'd foreseen our choices. Or perhaps she just knew us all well enough to know where we would want to sleep.

I stepped out into the hallway, listening for signs of life, and heard the soft slide of paper against paper. Following it into the living room, I found Shade reading on the smaller of the two couches, his upper body exposed as he wore a pair of pajama pants similar to mine.

His icy eyes remained on his book as he said, "She's outside."

"You should be sleeping," I told him.

He lifted a shoulder. "I wanted to be nearby in case she needed something."

It seemed I wasn't the only one with the protective gene engaged. "I'll keep an eye on her," I said, my voice soft. "Go rest, Shadow. You've done enough these last few days, and we all need your reserves fully restored."

Aflora's training would officially begin tomorrow. I'd developed an intense curriculum—one Zephyrus had fortified and Kolstov and Shade had perfected. It would require all of us to be at our best, not exhausted.

Shade set his book on the table. "She needs rest, too." He stood and stretched his arms over his head. "Perhaps you'll be better suited to convince her."

"I'll do my best."

His lips twitched as he stepped up to my side. "You'll have to do better than that. She's stubborn."

"I know how to handle her stubborn side," I promised.

He huffed out a dry laugh before heading down the hallway toward his room. When the door snicked closed, I wandered over to the table, curious to see what he'd chosen to read. I smirked at the title, familiar with the fictional trilogy from the Human Realm about hobbits.

It seemed just like Shade to indulge in such an epic tale.

Leaving the book alone, I redirected myself outside to the beauty lying on the ground. It seemed she'd ceased her pacing and had chosen to admire the sky instead. "It isn't real," she said to me as I approached. "But it certainly looks real."

"It's real to an extent," I replied, sitting down beside her on the soft bed of green grass.

The firm texture and vibrant life told me she'd bolstered it with her power, ensuring its strength beneath our bodies. I leaned back to join her in the prone position, my knuckles brushing hers as I aligned our arms alongside one another. Her fingers flexed toward mine, curling around the tips to hold me in her own way.

"Does the Hell Fae realm have stars?" she asked.

"I imagine it does in certain areas, but I've not explored it to know for sure." My paradigm was in the Human Realm, in Antarctica, which definitely had stars at night. Not that one could actually venture outside to admire them.

She tilted her head toward me, her blue eyes full of questions. But she didn't voice any of them. Instead, she just studied my features, content to coexist for a moment in silence.

Seconds turned into minutes as we watched each other, thousands of unspoken words and memories floating between us.

Then she leaned in closer to brush her lips against mine.

A token of trust.

A gift of gratitude.

We had been best friends once upon a time, our lives filled with a childish innocence that neither of us had ever fully understood. We'd bonded and loved each other in a way meant for children. And now we were very much adults, our connection shifting and growing into something very different.

It was a tentative link founded in confusion.

Aflora hadn't understood my motives or my purpose, just as I hadn't fully grasped her desires in life. But a few weeks together had opened our eyes to a whole new world of existence, one where our goals learned how to intertwine and grow as a unit rather than as separate strands.

My sweet little star had fused us together, tied our roots in a love-knot at the source of our beings, and ensured we were forever bound.

In essence, she'd captured my heart. I wasn't sure how or when it had happened. Perhaps in our childhood. Perhaps during that first dream when she'd demanded I please her without even asking my name. Perhaps when she'd fought me in my bedroom shortly after waking up.

Perhaps she'd always owned me.

I rolled onto my side to more properly face her, preferring to admire her over the starry night. Tucking my arm beneath my head, I placed my other hand on her abdomen, my pinky sliding beneath the fabric of her tank top to stroke the warm skin below it.

She didn't move, her eyes holding mine while we continued to stare at each other.

No words.

Just the sound of the perpetual night and the slight rustle of leaves and flowers, responding to the queen among them.

Her eyelashes fanned over her cheekbones as she blinked, her gorgeous features captivating my full attention.

I could gaze upon her for hours and never tire of it.

She possessed so much power and strength, the source's mark properly branding her as royalty. Cerulean ribbons glowed in her dark hair, lighting up her features and proclaiming her as my mate. I lifted my hand away from her stomach to draw my fingers through her soft strands, smiling as her energy kissed my skin.

"You're so beautiful that it almost hurts," I marveled, completely consumed by her and the vitality pouring off of her. I drew my thumb along her jaw, my touch instinctively reverent. "I know you're worried about the trials and marrying your power sources, but you were born for this, little star."

Her confidence continued to waver through our bonds.

It wasn't that she didn't believe in herself so much as she questioned whether or not this was the right path.

"You grew up being told that abominations are evil," I continued softly. "I grew up knowing that abominations can do good, too. Look at the Academy around us. This is here because of Zenaida, who, by all rights, is an abomination herself, and she worked with Lucifer, the unequivocal king of abominations, to create it. Does it feel wrong here? Evil? Dark? Nefarious? Or do you sense the life and love in this paradigm like I do?"

Similar sensations existed in my own paradigm, the one I'd created for those who favored retribution. But beneath that life had been a sense of anger and resentment toward other fae.

What I felt here was an underlying promise, a true sense of purpose for the future.

No violence or desire for bloodshed.

Just a desire to learn and work together.

A show of unity—something I hoped would be useful to Aflora later on.

"Peace," she whispered. "They feel at peace here. Protected. Safe. Like they can be themselves without worrying about punishment for doing so."

I nodded. "Because they're allowed to be themselves here. Abominations who just want to live, not fight. And it's not just within this paradigm, Aflora. You're picking up on it from the Hell Fae, too. They're a race of beings who have been shunned for so long that they built their own society to escape the others."

"Some of them are angry," she said softly. "I feel their ire like a weight against my soul. But others are just tired. They want to be accepted."

"And you can help them in that quest," I told her, my thumb tracing her cheekbone on my way to fondling her hair once more. "Being an abomination doesn't make one evil, little star. The soul is corrupt with or without power. Constantine is proof of that. He's a Midnight Fae who will destroy anyone and everything that stands up to his methodology for order. Hell, he took an inclusive council that worked positively together and turned them against their own hearts—the women who are the true figureheads."

It was despicable and wrong and so expertly crafted that I couldn't help developing a smidgen of respect for the bastard.

My father used to tell me that admiring one's enemies was to understand and never underestimate them.

I understood that now.

And I would never underestimate Constantine again.

"Constantine succeeded because he knew what weakness to exploit," I continued. "Emotion. What we need to do is show him how powerful emotion can be, by demonstrating how powerful our bonds are together."

I pressed my palm to the ground on the other side of her head, using it to balance myself as I leaned over to graze my lips across hers.

"We're going to train you, little star. We're going to help you through each trial. We're going to ensure you become the most powerful queen the fae have ever seen." I pressed my mouth to hers once more, my voice lowering to a whisper. "And when you fully ascend, we're going to kneel at your feet and show those Elders what a real council looks like."

She stared up at me for a beat. "Kiss me."

I brushed my mouth against hers, lingering for half a second before pulling back to study her features.

"Again," she whispered.

A variety of comments populated my thoughts, several of them taunts regarding her other mates leaving her needy for more. But rather than voice them, I adhered to her sensual command, this time parting her lips with my tongue to properly taste her.

We'd engaged in dreams, all of which resulted in me wearing something very similar to this while I pleased her with my hands and mouth.

But I wanted to experience the real her. The physical being. My *mate.*

Feeling her beneath me, her hands roaming up my back, was so much better than a fantasy. She knew me now. She accepted me. She trusted me. She could *feel* me, not just on top of her, but inside her.

And she wanted me.

I sensed her yearning, her innate recognition of what we meant to each other, and her subsequent happiness with our connection.

No dread. No doubts. No refusal.

Just pure, unadulterated acceptance.

It was the most amazing realization to learn that my mate desired me as I desired her, to know she considered me hers just as I considered her mine.

"Aflora," I whispered, deepening our kiss with my palms pressed to her cheeks to angle her appropriately.

Her nails drew down my back, her touch impatient yet adoring.

She wanted more.

She wanted me.

She wanted this.

I'd been with a few other women but had never felt connected to any of them. They weren't mine. They weren't Aflora. It was something I hadn't understood at the time, my intent always having been to only bond with Aflora for her protection and as a debt to be repaid to her parents.

Then I saw her again.

Felt her.

Worshipped her with my tongue.

And I'd never experienced such completion as I had in that moment.

Until now.

Until settling between her thighs and feeling her legs wrap around me in warm welcome.

Until tasting the craving on her tongue and feeling her dampening center against my growing arousal. Even through my pants and her shorts, I knew she was ready for me, that she wanted me—her mate—her Kai.

I never knew sex could feel like this, so much passion and heat and desire.

I'd watched her with her other mates, had seen how they'd pleased her, how she'd come undone with them with such devotion and grace.

I wanted to do that to her now, to be the one she cried out for, to finally claim my mate in the most traditional of manners.

"Yes," she whispered against my lips. "Yes."

I hadn't asked her. Hadn't voiced the desire. But she felt it in my mind, our bond, her heart responding to mine on instinct alone.

However, I didn't want to do it here. I wanted to be alone, to cherish her behind closed doors, to make it just us.

I stood and pulled her up into my arms, carrying her inside and to the room I now called my own. Zimney was nowhere to be seen, the wolf probably sensing my intentions and running off to frolic somewhere else.

The door shut quietly behind me, my steps silent against the white carpet.

I set Aflora on the bed, her legs hanging off the edge as she sat up with her hands on my hips. I stood between her thighs, staring down at her in wonder. Then I bent to capture her mouth once more.

Her fingers drifted across my lower abdomen, her quest clear as she unfastened the tie at my waist to push the soft fabric down over my groin to my thighs.

I righted my spine, allowing her to finish the task of removing my pants.

Then I stepped out of them and back between her splayed legs.

Her pretty eyes ran over me in deep appreciation, her pupils dilating as she took in my thick arousal.

She licked her lips and pulled her tank top over her head, presenting me with her beautiful breasts. Then she leaned forward to take my cock into her addictive mouth, her tongue running along the bottom of my shaft in clear and obvious invitation.

I threaded my fingers through her hair, a curse slipping from my mouth as I pushed myself deeper, loving the way she eagerly accepted me into her. Almost as though I'd always belonged. And I likely had.

But this wasn't the claiming I'd had in mind.

I needed to be inside her in another way.

To complete our coupling by fucking her to oblivion.

A very masculine, competitive part of me needed the

others to hear it, too. To know she was mine just as much as she belonged to them.

Her blue eyes sparkled knowingly as she released me from her mouth.

She scooted back onto the bed, hooked her thumbs into the fabric of her shorts, and pulled them off her long, athletic legs.

I stood beside the mattress, watching the show.

All of this was done without words, our bodies speaking for us.

An erotic dance of knowledge and passion and intensity.

And just pure need.

I braced one knee on the bed, watching as she found a place in the middle of the comforter. Her dark strands decorated the pillow in a welcoming gesture, her thighs parting to allow me to see her beautiful, sweet, wet pussy, the heart of her aching for me to take her.

My mouth watered, my desire to taste her almost overcoming my need to be inside her.

But the latter won out.

I could taste her later, indulge in her sweet flavor for hours, and ensure everyone heard her screaming my name.

Tonight, I needed to complete us.

I prowled forward, crawling over her and caging her beneath me. "This is about our union," I told her softly, lowering to press my groin to hers as I balanced myself on my forearms on either side of her head. "I'm not usually this gentle, Aflora. But something about the moment requires it."

She reached up to draw her fingers through my hair, the white strands loose around my face and falling around her like a curtain of false purity. "I'm not fragile."

"I know," I whispered, pressing my arousal into hers to feel her welcoming heat. I slipped through her folds, my head nudging her clit before drawing downward to the heart of her. "But I want to make sure you remember this," I told her, lining up with her entrance. "And I want to hear you scream my name."

She began to speak, but her words cut off on a cry as I drove into her, giving her a brief introduction to the power in my hips and my ability to dominate her entirely. Then I slowly withdrew and entered her again, gradually now, softer, ensuring she felt every inch.

Her mind rolled with comments, comparing sizes and strengths and girths, and my lips curled when she admitted I was the largest of her mates.

I already knew that.

However, she hadn't. Because she hadn't properly felt me yet.

Zephyrus certainly rivaled me in some ways, his propensity for being in charge equal to mine, but unlike him, I knew how to be gentle.

Which I showed Aflora now as I set a sensual pace meant for this moment, the one where our bodies declared themselves to one another.

She grabbed my shoulders, a soft moan leaving her lips as I tortured her with my unhurried pace.

Her little growl made me smile.

She responded by digging her nails into my skin, demanding with her body that I do more.

"You can't have it hard every time," I whispered, taking her mouth in a kiss meant to silence. She started to argue in my mind, only to cut off on a groan as my tongue engaged hers in the battle she craved.

All the way in, I said to her. *And almost all the way out.*

I repeated the action over and over, drawing out each thrust and ensuring I nudged that spot deep inside her with every downward stroke.

She scratched a path down my back, her legs wrapping

around my hips as she tried futilely to press up into me and dictate a faster pace.

But this wasn't about a quick fuck. This was about unleashing an experience for our *souls*.

I rolled onto my back, bringing her on top, and allowed her to drive. She sat up, eager to comply, her thighs straddling my hips as she began to ride me. Her breasts swayed enticingly with each hurried shift of her hips, her lips parting on a moan of excitement. However, after a few more urgent swivels, she caught her lip between her teeth and stared down at me, her dark hair framing her beautiful face.

Understanding seemed to light her up from within.

I sat up to join her, my lips ghosting over hers as I braced myself on one hand behind me and wrapped my opposite palm around her nape. "Tender can be just as good," I told her, my tongue licking the seam of her mouth before sliding inside.

She shifted, her legs moving to wrap around my back as she more firmly sat astride my thighs. A little mewl caught in the back of her throat as she realized how deeply I penetrated her in this position.

And then we both began to move.

Not hurriedly, but languidly, indulging in the sensations and bringing ourselves closer and closer to the precipice with long, thorough movements.

"Oh, Kai," she breathed, her nipples hard against my chest.

Sweat covered us both, the effort with which we fucked driving us both to a point of near madness. It was just so fierce, so utterly exhaustive in each glide and calculative stroke, that we were overwhelmed and fatigued by the sheer intensity of it all.

I felt her starting to come undone, our magic dancing together as one as cerulean sparks graced the air.

This was the culmination of a mating years in the making. Our paths finally intersecting after wandering off course. Our souls rejoicing in returning home, *together*, in a beautiful moment of bliss and harmony and absolute perfection.

I kissed her, confiding my deepest, darkest histories in the blink of a second, unlocking my mind to her and throwing away the key.

She responded in kind, her faith in me resolute.

And together we fell over the edge into a rapturous beginning that went on for what felt like hours, our bodies locked together in harmonious bliss and refusing to stop.

She cried out, my name a beacon that caused my heart to soar.

I followed her in kind, chanting *Flora* on repeat, my little star finally lighting up the dark, cruel night of my spirit.

Her lips whispered against mine, her body moving, taking, repeating, writhing some more.

And eventually we collapsed onto the bed, only to continue our sensual dance, our groins locked together in a kiss meant to last a lifetime.

She destroyed me.

She completed me.

She ensured we would remain forever together.

I sank my teeth into her neck, desiring that promise in blood.

She responded in kind, taking my essence deep into her mouth and swallowing before slamming her mouth over mine once more.

My Kai, she breathed.

My Flora, I returned. *My gorgeous, bright star.*

Our sensuality followed us into our dreams, the riddles fracturing between us and creating new, complex locks— ones no one would ever be able to break.

When night finally came, the sunset of our new life, I woke her in the same way we'd fallen asleep. Then I finally tasted her, and I confirmed that our dreams had nothing on our reality.

This is the real dream, I told her. *My life with you. That's the dream, Aflora. And I hope I never wake up.*

She smiled, her heart in her eyes. *Neither do I, Kai. Neither do I.*

"ALL RIGHT, NEW SCHEDULE," I said, standing at a stone board with my wand. I pointed the end at the obsidian marble. "Today is defensive training." The words scrolled across the rock in a fiery scrawl.

The action repeated as I said each new course by day.

Defensive magic.

Death magic.

Offensive magic.

Crash course into royalty affairs, including ascension with historical references, and general strategy.

Quandary magic.

"We'll go day by day, taking turns in the demonstrations. But we'll all be attending and learning together." That final sentence was for Zakkai, who sat beside Aflora with his arm lazily draped over the back of her chair. He cocked a white brow, his arrogance grating on my nerves.

Because I'd just spent the better part of the last twelve hours hearing him pleasure Aflora on repeat, all damn day. Which meant she hadn't slept well.

And neither had I.

Fucking prick.

Our only saving grace was the fact that we had bought ourselves some time by coming here, because I highly doubted Lucifer would strike a deal with Constantine anytime soon.

"This is our training facility." I glanced at Shade for confirmation, and he nodded.

"The gargoyles are ensuring the other students don't bother us," he added out loud. "This area is used for advanced courses, but the headmasters agreed to move them elsewhere for the time being for safety purposes."

"Good." Because we were about to unleash some intense and dangerous spells. Best not to be interrupted, especially should I decide to do a defensive demonstration with Zakkai. "Then let the fun begin."

Aflora didn't hesitate, her willingness to learn evident in the way she responded to our first day of training. She was tired by the end, her body and mind sore from everything I threw at her, but she didn't break or bend or beg me to stop. All she said was "More."

The next day, in our defensive magic course, went much the same way with her memorizing, manipulating, and regurgitating spells. She even put me on my ass a few times— a feat very few could claim. Of course, I was distracted by her mouth because all I wanted to do was kiss her when she managed to replicate an advanced shield using her hands instead of a wand.

The courses continued, Aflora never once wavering or

complaining. She was focused and the definition of determination, doing exactly what we told her and adding a few twists of her own.

By night, she was an apt pupil, learning and excelling and perfecting her skill.

And by day, she engaged in a similar routine… in the bedroom.

Constantine remained quiet, the trials lurking somewhere on the horizon. Shade met with his grandmother often, seeking updates. But aside from ensuring that all of Midnight Fae kind hated Aflora, he hadn't given anything away regarding his next trial.

However, we all knew something was coming.

He would be furious that she managed to pass two ascensions with such efficiency, and so quickly, too.

"He's strategic," Kols was saying now as we watched Shade and Aflora practice offensive magic. It was her third course in the topic, as we were well into our third week here at the Academy. "And the longer he takes, the more nervous I get."

Zakkai nodded, his silver-blue eyes on Aflora. He'd tied his white hair back at his nape today, displaying his long, athletic neck. And the bite marks Aflora had left there during her time in his bed today before class.

We'd developed a routine on sharing her, with our mate choosing to sleep in a different room each night. She never slept in her own space. I wasn't even convinced she knew a fourth bedroom existed.

Twice, Shade had chosen to join Kols, me, and Aflora.

Zakkai never did, preferring his solitary time with her.

It was different, but it worked. Because I wasn't sure I could share her with him. He would try to dictate the show, and I refused to submit to him.

Shade didn't exactly roll over for me either, but he seemed content to follow my lead.

Zakkai would sooner bite me than follow my direction, something he proved weekly during the Quandary magic classes. I told him not to push our mate too hard, and he translated that as *Put Aflora in the most dangerous position possible and see if she can survive it.*

Dick, I thought, not for the first time.

At least we agreed on Constantine. "He's definitely planning something big," he said. "Either Zenaida can't see it coming, or she doesn't want to risk the outcome by warning us." He ran his hand over the stubble dotting his jaw, then reached around to roll and pop his neck. "Regardless, we need to be ready."

"Yes," Kols agreed. "We do." He folded his arms and observed Aflora dismantling one of Shade's resurrection spells with a bout of life from her earth magic.

"Impressive," I murmured, grinning as she created a root from the figment and wrapped it around Shade's leg. She yanked on it, dropping him to the ground on an *Oomph.* "Ready to duel with someone stronger?" I asked her.

A shadowy figure flew at me half a second later, the Death magic stealing my breath and taking me to my knees.

I called up a defensive disfiguration spell, dismantling his enchantment and freeing my lungs. Then I shot an offensive charm at him meant to blister his eardrums—that he blasted away with his wand.

"You were saying?" the Death Blood drawled.

"That he wanted me to play with Aflora," Zakkai replied, sending a net of magic over her that sizzled and sparked and drew a surprised yelp from her. "Figure that out, little star."

She growled in response, making the hairs along the back of my neck stand on end. "What did you do?" I demanded.

"We're reminiscing." Zakkai cocked his head. "Stop snarling, little star. You need your oxygen."

I stepped forward. "Take it off her."

"No." Zakkai looked at me, his stance defensive. "And I don't recommend trying to help, or it'll make it much worse for her."

I lifted my wand at him. "Undo it, Zakkai."

He glanced at my hand and snorted. "Try and you'll definitely regret it."

I'm. Fine, Aflora snapped into my mind, drawing my attention to her on the ground, where she appeared to be paralyzed beneath a layer of cerulean magic.

You don't look fine, Aflora.

"Trust her to undo it," Zakkai interjected. "She might not have us all for her trials. She needs to learn how to work on her own without handicaps. Give her a moment to solve the puzzle."

He won't let anything or anyone hurt her, Kols added in my mind. *This isn't just about trusting Aflora to fight her own battles, but also having faith in her mates to keep her safe.*

She doesn't look fucking safe, I snapped back, wincing as she whimpered inside the net. *She looks pained, Kolstov.*

She does, he agreed. *But I have faith that she'll figure it out. And if she doesn't, I know Zakkai will step in.*

What if it's too late when he does? I countered. *What if she gets hurt?*

Then he'll feel like hell afterward, similar to how you did when you killed Clove. His burnt-bronze irises met mine, his auburn brow arching. *What happened to the headmaster who wanted Aflora to blossom and grow?*

He fell in love.

Kols grinned. *Yes. Yes, he did.* His focus returned to Aflora, his amusement disappearing behind a mask of concern as she struggled across the floor.

I took a step forward, only for Shade to step in front of me. "Let her learn," he encouraged, his hand wrapping around my wrist to lower my wand to my side. Then his icy gaze flickered to Zakkai, telling me with a look to check out the Quandary Blood.

When I glanced at him, I found his expression tight with concentration, his silver-blue gaze intense as he watched Aflora work.

His distraction could work to my advantage. I could knock him out and help Aflora.

Or I could fuck this all up by not trusting him and risk hurting her more with him unable to assist due to a magical coma.

My jaw clenched, my irritation over the situation making my heart beat a little faster.

I did not appreciate having my control taken away and a random lesson being inserted into today's plans. This was not what we were meant to do here.

But Zakkai was the wild card, the one I couldn't rely on or trust.

And instances like this only made that lack of faith worse.

Aflora gasped, seizing my entire focus.

Then she uttered a long, wicked enchantment and sent the web flying back at Zakkai.

But it didn't engulf him. He caught it instead and absorbed the magic back into his wand. "Beautiful," he breathed.

Aflora narrowed her gaze and hit him with another strike of blue magic, then spun a ball of WarFire into her palm. It whirled with a multitude of colors, the intoxicating mix clearly deadly.

"Do it," Zakkai dared.

She released it, throwing it right at him.

Where it landed against his chest.

Aflora shrieked, jumping up to her feet and running to him in a daze of concern. Only for the fire to sizzle and disappear, his clothing and chest fine. But he caught her by the back of the neck and drew her in for a kiss, one that ended in her biting his tongue.

He chuckled as she slapped him. "What was that?" she demanded.

"Defensive magic," he drawled, glancing at me. "Just the upgraded variety."

I narrowed my gaze. "Are you trying to piss me off?"

"I don't think I have to try, Zephyrus," he replied. "You're in a constant state of *pissed off* around me."

"Hmm, I wonder why that is?" I pretended to think about it. "Maybe because you don't know how to be a team member and fucking communicate."

"No, I'm rather certain it's because I won't get on my knees and suck your cock like all the others," he returned. "I'm not one of your students or your lover. I'm your *better*. Yet you attempt to dictate to me like I'm one of your pupils, when in reality, I've been playing with your spells since I was five years old. So if anyone is going to kneel for anyone, it'll be you on your knees for me."

"Okay, maybe—"

"That's never going to fucking happen," I snapped, cutting off whatever Shade was about to say. Because fuck this. "Those spells I'm teaching Aflora are ones I learned as a boy, too. But she's a new Midnight Fae. I can't just throw advanced enchantments at her and expect her to learn."

"And yet that's exactly what Constantine is going to do," he countered. "We can't baby her. We can't go easy on her. We have to go hard. Because the dark source sure as fuck isn't going to treat her like a child with training wheels." He stepped up into my space, his silver-blue irises swirling with power. "I'm ensuring she survives. What the fuck are you achieving by coddling her?" He lifted an eyebrow, daring me to argue.

But I didn't know what to say.

Because the bastard was fucking right.

I focused so much on protecting her—because my natural instinct was to *guard*—that I'd forgotten how to truly prepare her. How to *teach* her.

I took a step back, needing my space from him… from them all… to *think*, to process what to do next.

"Zeph," Aflora murmured, moving toward me.

"No, Aflora." I looked at her, a shield of magic immediately encasing me, my desire not to be touched clear, and perhaps not fair to her, but necessary nonetheless. "He's right. The bastard is fucking right." And I hated admitting that. Hated him for pointing it out. Hated him for *existing*.

I shook my head. "I just… I need a minute." I backed away, heading toward the room's exit.

I needed to rethink everything.

To create a new plan.

Three weeks wasted.

Three weeks of elementary training.

Preparing for a war that would destroy my mate if *I* didn't properly prepare her. No, we. If *we* didn't properly prepare her.

This was why Zakkai had created the original training plan; he'd known we would have to be harsh on her. But I'd pushed back.

We couldn't hold back anymore.

We had to drive her harder. Test her limits. All but destroy her.

Because Constantine would certainly try.

Now I just needed to decide if I was strong enough to do this—strong enough… to hurt my mate.

I FOLDED my arms and fought the urge to wince as Aflora fell to the floor on a gasp.

"Again," Zeph demanded.

He'd escalated Aflora's training to a whole new level after Zakkai's pep talk the other day. No more coaching. No more words of praise. Just harsh spells and commands to keep going.

Aflora didn't complain.

She merely stood back up and started over.

Again. And again. And again.

I admired her tenacity and drive, but I also wanted to kill Zeph and Zakkai.

Phoenix fires, Kols whispered into my head as Zeph nailed Aflora with a particularly painful spell. *He's taking this a bit far, yes?*

Yeah, he's being an ass. I understood why. I even agreed that it had to be done. But that didn't mean I enjoyed watching it happen.

"*Atlaqi Sarahee.*" Aflora breathed the words and made a circle with her finger.

They were practicing defensive spells without wands today—Zeph's idea to prepare her since she didn't have a magical conduit of her own.

The snakelike enchantment from Zeph dissolved, allowing her a sigh of relief.

Until he followed it up with an even more powerful charm that slammed right into her chest.

Kols stepped forward, but a glare from Zeph kept him from interfering.

He's in quite a mood, Kols muttered.

I'm taking Aflora later, I replied. *I don't trust him to give her what she needs after this. Not in his current mood.*

No. He needs someone who can withstand his aggression and return it. Kols's bronze irises flared. *I will gladly be that partner, as it'll provide an excellent opportunity to kick his ass.*

I smirked. *Good.*

Zakkai leaned against the wall, his hands in the pockets of his black pants. He was shirtless like the rest of us, dressed to spar. Aflora had on another tank top and pants of a similar stretchy fabric. She was barefoot and sweating, her dark hair pulled up into a ponytail at the back of her head.

"*Dayani Adhabat,*" she snapped, her finger drawing a dash across the air to dismantle the strangulation charm Zeph had released. "*Asqati Mayatun.*" Her hand flexed with the words, a dark ball appearing in her palm. She threw it at Zeph, the deadly ball disappearing before it could hit his face.

She followed it up with another sphere right after it,

aiming for his abdomen, then added the strangulation charm on top of it all, bringing the Guardian to his knees.

Zakkai grinned in amusement.

Aflora growled and hit Zeph with a fourth spell, one meant to be a punch to the gut.

Zeph deflected most of the power with a few defensive shields.

Then he lashed out with another offensive enchantment that knocked Aflora on her ass again.

She released a frustrated noise but didn't otherwise speak. Cerulean flames engulfed her from head to toe as she fought his new spell.

Then Zeph cursed as a burning thwomp shot up from the ground beside him. "No thwomps," he reminded her.

He dismantled the tree before it could set the room on fire. Given that the floors and walls were all obsidian, I doubted it would do much damage. But better not to tempt fate.

Their lethal dance continued, Aflora's outfit tarnished and nearly destroyed in the process. By the end, all I wanted to do was pull her into my arms and hold her for hours.

Zeph vibrated with irritation. He hated doing this to Aflora, but he and Zakkai were the best suited among us to teach her.

I'll distract him, Kols told me. *Take Aflora.*

The agitation pouring off Zeph suggested he wanted to soothe Aflora, but in a violent way. He needed to console himself as well, to know he hadn't actually hurt her. However, the anger he felt at himself for hurting her would end up translating to aggressive sex.

And that wasn't what she needed right now.

Aflora deserved some tenderness after the last few days of roughness. Yes, this all helped prepare her to face the inevitable, and Constantine wouldn't go easy on her. But having her mates grounded her and gave her an advantage that the Elder would never understand.

Therefore, she needed both harshness and love.

Zeph and Zakkai could focus on the former, as they excelled in combat.

Meanwhile, Kols and I would offer her the emotional support she required to truly flourish.

Zeph stepped toward Aflora, his expression lined with intent. Kols moved between them, and I shadowed to Aflora's side. Zakkai caught my gaze and gave a slight nod, aware of my intention. Then I wrapped her in a cloak of darkness and took her to our meadow.

She trembled against me, her head finding my shoulder as she silently cried in frustration. I held her, my hands roaming over her tattered tank top and offering her my touch and support.

You're magnificent, little rose, I told her.

There's so much violence, she replied, shuddering.

Her tears weren't a sign of weakness or sadness. They were about her difficulty in accepting the darkness of being a Midnight Fae. Her heart was all light and joy and sweet elements. This world that she'd fallen into blackened her soul, and only the strongest of fae could accept such a thing.

But even the strongest of fae needed a soft moment to reflect.

I pulled Aflora with me to the ground, her petite frame curling into my lap on instinct. Then I held her beneath the shade of the tree until the sun began to rise over our meadow. We didn't speak. We just basked in her earth, her life, her desire to create.

As the heat touched her skin, she lifted her head on a sigh and admired the rising sun. She knew it wasn't real, that the paradigm manufactured it, but that didn't stop her contentment from flowing through our bond.

"Can we stay here today?" she asked softly. "To sleep, I mean."

"We can do whatever you want, little rose," I promised her.

Her lips curled a little. Then she began to fashion a bed of flowers, the petals soft and colorful and filled with her strength.

I watched as she worked, content to lean against the trunk.

Sometimes Aflora just needed a day to play. And I gave her that, allowing her to flourish in her earth magic and giving her a chance to reinvigorate her soul.

Floral scents surrounded us, her element in full effect as she gave herself over to her Earth Fae heart.

Then she sprawled out on her bed, lost the tie in her hair, and allowed the strands to flow over the ground in cerulean and black waves.

I smiled, admiring the sight of her all content and warm and happy.

"Join me," she whispered.

I replied by pushing away from my tree and crawling to her. She grinned when I reached her side, then she wrapped her palm around the back of my neck to gently guide me toward her for a kiss.

We remained like that for hours, just letting our mouths do all the talking.

No sex.

No physical need.

Just a moment for our souls to heal, to love, to indulge in each other.

I told her with my mind how much I adored her. How much I respected her. How proud I was of her for embracing this new path.

And she told me how thankful she was to have me as her

mate. How she forgave all my secrets. How she wanted to live a lifetime together to heal all the previous ones I'd endured.

It was an intense, beautiful moment, one that left both of us replete in an entirely different way than ever before.

As the sun reached high noon, she snuggled into my chest.

And together we slept on the mound of flowers she'd built, the sky providing a natural blanket of heat that allowed us to dream.

Although, as I closed my eyes, I lost myself to a vision where the darkness of my world threatened to engulf Aflora whole, dismantling her light.

Something's coming, I thought, asleep yet very much awake. *A new trial is brewing. And this one will bring death.*

ZEPH AND ZAKKAI were being particularly cruel today.

We'd been living in this paradigm for five weeks now, almost six, and they'd decided it was time for me to face them collectively.

Which meant they were attacking me from both sides.

Kols and Shade hadn't been able to watch, their instincts to protect overriding the cause of today's session. But as the hours drew on, I started to wish they'd return and whisk me away from this hell.

I understood the purpose of this test, that Zakkai and Zeph were merely trying to prepare me to handle the ascension on my own, but that didn't make it hurt any less.

They were both lethally serious, their spells ones that would have killed me a year ago.

Fortunately, the dark source leapt to my aid, consistently allowing me to dismantle each enchantment thrown my way.

I tried to engage my earth side as well, but today's exercise required me to use my Midnight Fae powers instead.

Which I suspected was the point.

They wanted me to learn how to rely on the Midnight Fae part of me over the Earth Fae part, as they assumed Constantine would do the same.

I shivered as Zakkai's silver-blue eyes flared with power, his long white strands billowing in a magical breeze off his shoulders. The calculating edge to his cruelly handsome features told me I wasn't going to like whatever he did next.

Zeph attacked from my side, his fiery incantation wrapping around my leg as Zakkai hit me with a strategic web of magic that rendered me speechless.

I fell to the ground beneath their joint assault, wincing when they didn't stop.

Shield, Zeph demanded.

I threw up a mastery of defensive arts, the barrier invisible yet studiously deflecting their spells while I attempted to undo whatever they'd incapacitated me with.

It burned through my veins, stealing my breath and drowning me in a toxic chemical that fractured my ability to think.

Instincts, I thought numbly. *They want me to rely on my instincts.*

Zakkai had warned me that today's lesson would be difficult. I understood now—they'd purposely dismantled my ability to recall spells by verbal memory.

This was about relying on physical reactions.

I hated them.

Loathed that they struck my shield repeatedly while I futilely tried to undo the harsh restraint on my mind.

We were beyond kindness today. Hell, *this week*. They'd

been on me repeatedly, barely letting me sleep, forcing me to learn, learn, learn.

There were so many spells, *too many spells.*

I was being given a crash course in five weeks that should have been delivered over twenty-five years. As Kols had pointed out, I wasn't even of age to ascend. At least not according to previous Midnight Fae rituals.

All of this was being thrown at me because of a devious, underhanded, wicked male who wanted to use me to make a point.

I refused to let him win.

But in moments like this, it was easy to see how effortlessly he could best me. Because I couldn't fight this. I didn't know how. They'd handicapped my mind, leaving me defenseless beneath my deteriorating shield.

Stop feeling sorry for yourself and fix it, Zeph berated me. *You're more powerful than you realize.*

I hate you, I seethed.

Good. Then I'm getting through to you. Now fucking dismantle the charms.

I growled at him.

He snarled back.

And I suddenly wanted to cut through his magic just to return the favor.

There'd been this weight of darkness hanging on my shoulders for weeks now. A sense of foreboding. A thick feeling of dread.

I tapped into it now, wrapping myself in the black web of magic and allowing it to flourish through me. Ice drilled through my veins, dismantling my inner warmth yet bolstering my resolve in the process.

It coiled.

Strengthened.

Coiled some more.

Until I couldn't hold on to it for another second, the magic too intense and terrifying to maintain.

It exploded out of me in a cerulean flame, eating through all the enchantments in the room, including my shield, and seeking the two males attacking me.

Zakkai absorbed the tension with a wave of his hand.

Zeph created a shield that deflected the blast.

Then the two of them stared at me on the floor. The power had destroyed my clothes.

Zakkai walked over to a bag on the floor, found a new pair of pants and a tank top, and tossed them to me. "Get dressed. We're doing that again."

I shivered, my body too weak to repeat all that. "No."

"Yes," Zeph interjected. "Now, Aflora."

"*No*," I repeated. "I'm done for today." That power had been too much. Too dark. Too destructive. Too *not me*. It'd overtaken my earth, leaving me without a single glimpse of light. I refused to accept that. Refused to embrace it. Refused to allow it to happen again.

But Zeph wasn't having it. He slammed me with another bolt of power, this one sweeping my legs out from beneath me and pinning me to the ground. "We're not done."

A rumble started in my chest, my irritation mounting. He wasn't hearing me. "I'm. Done. For. Today."

"That's too bad, little star," Zakkai said, tossing my clothes to the side. "Because I agree with Zeph. We're doing that again."

I wanted to scream. To maim. To kill them both. I needed a break. I *deserved* a break. We'd been at this for hours. Days. Weeks. I hadn't complained once, taking everything they'd given me and memorizing their rules.

I'd put up with their treatment, Zeph's volatile behavior

and Zakkai's wicked spells, and I wanted to take the rest of the night off. Right now.

I took in Zeph's offensive spell, copied the general structure, and sent it back at him. He deflected with his wand, already preparing another enchantment. "*Enough*," I said through gritted teeth. I was too tired. Too done. Too—

"Do you think Constantine would listen to you right now?" Zakkai asked. "Because I think he'd revel in your show of weakness and drown you in it."

"I'm not weak!"

"Your current situation suggests otherwise," he countered.

Then he slammed me with another of those webs meant to dismantle my thoughts.

And Zeph followed up with another spell.

And another.

And another.

I tried to build a shield, to counter them, to protect myself, but my energy reserves were depleted from the darkness I'd allowed myself to release.

However, it still lingered.

Hovering on my shoulder, waiting for me to embrace it once more.

But I couldn't. It made me feel too cold. Too wrong. Too *powerful*.

I curled into a ball instead, denying that flicker of energy and absorbing the brunt of Zeph's and Zakkai's hits instead.

Aflora? Kols whispered into my mind. *Are you all right?*

No, I replied, trembling beneath the pain and agony of having my own mates attack me when I'd told them to stop. They were trying to make a point. I understood it. But that didn't make me accept it. *They won't stop.*

I sounded so weak. So pitiful. And I could almost hear

Zakkai and Zeph taunting me for it, calling me out for giving up.

They wanted me to be strong.

To stand up to them.

To give them a display of power meant to destroy them all.

I hate them, I told Kols. *I hate them.*

I could hear the sadness in my voice, a perpetual moping that I loathed.

I'm stronger than this, I thought in my next inhale. *So much stronger.*

But it required me to block an important part of me. My earth. My tie to the element I loved and adored. Choosing strength meant I had to welcome the darkness.

I shivered, abhorring the choice.

However, the electricity roaming over me, as well as Zeph's shouts to fight, left me no choice.

I tapped into that black hole, pulling it into me once more, and released it on a wave of energy that had tears falling from my eyes.

Everything stopped.

Inky flames engulfed the room.

Then Zakkai cut through it with a blast of cerulean magic that tamed the darkness back into a little ball of spinning power that seemed to seep back into me, inch by inch.

I didn't move, my arms locked around my legs as I remained in the center of the room.

The spells were all gone.

But the aggression remained.

"Aflora?" Zeph asked, his deep voice holding a touch of concern.

I ignored him.

"She's fine," Zakkai said. "Or she would be if she accepted the dark source the way she needs to."

"Does she look fucking fine to you?" Zeph demanded. "Because she looks broken to me."

Zakkai snorted. "You're allowing emotion to cloud your judgment. That's why she's not as prepared as she should be —because you've wasted all her time by coddling her. So now we have to resort to this to ensure she's ready because *you* failed to train her."

"I failed to train her?" Zeph's deep voice reverberated through the room, making my skin crawl with goose bumps. "You're the one who mated her first, Zakkai. Then you left her in the Elemental Fae realm to be raised by a bunch of Earth Fae. And you're blaming me for her lack of preparedness?"

"She wasn't ready then."

"And she wasn't fucking ready when she started at the Academy, either," Zeph retorted. "But I did the best I could with what I had to work with. She couldn't even make a damn sandwich right when we started."

I flinched at the way he said it, like my lack of dark-magic skill made me somehow weak in his eyes.

"Maybe things would have been different had you been the one to take her that day instead of Shade," Zeph continued.

"Oh, they absolutely would have. You'd all be dead right now. Instead, I'm stuck putting up with your arrogance on a daily basis—an arrogance you have not *earned*."

"You say these things like you know what I can do," Zeph replied, a lethal edge in his tone. "But how about you put that *arrogance* of yours to the test, hmm?"

"Happily," Zakkai replied, a bolt of magic singeing the air.

Zeph responded in kind, causing the hairs along my arms to dance on end.

What's happening? Shade demanded in my head.

But I was too consumed by the growing power in the room to reply. *Danger,* my instincts whispered to me. *Protect.*

I lifted my head to see Zakkai and Zeph engaged in an all-out duel, their aggression mounting with each strike.

They refused to yield.

Refused to acknowledge the other as superior.

Because they were the same—both dominant and proud and powerful in their own ways. Zakkai had the edge as the Source Architect, but Zeph had spent his entire life training for a battle like this. He was a Guardian, one assigned to protect the incoming Midnight Fae King. And he demonstrated that now by unleashing all his power into Zakkai.

My eyes widened, realization striking me in the chest.

He *had* been going easy on me. Even when I thought he was giving me his all, he'd never fought me like this.

And for some reason, that angered me.

They were supposed to be training me to fight Constantine. He wouldn't even consider lessening his blows. Yet Zeph had held back, afraid that I couldn't handle him in his full force of power.

Which was precisely what Zakkai had kept arguing, that Zeph needed to remove the emotional filter and test me. *Really* test me.

And I'd reacted like a brat today, telling them to stop. Just when we were on the cusp of unleashing my greatest power.

The chip on my shoulder… that inky spot that weighed me down… was my connection to the dark source.

I understood that on a level but hadn't *accepted* it. That'd been the reason for Zakkai's pushing. He wanted me to allow the darkness out to play so we could realize my true potential.

We'd spent five weeks going through trivial spells and historical potentials and studying scenarios meant to help me pass my trials.

But today was the first time I'd experienced the real power flourishing inside me—the one that would guarantee I excelled.

Zeph snarled as Zakkai hit him with a cerulean spark. Then he volleyed a green one underlined in black back at him.

I sat up, my eyes widening. *They're trying to kill each other.*

There was no going easy here. No submitting. No *acceptance.*

They were part of the problem—the harsh point in my bonds. They didn't trust each other. Nor did they like each other. And it was coming to a head now as they dueled in a way only alpha males could.

I had to stop them. To force them to see reason. If one of them was injured in this aggression, I'd never forgive myself, or them.

"*Stop,*" I told them.

They were too lost in their furious energies to hear me, their duel intensifying with every passing second.

I went to my knees, calling on that power once more and allowing it to consume me entirely, needing it to protect me *and* my mates.

It culminated, curled, and grew inside me.

Zeph cursed as Zakkai struck him with something harmful. It only seemed to enrage both men more, heightening their need to declare victory over the other.

"*Enough!*" I shouted, releasing my energy into both of them and knocking them to the ground.

They weren't prepared for my reaction, too focused on

each other to notice me. I used the final vestiges of my strength to stand, my hands on my hips as I glowered at them both.

"No more," I stated, power flickering around me in warning as I replenished my depleted reserves directly from the dark source. It was foreign and cold, but necessary because my earth magic couldn't refuel the blackened part of me.

Zakkai's lips curled faintly, his white hair a tangled mess around his shoulders. "Well done, Aflora."

"That was a fucking test?" Zeph sounded pissed.

Zakkai merely lifted a shoulder. "Does it matter? It worked."

"I'm going to kill you," Zeph threatened.

Zakkai pushed up to his feet and shook his head. "You'll try," he taunted, moving to stand behind me. "You'll fail." He kissed my neck, his lips going to my ear. "You're burning so bright right now, Flora. Just like a star."

I shivered beneath his praise, but a bolt of irritation still lingered in my veins. "You pushed me too far today."

"I pushed you just far enough," he countered against my ear, his tongue licking the shell before pressing another kiss to my thundering pulse. "And you were magnificent."

Zeph left the floor and positioned himself across from us, his fury a palpable spike against my senses. "You need to learn to fucking communicate."

"I've been communicating. You've not been listening," Zakkai murmured, his mouth drawing a path to my shoulder. "You taste like darkness, sweet star."

His touch sent a shiver down my spine, his hard body cradling my back as he more firmly pressed against me. He was shirtless—something all my mates seemed to do daily now for training—which allowed me to feel his heat directly against my skin.

"So decadent," he hummed, licking back up my neck to my ear. "You feel it, right? The power? The intensity?"

"Yes." I swallowed, my gaze on Zeph. "But I'm not sure I forgive you for provoking it."

He chuckled against my neck. "I know. However, you will." He slid his arms around my abdomen, holding me to him. "Would you like me to worship you with my tongue, my queen?"

"I…"

He nibbled my pulse. "We can make the Guardian watch," he suggested.

Zeph narrowed his gaze and took a step forward, his hand finding my hip. "Or maybe I'll make *you* watch."

My heart skipped a beat at the intensity pouring off of them.

Zakkai might have provoked that duel to test my resolve and power, but Zeph had eagerly engaged back with the intent to kill.

A dangerous game.

A lethal provocation.

They were too strong, too dominant, to share. Yet I couldn't pick between them. They were my mates. My future. They owned equal parts of my heart, and I needed them to accept that, to accept each other.

I went to my toes to kiss Zeph before he could speak again, my teeth dragging along his lower lip and demanding he reciprocate. He didn't right away, his grip tightening against me in warning. Then my tongue slipped into his mouth, and some of his tension left his jaw.

Zakkai didn't release me, his arms locked around my abdomen as Zeph stepped closer to press against me, sandwiching me firmly between them.

I reached behind me to grab Zakkai, ensuring he didn't leave.

And used my opposite hand to wrap around Zeph's nape.

You're both mine, I told them through my wide-open links. *I claim you equally.*

Zeph growled in response.

Zakkai matched the sound with a vibration of his own.

I released Zeph's mouth to meet his blazing green eyes. "I will not choose."

THE INTENSITY in Aflora's features gave me pause. "You think I want you to choose?"

I would never ask for such a thing. It would be akin to asking her to kill a piece of her soul. We were all part of her, whether we liked each other or not. And while I certainly did not care for Zakkai, I acknowledged who he was to her.

I could also admit his use to her as a protector as well.

There wasn't anyone else in this world better suited to guard Aflora than Zakkai.

"I would never want you to choose, pixie flower," I added in a low voice, my hand cupping her cheek while my opposite palm remained against her hip. "We're your mates, even when we hate each other."

"*Hate* is a little strong," Zakkai replied, his lips ghosting along her neck to settle over her pulse. "Dislike, maybe. Hate, no. I just wanted to make a point. *Again*."

My jaw clenched at his words, mostly because I understood them. Respected them, too. Because his point had been needed.

And admittedly, I hadn't possessed the ability to push her the way he had.

She wasn't the delicate flower I'd first met, but a being of superior magic and strength that I admired to the depths of my soul.

However, it was hard for me to see that part of her. Because it required me to hurt her to ignite the power within her, and I had learned over the last few weeks that harming my mate was not a natural skill of mine. In the bedroom in a fun way? Yes. In reality, where she could seriously be injured by things outside my control? Absolutely not.

Zakkai seemed able to provoke her without regret. Like he was somehow programmed to mete out dangerous training.

I envied that about him. It granted him a measure of control over our situation that I couldn't attain. And I did not handle a lack of control well.

I met his gaze over her shoulder. "I may not agree with your methods," I said slowly. "But I can't deny the outcome of those methods."

His responding nod was short and to the point. Then he returned his focus to Aflora's neck, his lips worshipping her skin. "I don't hate your Guardian lover, little star," he informed her. "I just refuse to kneel to him."

I snorted. "Likewise."

Aflora sighed. "You both are going to be the death of me." She relaxed between us while she spoke, her fingers tracing my nape near the edge of my hairline. "Can I please be done for today?"

Zakkai's eyes met mine once more, a foreign understanding passing between us. "No," he said softly. "We still have another lesson to deliver."

His palm slid up her side to her breast, squeezing her flesh while holding my gaze.

A new activity.

One about unity and understanding.

He was inviting me in his own way to help deliver that lesson. We might fight one another on many things, constantly striving to best the other, but at the end of it all, we were still her mates. And we would never make her choose.

"You did well today," I told her.

"Extremely well," Zakkai added. "But you failed to understand something important, Aflora."

"Yes," I agreed, drawing my thumb along her lip.

"What?" she breathed. "What did I miss?"

"The fact that we will never make you choose," I told her, leaning forward to kiss her.

"But we might make you take us both," Zakkai murmured at her ear.

"B-both?" she stammered against my mouth.

"It's a suitable lesson, isn't it?" I studied her eyes, noting her flared pupils. "You doubted our intentions. Now we'll demonstrate them thoroughly."

"By not letting you choose," Zakkai finished for me. "And neither of us will submit, Aflora. Which means you'll be forced to handle us together."

"At the same time," I said.

"Indeed."

Aflora shivered. "I… I don't…"

"No choosing, remember?" I skimmed my teeth along

her lower lip, then bit down gently. "You'll take us and accept us. As one."

She inhaled heavily, her cheeks turning an adorable pink shade.

Zakkai's palm left her breast to explore downward to the sweet apex between her thighs. His growl of approval told me what I already knew.

"You're soaked," he whispered, his finger gliding through her folds to pierce her deep. "You want us inside you, don't you, little star? All that power turned you on just like it did to us. And now you want to expel some of that residual energy by taking us into this sweet pussy and screaming out our names."

Kols and I had done this once before, but not with Aflora.

Her eyes widened at what Zakkai had implied, her mind whirring with impossibilities. I silenced her with a kiss while he stroked her below, his arm brushing my abdomen as he taunted her lower half. She gasped as his teeth pierced her neck, his throat working to draw her essence from her vein.

I speared her mouth with my tongue, distracting her while he lit her internal fuse with his vampiric kiss and clever touch.

She moaned, shivering between us as he drew her closer to a climax. It would take some of the tension out of her body, making her more pliant as we prepared her.

I let go of her hip and drew my touch upward to her protruding nipple. She released a breathy sound as I pinched the hard peak, massaging it in time with Zakkai's ministrations below.

He released her neck, his gaze flashing to mine. I took over his bite, sinking my teeth into the same grooves he'd created, providing Aflora with a demonstration on how we intended to share her as equals.

She belonged to us just as much as we belonged to her.

Zakkai threaded the fingers of his free hand through her thick hair and guided her head to the side and slightly up so he could kiss her. It exposed her neck to me even more, the column of her throat stretched to accommodate us both. Just like we would soon do to her tight little body.

Aflora canted her hips into Zakkai's touch, her skin fevered with arousal as she strove to find her release. *Zeph,* she whispered. *Zeph, please…*

I grinned against her neck, enjoying that it was my permission she sought while Zakkai penetrated her.

Then he pinched her clit, causing her mind to fracture as she came undone beneath his command, not mine.

He didn't look at me while he did it, but I sensed his pride nonetheless.

She was his, too.

And if he wanted her to come, she would. With or without my permission.

I fought the urge to growl in response and instead focused on Aflora's euphoric blood. I could taste her orgasm in her essence, her excitement an aphrodisiac to my senses and drowning me in her heady scent.

Her fingertips remained against the back of my neck, her nails digging into my skin as she writhed in pleasure.

Then Zakkai added more pressure and she stilled.

"You can take it," I said against her neck. "Just relax and let us guide you." It was an act between me and Aflora that I always assumed would be shared with Kols first. But the significance of this with Zakkai wasn't lost on me.

Aflora needed this.

Our circle needed it.

Because it would join him and me in a way we couldn't undo, while also showing Aflora what she meant to us. This wasn't just about sharing but about teaching her what we were prepared to sacrifice for her.

Zakkai wasn't the type to share.

And I wasn't the type to bend.

We would have to rely on each other to control the situation, to read her cues, and to ensure her safety and pleasure throughout.

That wasn't an easy task, but it was a necessary one.

"Take off Zephyrus's pants," Zakkai said against her mouth, releasing her in the next breath. "Now."

I swallowed down the urge to correct him and issue the command myself. Instead, I focused on her gaze as she looked up at me.

Do what he says, I whispered into her mind.

Her throat worked as she licked her lips, then she reached for the drawstring at my waist.

I kissed her forehead, thanking her without words for acquiescing. This had to be an intimidating lesson for her, but she showed her faith in us by doing exactly what we'd told her to do.

She pushed the fabric from my hips, causing them to drop and leaving me naked before her. We never wore shoes while dueling, and I rarely wore a shirt. Zakkai was the same, his pants the only clothing remaining between the three of us. He removed them himself, kicking them off to the side before licking Aflora's essence from his fingers.

Then he did something I would never have anticipated.

He created a bed with a spell and sat down in the middle of the black sheets.

I arched a brow.

He merely said, "Come over here and straddle me, little star."

He was offering to be on the bottom, at least in a mild

manner. He was still sitting and very much in charge, but he wouldn't be the one driving into her from behind.

Which meant he expected me to set the pace for her after he finished preparing her for my entry.

I stroked my shaft in anticipation. *Go to him, pixie flower. Take him in that tight cunt so I can hear him tell me how wet you are for us.*

Aflora visibly shivered, then followed our orders without an ounce of hesitation.

Zakkai entered her with ease, her body more than ready to receive his cock. But mine would be another matter entirely. "Not ready yet," he said, reaching between them to stimulate her clit with his thumb as he slid another finger into her alongside his shaft.

She moaned in response, her breasts flushing with color. They were all signs of a needy, expectant woman. Not one fearing what we were about to do, but one looking forward to our intentions.

"Think you can suck my cock while he prepares you?" I asked, stepping up to the side of the bed. "I'm feeling a little *dry.*"

Zakkai chuckled, the sound deep and languid. "You won't be in a few minutes."

"Mmm," I hummed, agreeing. Then I lightly took hold of Aflora's chin and drew her focus to me. She was at the perfect height while sitting astride Zakkai, her lips level with my groin. "Part your lips for me."

The flaring of her nostrils told me she approved.

Then her mouth confirmed it as she took me deep, her tongue a velvety touch against the underside of my shaft. "Fuck," I breathed, loving the way she sucked me.

She knew everything I liked, her actions all ones I'd taught her, with a few moves tossed in that were just pure instinct.

Such an apt pupil.

The perfect student.

She murmured something against my shaft as Zakkai flexed below, her eyes rolling into the back of her head.

I grinned, seeing all the signs I craved in her—appreciation, excitement, arousal.

She wanted us.

We wanted her.

And we were about to embark on something that would change the landscape for all of us.

Zakkai had yet to embrace her other mates, choosing to watch rather than play. Tonight, he opted to engage in the most intimate way imaginable—all to show Aflora that he could share in his own way.

If she'd said no and meant it, we wouldn't do this to her. That wasn't what we meant by this lesson and her not having a choice. We were telling her that *we* accepted the dynamic and that we would never allow her to choose between us. Instead, we would ensure she could always take us both.

Even if that meant a little pain with her pleasure.

Which she seemed to be enjoying now as her hips undulated against Zakkai.

He braced himself on one hand while his other continued to prepare her, his thumb circling her clit and stimulating her the way he should.

It was exactly what I would do.

Although, I'd probably have her take Kols first, then position myself behind her and prepare her that way so I could intimately feel our Elite Blood mate penetrate her with my fingers.

An activity for later.

This lesson was about Aflora indulging the two dominant males in her life.

And about us accepting each other.

Her teeth skimmed my dick in a taunting caress, her blue eyes flickering up to mine.

"Siren," I whispered, brushing my knuckles across her teeth. "But I'm not coming down your throat, pixie flower." I wrapped my palm around the back of her neck to encourage her to take me deeper while I spoke, my hips forcing her to take as much of me as her mouth allowed.

I waited a beat before withdrawing, smiling as her irises glistened with erotic need.

Her tongue licked my tip, kissing me in her own way, just as Zakkai confirmed her readiness with a look.

No words, just a knowing glint.

I released her nape and went to kneel on the bed behind her.

Zakkai didn't lie back the way Kols would have. He chose to remain seated, his gaze holding mine in a war for dominance as I found my position against Aflora.

His hand blocked my entry, his fingers still lodged deep inside her.

Then he slowly withdrew but kept his cock inside her.

This would be undeniably intimate, an act neither of us likely ever intended to share together. Yet it was oddly appropriate given the circumstances.

His damp fingers went to the back of her neck, claiming her as he pulled her in for a kiss meant to distract her.

This would hurt at first.

And this was his way of saying he'd do his best to keep her preoccupied.

I reached around her to resume his ministrations with her sensitive nub, my thumb finding the swollen flesh with ease. She shuddered between us, another orgasm lurking on the horizon of her thoughts.

He'd properly stimulated her.

Now we were going to utterly annihilate her, blacken her senses, and show her an ecstasy few had ever experienced.

I lined myself up with her entrance, my head touching Zakkai's shaft.

Neither of them reacted, Aflora lost to his kiss.

But I knew he felt me.

And I suspected this was unlike anything he'd ever done before.

I kept one hand against her center while I used the opposite to guide myself toward her entrance.

She froze as I started to slide inside, causing Zakkai to growl and bite down on her lower lip.

You can take it, I assured her as I pressed in slowly, my patience and control resolute.

Zakkai remained equally still, his cock pulsing in response to the added pressure but otherwise staying firmly lodged inside her.

Aflora whimpered a little, her body tensing between us. I kissed her shoulder and then her neck before pressing my lips to her ear.

"You feel amazing," I praised her. "So good. So tight. So wet." I rocked into her a little more, easing her into this intensity, knowing how easily we could accidentally hurt her like this.

"Oh," she moaned, arching into me and tilting her head back to find my mouth.

"Perfect," I whispered against her lips. "Fucking perfect." I penetrated her with my tongue, taking full advantage of our kiss as I slid the rest of the way inside her.

Zakkai groaned, his palm skating up her side to capture her breast as he continued to brace himself on his opposite hand.

Aflora whimpered, the sound one of pleasure underlined

in torment. I massaged her with my thumb, renewing her ecstasy in hopes of drowning out the pain.

Her tongue sensuously touched mine, then Zakkai did something to her breast that had her gasping.

She whipped around to face him, and he took her mouth in the next breath, demanding her attention as he tweaked her nipple.

We didn't move or thrust, giving her the time she needed to accept our joint size.

Zakkai wasn't small and neither was I.

However, Aflora took us both, her body seeming to expand to accommodate her mates.

Elemental Fae were known for their sexual appetites, something I'd indulged in thoroughly these last few months. And we had a lifetime to explore her true limits.

This certainly wasn't one of them.

Something she demonstrated as she began to tentatively move between us, her soul firing to life at the sensation of being so utterly filled by her men.

I allowed her to dictate the pace at first, wanting her to enjoy the experience as much as we were.

Zakkai clearly felt the same way, his body tense with control, giving her time to explore and feel and indulge.

Her nub pulsed beneath my thumb.

Her breathing escalated.

Her heart beat loudly.

And her moan reverberated off the walls.

"Fuck me," she panted, her words going straight to my groin.

She never cursed unless we were in bed together, and she only did it to provoke my passion. Now was no different, her demand one I happily accepted.

Zakkai clearly agreed because he thrust upward into her,

his shaft stroking mine in tandem with her and sending a jolt through my system.

Because fuck, that was intense.

His eyes met mine as he pulled away from Aflora's mouth, his expression telling me he felt the same way.

So he did it again.

Then I repeated the motion.

And we found a rhythm together that had Aflora singing between us, her body breaking beneath a rapturous typhoon of hot sensation.

We all felt it, her exuberance gracing the bonds and spilling into our own pace. I groaned, my blood on fire from her reaction to being filled to the hilt by two of us.

Then Zakkai let me set a pace, my position on my knees giving me greater momentum.

He kissed Aflora again, his hand leaving her breast for her hair as he tugged her into him with a need that was borderline feral. I felt it *through* her, his power a whiplash to my senses that drove me onward, compelling me to take us all over the edge in a ferocity of movement that would either kill us or take us to the brink of death and back.

It no longer mattered.

We were beasts fucking and reveling in the shared energy rolling between the three of us, Aflora a beacon of power we could only worship and praise.

I kissed her neck, her shoulder, her cheek, and eventually her mouth as Zakkai released her lips to feast upon her breasts.

I lost track of time, my control slipping into a vortex of consuming passion.

Aflora's walls began to tighten, her body strung tight as her clit pulsed beneath my thumb.

One more flick, a single circle, and it sent her off into the stars on an explosion that pulled me right along with her. I cursed, my orgasm so intense it sliced through my insides and left me paralyzed against her back. I was only vaguely aware of Zakkai shooting off with us, his growl one that seemed to echo through the room.

And then the three of us collapsed in a pile of limbs with Aflora limp between us.

"Power expulsion," Zakkai said, his voice hoarse.

It took me a moment to understand, then I felt her energy thriving through my veins. Another one of those dark balls of power had erupted from her, but not in a fight this time… in ecstasy.

And she'd released it directly into our bonds.

That was what had taken me over the edge with her, along with her tight cunt squeezing my shaft in that addictive pulsing motion. My balls tightened at the memory, my lower abdomen clenching. We were no longer inside her, my cock against her damp thigh and Zakkai's against her abdomen.

He drew his fingers through her hair, his expression reverent.

"Kols," he said softly.

"What?"

"Kols," he repeated. "She'll need someone to take care of her when she wakes up. Shade and Kols are best for that."

I wanted to argue because I very much excelled at aftercare, but with how destroyed I felt right now, I realized he was right.

Kols, I said, opening my link to him.

I'm already here, he replied, drawing my attention to where he stood leaning against the doorway.

Oh. That was why Zakkai had said his name—he'd been calling for him to join us. I'd been so lost to Aflora that I hadn't even noticed Kols was here, something that should have concerned me, as I was always aware of my surroundings. But that joining with Aflora had removed my ability to focus on anything other than her and the act that had followed.

You all right? Kols asked, clearly sensing the direction of my thoughts. Zakkai calling to Kols suggested he hadn't lost his awareness at all, not even when we all detonated. I wasn't sure if that impressed me or annoyed me.

Zeph? Kols prompted when I didn't reply to his question.

I'll live.

Will she? he countered.

She's fine, I replied, brushing my lips against her temple. *Just lost in subspace.* She'd been dominated by two men and had erupted on an avalanche of power. I wasn't surprised that she'd passed out afterward. Hell, I felt like I was on the edge of unconsciousness, too.

Kols snorted into my head. *Dangerous game you two just played.*

She loved it.

I know. His words implied he'd witnessed her falling apart.

Are you upset? I'd never shared women with other men, only with Kols. But this situation was unique.

No. I enjoyed the show. He pushed off the door and sauntered toward us. "I'll take her from here." He lifted her into his arms and cradled her against his shoulder. "Try not to kill each other while she's gone."

With those parting words, he left.

And all I could do was laugh.

Because killing Zakkai was absolutely not what I wanted to do at the moment.

He seemed equally against the idea as he sighed in content, his arm falling over his eyes. "I'm taking a nap."

I considered leaving him to it, then rolled my head against the bed beneath us. "Yeah. Me, too."

Right here.

Next to him.

"Class dismissed," I added on a yawn.

Because after that performance, who the hell cared anymore?

He snorted in agreement.

I closed my eyes, forgetting his presence beside me. And let sleep take me under.

Shade met me outside, his expression giving nothing away as I carried a naked and replete Aflora toward him.

Several Midnight Fae had gathered around the area, the energy radiating from the building behind me an electric spire everyone had sensed. Aflora had detonated four times over the last few hours, the first three during combat and the final one during sex.

I hadn't witnessed the others, only the fourth.

And it'd been a sight to behold.

But she would not approve of everyone looking upon her now in this state, something I whispered into Shade's mind as I approached.

He responded by wrapping us both up in a black cloak

and shadowing us to a meadow bathed in moonlight. I frowned, glancing around.

"It's my place, the one I keep taking Aflora to," he explained. "Still within the paradigm, but not on Academy grounds." He cocked his head. "I'll show you." He led the way toward a tree… and stepped through it.

With a raised brow, I followed and found myself in a modest room with a big bed, a living area, and a small kitchen. "Ah, this is where you've lived when not on campus, too." I could tell because it smelled like him. Which meant he stayed here often.

He shrugged. "My grandmother is nearby. I visited enough over the years that she decided I needed my own place." He started toward the bed but passed it on his way to a set of double doors. "I think she also foresaw my desire to share a private space with Aflora, but I really don't want to think about what prompted that vision."

I smirked. "We all know what prompted it."

"Yeah, like I said, that doesn't mean I want to think about it." He disappeared through the doors.

I trailed behind him, pausing on the threshold as he bent over a large bathtub—that was the size of a small pool— rimmed with marble benches for seating and a stone exterior for decoration. He turned on the water, then tested it with his hand before clicking a button that increased the flow of water and stopped it from draining.

Aflora remained unconscious against me while he worked, completely oblivious to the salts and scents he added to perfect the bath.

It took nearly fifteen minutes, his work studious and meticulously planned.

When he finished, he stripped off his clothes.

Then he stepped into the water and sank down into it before turning on the soft purr of the jets. He didn't turn off the faucet, but it changed to a more subtle flow, the drain seeming to work in tandem with the incoming water. It appeared to be cycling somehow, which made it ideal for bathing because the bath would continue to refresh itself.

Give her to me, he whispered into my mind, holding out his arms for her.

I walked over to do as he asked, mostly because it was clear he intended for me to join them. The tub could have fit Aflora and all her mates, making it ideal for whatever he had in mind.

I removed my button-down shirt, slacks, and shoes in the closet beside the bathroom. Then I returned to join Aflora and Shade in the tub.

He had her head on his shoulder, his arms around her to ensure she stayed above the water.

"There's a comb over there," he said softly, gesturing with his chin to some of the supplies he'd set beside the tub. I hadn't caught all the items he'd grabbed, but noted now that they were all things meant to help cleanse and care for Aflora.

I picked up the item he'd mentioned and used it to brush through her knotted strands.

The jets kept the water warm and moving, the scents all relaxing and obviously meant for healing.

Aflora slowly came to while I drew the comb through her dark hair, her eyes going to Shade and then to me. She stretched her legs a little, then lifted her head to give me better access to her strands.

No words were spoken, just emotion as she let us take care of her.

We all knew what had happened, how Zakkai and Zeph had joined inside her. I'd detailed it to Shade while I'd watched, wanting him to know what they were doing to Aflora and how she was taking it.

He'd been concerned at first—as had I—but I'd trusted Zakkai and Zeph not to truly hurt her. And they hadn't. If anything, they'd taken her to new heights.

It'd been strange to see Zeph with another man, but I'd felt his emotions the whole time. He hadn't been with Zakkai out of love or desire, but out of a need to prove to Aflora that he accepted all her mates.

It'd been their way of ensuring trust within our circle.

I'd accepted that.

As had Shade.

"How are you feeling?" he asked Aflora after several minutes of soft silence.

She didn't answer for a moment, her focus on stretching her legs and arms once more as she languidly lounged against him. "Relaxed," she said. "Used, in a good way. Sore."

I set the comb down and picked up some bodywash that Shade had procured. It would dissolve into the bath, but with the way the jets seemed to work, it'd cycle through and replenish with clean water.

Aflora allowed me to run the soap over her arms and along her torso, down to her legs. It wasn't as precise as a shower, but it worked, and it gave me an excuse to check her thoroughly for bruising and any pain points.

She didn't flinch at all, her body seeming to be utterly relaxed between us.

I sensed her reaching out to check on Zeph and Zakkai, her lips curling slightly at finding them passed out.

Well, I assumed they were both asleep, anyway, because I could sense Zeph resting contentedly. He and Zakkai had been in charge of most of Aflora's physical training, leaving both males more exhausted than me and Shade.

I'd led more of the open dialogue on what Constantine might plan, providing as much background and detail of my own trials as possible. I'd also instructed her on how to listen to the source, something she seemed to be doing more and more. Today's episode was certainly proof of that—or at least, it'd been the first time I'd seen her accept power directly from the source itself.

Shade had assisted her in other ways, mostly teaching her escape mechanisms and helping her to master shadowing.

He kissed her cheek as she moved off his lap to sit between us. Then she sighed as her head fell back. "This bathtub is better than spritemead."

I chuckled at her drunk-like comment.

Shade merely smiled. "Glad you approve, little rose."

"Definitely approve," she murmured, her legs lifting to kick slightly. "This has to be a Water Fae's wet dream." She snorted a laugh at her own joke, then covered her mouth as she giggled.

"I'll have to send Cyrus notes," I drawled. The Water Fae King would certainly enjoy playing in a tub like this. Although, I suspected he already had one.

Aflora giggled again, then slipped off her bench with a true laugh. Shade grabbed her arm to pull her back up onto the seat between us, and she shook out her wet hair with a happy sound that made my lips curl.

"You're quite fun while drunk on sex," I informed her, my palm going to her thigh to hold her in place beside me.

She stilled. Then her hand went to mine to draw it higher. I glanced sideways at her, grinning when I found her peeking at me through a curtain of dark, damp strands. Her pupils were blown wide, her plump lips begging to be kissed.

Even after all that she'd been through with Zakkai and Zeph, she still craved more.

That was what the dark source could do—it revitalized and recharged, providing ample energy to the one wielding the direct link. And she had the earth source inside her, too.

I cupped her tenderly between her legs, watching her expression as I drew my finger through her slit. She rested against me in response, her eyes closing.

Is she swollen? Shade asked, his icy gaze locked on her face.

I dipped a finger inside her and shook my head. *No, she feels like she always does. Wet and ready.* I leaned in to kiss her mouth, wanting to taste her. She opened for me, her tongue dancing with mine as I stroked her beneath the water.

Her hand rested on my wrist, her nails digging into my skin to encourage my movements. Then she released me and reached for Shade, pulling him to her and kissing him thoroughly.

He languidly indulged her, his palm on her thigh in a similar location to mine moments ago.

I nibbled her neck, my tongue skimming her pulse. It was steady and slow, her movements relaxed.

After her fevered experience with Zakkai and Zeph, it was clear she wanted something a little less hectic. Something more tender and sensual, and Shade and I were more than willing to give her that.

Whatever she wanted or needed, we'd provide.

Even if it was just holding her while she slept.

She shifted away from me to straddle Shade, her arms circling his neck as she continued to engage him in a tender kiss. Not hot or intense, just filled with emotion and love. I felt the emotions thriving through our bond, her contentment to just exist and hold him, her gratitude over everything he'd sacrificed, and her desire to worship him the way he always worshipped her.

She angled her hips to take him inside her, a soft moan parting her full lips as he filled her to the hilt. Then she pulled her mouth from his and focused on me.

"Kols," she whispered, begging me to come closer with

her passion-filled gaze. She held out her hand for me as well, ensuring I understood what she wanted.

I drifted toward them in the water, my lips finding hers on impulse as I pressed my palm to her lower back to push her back into Shade. She gasped against me, his hips sliding up at the same time, filling her once more. The water made us all buoyant, creating a languorous rhythm between them.

Her lips left mine to travel down my neck, where she nibbled my pulse.

Then I locked gazes with Shade, his irises smoldering as she rocked against him. His arousal touched our bond, his need an icy kiss to my senses.

I'd never really felt his desire.

He'd always hidden it from me before.

But I sensed it now, our bond wide open and accepting.

Aflora's teeth sank into my neck, drawing a surprised hiss from my chest. Then she swallowed my essence on a groan, her body seemingly possessed by dark magic.

She's learning to embrace her Midnight Fae inclinations, I thought at Shade.

Yes, he agreed, his palm lifting to cup the back of her head. *She's finally realizing who she is.*

Our queen.

Our queen, he echoed on a groan as she righted herself, my blood painting her lips.

He stared up at her through hooded eyes, his hunger spiking through our bond.

Then he pulled her down to lick my essence from her mouth, strengthening our connection to the next level.

It was impulsive.

Yet right.

And it sent a shock wave through my system.

"Take me to bed," Aflora whispered against his mouth. "I want you both to take me to bed."

I WAS drunk on my mates.

Kols kept kissing me, his touch soft and knowing.

Shade licked me, nibbled me, explored me with his hands.

One of them was between my legs, feasting on my needy flesh. The other was in my mouth, his cock hard but not demanding.

We kept switching positions.

Our limbs everywhere. Our mouths dueling. Our bodies gliding, roaming, owning each other.

I lost myself to the sensations, drowned in their combined passion, and gasped when I found them kissing each other. They were just as lost to the connections as I was, their tongues mastering one another before sinking their teeth into each other's necks.

I groaned, the image so erotic and beautiful and intoxicating.

Then Shade took my mouth again, Kols's blood lingering in our kiss. My Elite Blood mate kissed a path down the center of my body to lick me to completion again. I moaned their names, lost to the oblivion they created.

I watched as Kols went down on Shade, his mouth wicked and perfect and bringing the other man to climax after a few knowing pulls.

It all felt like a dream, a fantasy come to life, but the bite marks and bonds confirmed the reality of our intimacy. I felt Zeph and Zakkai in my head, their contentment palpable.

All my mates had bonded in some way, respecting our dynamic and completing our circle in a manner I hadn't realized we'd needed.

Kols slid inside me, his cock thick and pulsing with need. He hadn't come yet. But Shade had orgasmed twice. The first time had been in my mouth. The second time between Kols's lips. And now the Elite Blood—who tasted like my Shade—wanted to come.

I wrapped my legs around his waist, encouraging him to drive into me.

But he kept his pace slow. Loving. Tender.

I groaned, lifting my hips into him, demanding more.

However, his pace never wavered. He kissed me lazily while Shade nibbled at his shoulder. Then Kols guided Shade to my mouth, forcing our tongues to dance while he continued to slide in and out of me. *Slow. Purposeful. Strokes.*

It was the antidote I needed after a long few weeks of training.

The tenderness I hadn't realized I craved.

One of their thumbs—I thought it might be Shade's—

found my center, drawing out more pleasure from me. I clamped down around Kols, my ecstasy too great to hold back, and forced him to join me.

He never increased his pace, maintaining those thorough thrusts.

And after he finished, Shade licked me clean.

The two men had never indulged in each other this way, and I could feel their increasing interest through every intimate move. Shade kissed Kols once more, sharing the taste from our lovemaking, and groaned when Kols sucked his tongue clean.

Then they both looked down at me and kissed me at the same time.

It was erotic.

Hot.

Beautiful.

A fantasy I never anticipated.

And I lost myself to them all over again, allowing them to worship me and each other for hours. They kissed away my bruises, renewed me with fresh blood, and ensured I was physically perfect before finally lulling me into a dreamland.

I relaxed, more replete than I'd felt in a very long time.

Only to feel a prickle of heat in my mind, the dark source calling for my attention. *Something isn't right*, I realized, following the strand of discomfort.

No, it wasn't the source… but Midnight Fae.

I could sense them, the disruption, the agony rippling through the kingdom. *What is it?* I wondered, searching for the cause.

So much anger. So much hatred. So much *pain*.

The village.

I could picture it, the tavern up in flames, Anrika's body floating in the sky with a spell inscribed beside her. *Risaleea*.

I searched my memories and those of my mates for the

translation, then recognized the spell from Shade's psyche. It was a Death Blood charm cast by a dying Midnight Fae when someone wished to leave behind a message for a loved one.

Is this real? I returned to the village, noting the fires and billowing smoke from the buildings nearby. Everyone was silent, their focus on the stage.

Constantine stood at the center with a scroll in his hand, speaking.

I couldn't hear him, my vision not quite realized.

But all the onlookers appeared distraught.

What's happening? I longed to ask them. I whirled around, sensing the heat and embers of the attack.

Anrika's body looked so alive, her long white hair floating around her like an angelic cape. Her green irises flared with life, but her marbleized skin suggested death.

She didn't blink.

She didn't speak.

Her lips were parted, perhaps from voicing the spell.

And her clothes were singed with ash.

Two more Midnight Fae were on the ground, their skin holding a similar texture. But their eyes were closed, their hands clasped together in peaceful death.

I could sense through the source that they were dead. All of them. That this was real. That what I witnessed now was happening in real time.

Somehow, I was seeing this through the eyes of the crowd, like my link to the dark source had granted me access to all their minds.

I refocused on the stage, my lips parting as Emelyn appeared beside a stoic, dark-haired man. Tears tracked down her cheeks as she tried to plead with him, the word *father* seeming to fall from her lips. But I couldn't hear her, only see.

And then I gasped as Constantine struck her with a spell, yanking her soul from her body and turning her to marble like the others.

No, I thought. *No!* This couldn't be happening. This couldn't be real!

Before I even realized what I was doing, I'd engaged Shade's shadowing ability and I was flying through space to land in the crowd of silence. No one noticed my arrival, the onlookers too busy applauding Emelyn's death.

The sound reverberated through my ears, my arrival allowing me to hear.

But the cheers weren't what I wanted to experience. They were applauding Emelyn's death.

Her dark eyes looked out upon them, frozen in time, agony etched into her features.

He killed her.

Constantine killed *Emelyn.*

My heart stopped, my world crashing to a halt. I couldn't stop staring into her eyes, the lifeless orbs echoing a pain I felt to my very soul.

I was too late.

I couldn't save her.

She was already gone, taken from me, from this realm, by the Elder standing stoically on the platform.

My fingers curled into fists at my sides, my ire mounting by the second.

Only for my blood to freeze in the next minute as a familiar voice screamed, "Tray!"

My neck refused to work, my eyes locked on the stage. A fae approached to remove Emelyn... by smashing her body with a large hammer, shattering her marbled form into a thousand pieces.

I covered my lips, my gasp drowned out by the booming approval around me. *They're celebrating her destruction.* Tears smothered my vision, my soul screaming at the unfairness and wrongness of it all.

Then Dakota appeared, her dark hair styled in an elegant bun that somehow matched her too-perfect face. I nearly growled at the sight of her, the traitorous bitch having hurt more than one of my mates.

Except the wiggling blonde fae beside her captivated all my attention in the next breath.

Ella.

I stopped breathing, my heart no longer functioning, and I barely heard Constantine speaking above the roar in my ears.

"This Halfling traitor knowingly helped an abomination to escape our kingdom, her antics nearly taking the life of her mate, Trayton Nacht. Based on the testimonies of her male mate, the Midnight Fae Council finds her guilty on all counts and has hereby sentenced her to immediate exsanguination."

"He's lying!" she screamed, tears streaming down her cheeks. "Tray, tell them he's lying!"

But Tray did nothing.

He merely stood with the Council off to the side with an expression of indifference. A foreign energy wafted around him, rippling in hypnotic waves as though lulling him into a bizarre state of comfort. *This is just a nightmare. This isn't real.*

However, it felt real.

The dark source pulsed inside me, protesting these antics. It wanted me to act, to do something to stop this madness.

"Please!" Ella cried out.

Dakota laughed, the sound cruel and cold and grating my ears.

Constantine handed her his scroll and pulled a wand from his cloak. Then he began to murmur a spell, the chords of the enchantment underlined with death.

"*Tawaqweef!*" I shouted, blasting his incantation to literal pieces. Shard of rocks splayed across the stage, hitting Ella in the face, but keeping her very much alive.

Constantine didn't hesitate, his lack of surprise telling as he pointed to me in the crowd. "Seize her!"

I'd unknowingly shadowed in with a cloak around my shoulders and hiding my head, which was why no one had noticed me.

But they did now.

A horde of Warrior Bloods appeared from the shadows, the trap evident in the way they moved directly into sight, their focus on me.

Yes, this was definitely real.

Which meant Anrika and Emelyn were dead. Because of this monster. This *thing* that the Midnight Fae chose to follow. Several fae from the crowd pulled their wands and directed them at me, their propensity for violence a dark mark against my psyche.

Midnight Fae kill, I thought, looking around at these lethal beings and their love for drawing blood. *What is wrong with you?*

They all craved death.

They all wanted *my* death.

They all were okay with standing by to watch innocents die.

Unworthy, I thought. *You're all so unworthy.*

Midnight Fae in general weren't kind. They were bad. Evil. Vile. They didn't value life or joy or brightness. They craved the darkness inside their hearts.

I blocked all their incoming spells, the shield Zeph had taught me how to make nearly impenetrable.

And behind it, I growled.

I hated all of them. I hated Midnight Fae. I hated their desire for gruesome displays of torture.

They'd all been enraptured by Constantine's demonstration. Some of them had even *applauded*. Despicable. Wrong. Cruel beings.

I don't want to be like any of you. I don't want to be your queen or represent your kind. You're evil, all of you! I knelt to the ground, a spell lining my lips. I would destroy them all just the way they liked. Teach them all—

Aflora! Shade yelled into my mind, stopping me mid-spell and breaking through some sort of block I'd created in my mind. In the next breath, all my mates entered my thoughts, but Zakkai was the loudest among them.

It's a trial, Zakkai said, his urgency in my mind granting me a brief moment of clarity.

It's not real? I asked, hopeful.

It's real, he replied sadly. *But it's still a trial.*

Anrika… Emelyn…

I know, he replied.

He killed them.

I know, he repeated. *He must have felt you embracing the dark source during training, and he chose to act accordingly. He did all this to trap you.*

I'd already guessed that with the Warrior Bloods.

But I hadn't considered the trial.

Kols had told me the acting monarch could arrange the trials for the successor. This must have been Constantine's idea of an ideal test. *Sick bastard,* I thought, glaring at his smug face through my shield.

Spells continued to bounce off of it, the edges beginning to fray.

Shadow back, Zakkai urged.

I met Ella's frightened blue eyes on the stage and noted Tray's lack of a reaction again. *I can't.*

She'd become one of my closest friends. She'd accepted

me before everyone else had. I couldn't leave her. I'd already failed Emelyn. I wouldn't do the same to Ella.

Because there are good Midnight Fae, I realized. I was staring into the eyes of one of them and had four more yelling in my head.

Constantine had enchanted these fae. Or at least some of them, like Tray. Now that I'd removed my fog of fury, I could see that Tray wasn't relaxed at all but was fighting the essence surrounding him, trying like hell to save his mate.

However, whatever incantation Constantine had woven over him was too powerful for him to counteract.

I longed to help him, to dismantle the spell for him, but I didn't have time. The others were almost through my protective barrier. Taking him back to the Hell Fae realm wasn't an option. That spell around him would trigger all sorts of alarms within Lucifer's borders. They'd either kill Tray or deny him entry.

Either way, he'd suffer.

We'll return for you, I promised him, then winced as the final vestiges of my shield began to crumble.

There was only one option left for me now.

I tapped into the dark source, allowing it to consume me like I had several times already, and this time, I granted it access to stay. I didn't expel it. I didn't push it out of me. I *accepted* it as part of my being.

Something clicked inside, a proverbial crown circling my mind, as I stood up tall and stared Constantine right in the eye. "You will bow," I promised him.

Then I shadowed to Ella's side and yanked her away from Dakota before the dark-haired female had a chance to react.

And disappeared back to the paradigm within the Hell Fae realm.

AFLORA APPEARED IN OUR MEADOW, her cloak billowing in the smoke around her. Ella collapsed beside her on a scream that had Kols running right for her.

I grabbed Aflora, checking her for signs of injury beneath the dark fabric surrounding her smaller frame. "Where did you find this?" I asked, stroking my palm down the cloak along her arm. The foreign material contained an electric current, the magic running through it unlike any I'd ever felt.

"I don't know," she whispered, her blue eyes peering up at me from beneath the hood. "He killed Anrika, Shade. And Emelyn."

I flinched, having heard those details from her mind.

"There were others, too," she continued. "And they were

cheering. Happy. Reveling in the deaths of fellow fae." Her anger lashed at my senses, but her expression radiated pain. "How can they be so cruel and disrespectful with life?"

"Because they've been led to believe it's the only way," my grandmother replied from the tree line, her voice soft and carrying through the meadow on a subtle breeze. She stepped into view beneath the rising sun, her dark hair glittering with the light.

No cookies.

A good sign.

But my grandfathers were behind her, which meant they felt the need to protect her.

Not a good sign.

But as Zeph and Zakkai burst into the meadow, I realized why. While my grandmother admired and respected Zakkai, my grandfathers interpreted his abilities as a potential threat.

An apt reaction. Zakkai was fucking powerful. However, I trusted him with Aflora because I felt her faith in him through the bonds.

"Aflora," he said, his palm finding her face beneath the hood and pulling her to him.

Zeph studied her expression for a beat beside him, pacifying himself with her safety, before switching focus to the shrieking female on the ground.

Ella hadn't stopped crying.

She was telling Kols everything that had happened to Tray, how the Council had taken him and changed him into a dark figure of who he should be. She told him about his father as well, saying Malik was acting just like Tray. And she no idea what had happened to Kols's mother, either. She hadn't seen her in weeks.

"But they're not themselves, Kols. It's not Tray. And your dad isn't your dad," she was repeating again now. "I... I don't know what the Elders or the Council did... but he...

Tray told them to kill me. He gave them permission to… to…" She trailed off on a broken sound, and Zeph knelt beside her, his protective energy pouring over her.

"He was surrounded by dark magic." Aflora swallowed. "I could see it, the ropes binding him, but I didn't know how to free him. There wasn't time. And I wasn't sure if… if the Hell Fae realm would accept him like that."

"It would have triggered the wards," my grandmother confirmed.

"With Ella, I somehow knew the wards would accept her. It was instinctual," Aflora continued as though she hadn't heard anyone else. "But Tray… we need to go back—"

"Constantine will be waiting," Zakkai interjected, his thumb hooking beneath her chin to pull her attention to him. "He won't hurt Tray. He already has him on a leash. And if anything, he'll use him as bait. Which means he needs him alive."

Kols growled, not liking the sound of that at all.

He's right, I whispered to his mind. *Constantine won't hurt him any more than he already has. And we need time to formulate a plan. Reacting rashly is what your grandfather wants.*

You think I don't know that? the Elite Blood snapped back at me.

I met his burning irises.

He glared back.

I'm making sure you don't run off and do something that will hurt us all, I told him softly. *He's your twin, Kolstov. We don't always think rationally when it comes to those we love.*

My words and concern came from a tender place inside me that had only ever existed for Aflora. But my relationship with Kols had evolved over the last two months, becoming something I could never have anticipated.

I cared about him.

And last night, we'd shared something… different.

We'd also solidified our mating, having bitten each other several times during our sexual moments with Aflora. He was firmly inside me, just as much as I was inside him.

Which meant he could feel all my emotions, hear my concern, and understood the reasoning behind my words.

While the statements irritated him—his mind quickly telling me that he would never react without thinking through his actions first—he also appreciated my concern.

We'll work together to bring him back, I promised him. *We'll help your dad, too. And I'm sure your mom is okay, just locked up somewhere.*

He grimaced.

We're going to save them, I reiterated, ensuring he heard me.

I know, he replied after a beat, his glare softening to display a measure of understanding before his focus shifted to Aflora. His mind fought for a change of subject, his need for a distraction clear as he whispered, *That cloak is radiating dark energy.*

Yes. I could feel it beneath my fingertips.

Zakkai seemed equally enthralled by it, his palms roaming over the fabric in a similar way to mine moments ago. "This is a gift from the source," he marveled.

"Yes," my grandmother agreed, reminding us all of her presence. "And I have the matching staff."

We all looked at her. "Matching staff?" I repeated.

She merely smiled, then cocked her head. "Come. Breakfast is almost ready."

"Cookies?" I asked warily.

"Eggs," she replied. "And blood shakes. Aflora will need one soon. As will Ella."

"Will Lucifer be okay with her presence here?" Zakkai wondered out loud, voicing a concern I hadn't considered.

My grandmother's blue eyes sparkled knowingly as she glanced at him. "Yes, Kai. I cleared it with him already."

"Have you cleared anything else with him?" he pressed.

She blinked. "Why? Do you sense something?"

He didn't reply, just stared at her.

She studied him for a long moment, then turned toward the trees without another word.

His jaw ticked in reply. "She's not telling us something."

"Welcome to my world," I muttered.

"You mean other people keep secrets from you?" Zeph asked, feigning a note of shock. "How horrible for you. I have no idea how that feels." The sarcasm in his tone made me snort.

"Where are we?" Ella's soft tones drew our focus to her. She hadn't moved away from the ground, her pale features marred by tears. But she seemed to have stopped crying for now, her attention distracted by the meadow around us and the rising sun.

"A paradigm within the Hell Fae realm," Aflora replied. She pulled away from me and Zakkai to look at Ella. "And I'll get Tray back for you. Soon." She sounded so regal and confident, the dark source swarming around her with free abandon.

I glanced at Zakkai and then at Kols. Both of them were studying her cloak again.

Zakkai spoke first. "You accepted the dark source, passing your third trial."

"Yes," she confirmed. "But I'm still the Earth Fae Queen, too."

"Because you taught the sources how to play nicely together," Zakkai said, appreciation evident in his tone and features. "It's beautiful, Aflora." He stepped toward her again, his palm returning to her face as he tipped her head back for a kiss. "You're stunning."

She returned his embrace, her power flowing openly through all our bonds.

"Breakfast will get cold." My grandmother's voice carried to us on the breeze once more, her energy brushing my skin. "Aflora needs blood."

"I do," my mate confirmed, her voice suddenly tired. "The source… requires it."

"Yes," Kols agreed, his tone soft. "It's taxing and will need to be fed daily."

Aflora nodded, her hand reaching for mine. "Lead the way, Shade." Energy sizzled along her palm, crawling up my arm as I laced our fingers together. She'd definitely grown in power, her acceptance of the source subtly altering her.

She no longer doubts herself, Kols said to me. *That's what you're sensing. She finally sees herself as the rightful queen.*

I think it's more than that, I replied. *It's not that she sees herself as the rightful queen so much as she wants to help those who need her, to be the queen they deserve, and to remove the ones tainting the Midnight Fae realm.*

When I'd crashed through her walls earlier, I'd felt her uncertainty and her displeasure over the pain lurking inside the dark source. She wanted to fix it, to become the entity that righted the wrongs of others, that set the Midnight Fae on the correct path.

It was what made her the perfect queen—she always put others before herself. She understood the value of leading by example. And she would never allow the power to consume her.

Her blue eyes slid to mine from beneath her cloak, her expression warm and welcoming. *I love you, Shadow. I love that you see me.*

We all see you, little rose, I told her. *And we all love you.*

Her lips curled.

I stopped walking to pull her in for a kiss, my lips whispering over hers as I said, "And I more than love you, Aflora. You're my reason for everything."

They were publicly said words meant for her ears alone. But all her mates heard them.

No one commented.

No one interrupted.

They just allowed the moment to prosper for one beautiful second, then I resumed our path toward my grandmother's home. It came into view beyond the trees, the door open in invitation.

All six of us entered, the room expanding to accommodate us all as we stepped inside. "Clever," Zakkai murmured, impressed by the magic.

The table elongated as well, then several chairs appeared out of thin air. I led Aflora to one and took a seat beside her. Zakkai settled on her opposite side. Zeph, Kols, and Ella all sat across from us. Then my grandfathers took the heads of the table, leaving the chair across from Aflora available for my grandmother.

"I don't believe we've met," Kols said, looking at my grandfather Vadim. "But I can see the resemblance." He glanced at me and then back at my grandfather.

We both had dark hair, ice-blue eyes, and sharp cheekbones. He also somewhat resembled my mother, but Kols wouldn't know that, as my mother was rarely seen in public.

Grandfather Kodiak resembled a Fortune Fae with his bulkier build and alpha fangs. Although, his blue eyes weren't slitted like a true alpha, his transition having been paused in a unique way when he'd mated with my grandmother.

"King Vadim, yes?" Kols continued.

"I prefer Vadim, no 'King,'" my grandfather replied, his lips twitching as he glanced at his Fortune Fae Alpha mate.

"Not happening," Grandfather Kodiak murmured.

"Pity," Grandfather Vadim replied.

My grandmother snorted as she set a glass of blood in

front of my grandfather Vadim, then she passed an orange juice to Grandfather Kodiak. "Behave."

"Never," they said at the same time.

"I feel like this is my future," Aflora murmured, blinking at the two men. "Only multiplied by two."

My grandmother smiled at her. "A beautiful path, yes?" She reached for the blender to pour Aflora a shake, then brought it over to the table. Her blue irises landed on the rest of us, her gaze calculating. Then she went back to the blender to create more.

I magicked a straw for Aflora, sliding it into her drink before she could take a sip. *Thank you,* she whispered into my mind.

You're welcome. I kissed her temple and waited for my grandmother to finish serving everything. I would have offered to help, but I knew she'd scold me for trying. She liked to entertain. This house was her domain, something both my grandfathers knew and respected, so they didn't try to assist either.

Omegas were particular about their space.

Especially with a nest nearby.

She adorned the table with a platter of eggs, a dish of bacon, a basket of breakfast pastries, and more red-tinted shakes. Then she placed a floral fruit salad adorned with leaves in front of Aflora.

"Oh, look, mustard berries," Zeph said conversationally.

"I believe they're called mouseberries," my grandmother corrected.

"See?" Aflora arched a brow. "*Mouseberries.*"

"Hmm," he hummed, reaching across the table to steal one from her plate. "Delicious."

"Liar," she replied, grinning. "Thank you, Zen."

"Of course, dear. I didn't think you would enjoy the bacon." She sat down with a flourish as my grandfather

Kodiak began to assemble her plate. She might have served us all, but he would ensure she had the first helping.

We all waited as the Fortune Fae Alpha worked. He assembled a dish for Grandfather Vadim as well, then started on his own before handing the serving utensils to Zakkai.

It was a symbolic gesture, one that said he felt Zakkai was the unequivocal alpha of our circle.

Kols met my gaze with a smirk, having heard my thoughts. *Don't tell Zeph.*

Not today, anyway, I agreed, momentarily entertained. *But when this is all said and done? No promises.*

Deal, Kols agreed.

Zakkai, who was very well versed in Fortune Fae formalities, assembled a plate for me first, suggesting he saw me as the group Omega. I rolled my eyes at him. "Hilarious."

He just grinned and went about creating a dish for Kols, who was equally unamused by his antics.

Then he started assembling a dish for Zeph, only for the Guardian to say, "I'll get my own."

Whether he understood the significance of that or not, I wasn't sure.

Zakkai replied by finishing the plate and handing it to Ella.

"Thank you," she whispered, clearly overwhelmed by the table politics.

Zakkai didn't acknowledge her gratitude, instead looking at Aflora. "Do you want anything else, little star?"

She shook her head, already halfway through her fruit plate. "No, thank you."

He kissed her temple, slowly fixed himself a plate, and eventually passed the utensils to a quietly simmering Zeph. "Here," he said.

Kols bit his lip to keep from smiling.

I just shook my head at their dominance war. Apparently, the little fuck fest yesterday hadn't solved their alpha duel problem.

But it was a little less tense, like the two of them knew how to see eye to eye and work together now. At least where Aflora was concerned.

She sipped her shake through the straw, then watched as I took a bite of eggs with bacon. Her nose crinkled as she leaned forward to sniff my plate. "Troll fat?" she asked, making me choke.

"What?"

"Cooked troll fat," she replied, grimacing. "You call it bacon?"

My grandmother released a small laugh. "It's from a pig in the Human Realm."

Aflora blanched. "A *pig*?"

"You remember that brown crap on the bloody noodles?" Kols asked conversationally, causing Aflora's eyes to round.

"Ugh, yes. Don't remind me."

He chuckled, then shoveled a forkful of egg and bacon into his mouth with an "Mmm" sound.

She gagged and focused on her fruit salad again—a fruit salad that magically grew as Zeph discreetly hummed a spell. Some of her disgust seemed to melt at the sight of her colorful berries, her gaze flicking up to him in clear gratitude.

He winked in response.

Then the rest of us ate in silence.

Ella was the only one who didn't seem to share in any of our amusement, her expression melancholy as she forced herself to sip her shake.

My heart ached for her. "Have you seen or heard from Ajax?" I asked her softly.

Her blue eyes lifted to mine, the sadness in them making my stomach clench.

I swallowed. "What happened to Ajax?"

She shook her head, a tear falling down her cheek. "They... they separated all of us. He was in line behind me. In line to be..."

"Executed," Aflora finished for her, magic seeming to swirl around her being. "I have to—"

"He's safe," my grandmother said, reaching for her hand. "Trust me."

"Safe like Aflora's parents were safe?" Zakkai asked. "Or safe like Aflora is now, safe?"

"Careful," Grandfather Kodiak warned in a low growl.

Zakkai looked at him without an ounce of fear. "It's a fair question, Kodiak."

"Your uncle has him," my grandmother said. "With Kyros."

My shoulders sagged in relief. If Tadmir and Kyros had Ajax, then he was fine. Unless... "Does he know about Emelyn?"

"Yes." My grandmother's expression was sad. "That's why Tadmir has him. He's trying to calm him down."

"Does he know about his parents yet?" Zakkai asked.

"His parents?" I repeated.

Aflora gasped, dropping her fork. "The two bodies under Anrika..."

Zakkai cast her an apologetic look. "Yes, little star."

"Oh, Fae..."

My appetite dissolved, the food in my stomach beginning to turn restlessly inside me. *Fuck.* "I need a minute," I said, pushing away from the table to step outside. *Fuck. Fuck. Fuck!*

Ajax's parents had already been attacked once. Now they were dead? And Emelyn, too?

I felt Kols join me, his warmth a presence at my back.

Why would Ajax care about Emelyn? he asked softly, his mind searching mine. I didn't reply, but he found the answer he wanted lurking inside my mind. *Ah. I see.*

He leaned against the house, blowing out a breath. "Shit."

"An adequate summary," I muttered, pacing and running my fingers through my hair. Ajax was strong. He could withstand a lot. But this... "I need to find him."

"No," he replied.

"What do you mean, *no?*" He had to know me well enough by now to realize that I didn't adhere to authority. I managed my own life, made my own choices, and I wasn't about to bend to his will in the process.

"I mean, *no,*" he reiterated, his tone all regal elegance. "You can't go to him."

"Fuck off," I said, no longer interested in whatever he had to say. "Just because we're bonded doesn't mean you have a say in what I do and don't do now." Only Aflora had that right. No one else.

"Yet you felt the need to remind me of my purpose here when you felt my yearning to go to Tray, and that was all of, what, thirty minutes ago?" His bronze irises narrowed. "Is this truly so different, Shadow?"

His words hit me in the heart, the rightness of them drawing a curse from my lips. Because fucking Fae, he was right.

I gripped my hair by the roots and closed my eyes.

He pressed a palm to my lower back half a beat later.

Then he pulled me into his arms, offering me a hug that I hadn't realized I needed. Part of me wanted to punch him for touching me, for correcting my path before I could even walk down it. And a weaker part of me just wanted to collapse.

I'd played with time, nearly costing Kols his life.

And now Emelyn, Anrika, and Ajax's parents were gone. Never to return.

Dead.

Because of me? I wondered. *Because of my altering of fate?*

Because of my grandfather, Kols corrected, his opposite arm wrapping around my shoulders to squeeze me tight. *Not you, Shadow. Never you.*

I released a shuddering breath, my heart in my throat.

Then I buried my face in his neck and inhaled his spicy aftershave. It was underlined with roses, reminding me of Aflora. *You smell like our mate,* I mused.

So do you, he murmured. *But not roses. I smell power and mint.*

That could just be me, I drawled.

He chuckled and let me go with a shake of his head. "You wish." Then he clapped me on the shoulder. "You good?"

"No," I admitted. "But I will be."

He nodded. "When we kill my grandfather."

"When we kill your grandfather," I agreed.

"Sounds like the perfect date," Zeph said from the doorway, his shoulder propped up against the door frame. "Will there be chocolates and flowers afterward?"

"Depends on our mate," Kols replied, turning toward him with a grin. "Or maybe just some paste."

"Mmm, now you're speaking my language." Zeph pulled Kols in for a searing kiss before meeting my gaze in challenge. *Mine,* he was saying.

I rolled my eyes. "He's all yours, Headmaster." Except for when Aflora wanted to play with us again. Then I'd indulge her desires because they were secretly becoming mine, too.

I heard that, Kols murmured.

I wasn't exactly hiding it, I told him.

No. His auburn hair flickered like fire from the sunlight spilling in through the trees, the ash-tipped strands particularly bright. *No, you're no longer hiding at all.* A hint of emotion touched his bronze irises. *I can feel what you've sacrificed for us, Shadow.*

My first instinct was to shove him out of my head, but I was too tired to try. If he wanted to play in my memories, I'd allow it.

They don't understand what you've given up for us, but I do. As does Aflora.

I didn't reply.

Because there really wasn't much left to say.

We're on the right path now, he whispered. *Now come back inside.*

He turned to lead the way with Zeph beside him.

Zakkai glanced up as I walked inside. He had his arm around Aflora's chair, his thumb brushing her back through the cloak. She'd dropped her hood but remained otherwise wrapped up in it.

Which reminded me of why we'd come here in the first place. "Tell us about this staff," I told my grandmother. "Please."

THE POWER RADIATING off of Aflora seduced my senses, taunting my Quandary Blood abilities. I kept losing myself in her cloak, the tendrils whirling around her filled with delicious energy.

She leaned into my side, her strength waning despite the blood in Zenaida's shake. Aflora would need to properly feed soon. Yesterday's training and today's trial had left her replete and in need of more sustenance. I would ensure she received those nutrients just as soon as we finished up with whatever game Zenaida wanted to play.

She'd made a show of cleaning up the dining table, but Kodiak had insisted on helping her with the dishes, saying she needed to focus on the guests. I gathered from her pinched brow that she would be having a word with him on that later, her desire as an Omega to manage her space evident in the way she kept glancing over to inspect his work in the kitchen.

Her eyes took on a silvery gleam for a moment as the future presented itself to her. After a beat, her features relaxed and she led us to the living area—which expanded like the dining room to accommodate everyone.

I took a seat on a couch with Aflora. Zephyrus settled into the cushion on her opposite side, his arm stretching out behind her while I clasped her hand in my lap.

Shadow and Kolstov took over the love seat.

Ella, short for Isabella, sat in a solitary chair, her shoulders hunched. However, her eyes were vivid and very much alive. I'd never met the girl, but I knew of her through Aflora.

A Halfling.

Mate to Trayton Nacht.

Not all that powerful, but an Elite Blood with mortal qualities after being raised in the Human Realm.

Aflora liked her. They were friends. Therefore, I would protect her by default. Even if I didn't approve of her mating a Nacht.

Kolstov's twin, I thought, pinching my lips a little.

Well, if Trayton ended up like Kolstov, I would forgive it. Maybe.

Aflora laid her head on my shoulder. *Tray's a good Midnight Fae*, she told me softly, showing me a strand in her mind that blinked brightly within the dark source. *We will save him.*

As you wish, little star, I whispered, awed by how easily she pulled up the life strands of Midnight Fae within the dark source. She didn't seem to realize how advanced that was in terms of power. The dark source was already treating her like a queen, despite the four trials ahead.

"This is the staff," Zenaida said, pointing at the table.

I arched a brow at the flat, empty surface.

But Aflora gasped as something revealed itself to her exclusively. "May I?" she asked.

Zephyrus met my gaze over her head, his bemused expression rivaling my own feelings. *What do you see, little star?*

Magic, she whispered. *Beautiful magic.*

"Yes," Zenaida replied as she settled onto Vadim's lap. The chair he'd taken over was wide enough for them to share it side by side, but the Omega seemed to be craving the touch of her mate. Perhaps because her Alpha was still cleaning the kitchen and she needed someone to hold her back from taking over the task.

Or maybe she just wanted to be held.

He wrapped his arms around her, the adoration in his face reminding me of the way Shade often looked at Aflora.

Aflora leaned forward, her fingers curling around air— air that manifested in a vine as she lifted it from the table.

My eyes widened.

Not a vine. A staff.

But the obsidian rock curled around the long, dark pole like a snake-vine up to the impressive sphere at the top. Color glittered from the orb, flashes of cerulean, purple, red, and green, with the underlying core being as black as a starless night.

Magic hummed through the air, reminding me of a wand, the staff immediately taking to Aflora and alighting with powerful approval.

I pulled out the wand Aflora had been using to compare, noting how the magical conduit no longer acknowledged her as the owner.

Because she'd just inherited her true source—the staff. "Where did you find this, Zen?" I asked, using her preferred name only because I wanted her to give me a real answer, not a riddle.

"It's the royal staff," Kolstov whispered, awe in his tone.

I glanced at him, having never heard of such a thing. "Royal staff?"

"A relic." He admired the electricity swirling around the circle at the top. "It was rumored to have been stolen and destroyed by the Quandary Bloods."

Zenaida snorted. "Not stolen or destroyed, but rightfully mine as the Midnight Fae Queen. However, that cloak around Aflora's shoulders is a sign from the dark source. The staff has chosen a new owner. Which is why she could see it when the rest of you couldn't. Set it back down, Aflora, and show them."

Aflora bent to lay it on the table, and sure enough, the magical conduit disappeared.

However, the energy lingered behind it, my Source Architect power allowing me to identify the general makeup of the staff without actually seeing it. Sort of like looking into an electrical field and sensing the magnetic pulses but being unable to identify the unique layers themselves.

"That's fascinating," I said, impressed. "Who created it?"

"Who creates wands?" she countered.

A fair retort to a stupid question on my part. "The source." Of course. Just like the dark source had created the cloak around Aflora's shoulders and the choker at her throat holding it on her.

The clothes beneath the cloak were magical as well, but I suspected those were born of necessity for propriety more than the dark source gifting her magic. She would have been naked when she'd shadowed to the village. Just as I'd been naked when I'd started running toward the meadow earlier to find her.

A quick spell had gifted me a button-down shirt, pants, and proper shoes.

Zephyrus wore a matching outfit.

Kolstov and Shade were just in their sleep bottoms and T-shirts.

What an interesting pack we made, our magic all unevenly matched and yet complementary to each other.

I lifted my ankle to rest it on my opposite knee, my focus on Zenaida. "What else did you and Lucifer negotiate?" I asked her, changing the topic away from the staff because I knew that wasn't the only reason she wanted us here.

Zenaida adored her word games.

And I was a master at solving riddles.

Her blue eyes gleamed with amusement, pleased to have had her game spoiled. Of course, we both knew I'd been aware from the beginning that she was hiding something from us.

I'd just given her time to play hostess, had indulged in breakfast—which, thankfully, had not been poisoned, something I'd verified with magic before taking a bite—and had allowed her to give Aflora the staff because I'd assumed it would be beneficial for her next trial.

"Your father has requested entry," Zenaida said softly. "I negotiated it, and the request has been granted."

"Unity trial," I replied, looking at Kolstov and then at Aflora before refocusing on Zenaida. "How long do we have to prepare?"

The Fortune Fae Omega blinked. "Not long."

Meaning he was already on his way here. "Is he at the gates yet?" I asked casually, already mentally considering our options.

"Yes," Aflora replied, reaching for the staff, power rippling around her. "I can feel them." Her blue eyes met mine. "He's brought several Quandary Bloods with him."

"That's quite the negotiation, Zenaida," I muttered, glancing at the seer. "I assume you failed to give us notice for a reason?"

"There are no other paths, Zakkai. We were always destined to meet again. And Aflora deserved the break, regardless of how fleeting it could be." She clasped her hands in her lap. "So now the sides will either join forces or…"

"Destroy each other," I finished for her. "Thank you for the meal." That'd been her version of helping us rejuvenate before Aflora's next trial. My poor mate wasn't even being given days to recover, just hours. But now that the source had marked her with the cloak, it would want to accelerate her ascension—something Constantine had assured would happen with his antics today.

The Elder had out-strategized me again.

My jaw ticked at the knowledge, my veins flooding with anticipation. "Time to go."

"There's more blood in the fridge," Zenaida murmured. "Take it with you. Aflora will need it."

Rather than take the offer, I bit into my wrist and held it to Aflora's mouth.

My mate didn't hesitate, taking what she needed before Zephyrus followed suit.

Zenaida merely smiled, her gaze knowing. "We'll keep Ella here while you negotiate," she said softly. Then she looked at the woman, her expression brightening. "I'll make you cookies, dear. You'll love them."

Shade glanced sharply at his grandmother, but she was already on her way back to shoo Kodiak out of her kitchen.

His icy eyes met mine, his concern palpable.

"We approach them as a unit," I said as Aflora finished drinking from Kolstov's vein. Shade was last.

Then the five of us left with Aflora carrying her new staff and leading the way, her confident strides a novel behavior that I hadn't seen from her before.

It was a definite improvement.

And befitted a queen.

My lips curled at the sight, and I realized all the others wore similar expressions.

Because they were all thinking the same thing as me.

She's ready.

THE STAFF REMINDED me of a wand in weight, the magical conduit fitting in my hand and moving with me like an extension of my arm.

Magical swirls danced around it, tickling my skin as the source embraced me with fiery little kisses that disappeared into my cloak.

It all felt so natural, like my connection to earth, the life and darkness swirling through me with renewed vigor after having taken blood from all four of my mates.

The act of drinking from them didn't bother me.

But I would absolutely not be indulging in their cuisine choices.

Pig Yuck.

I'll make you all the shroom loaves you can eat, pixie flower, Zeph vowed, having caught my thought. *I'll even add your favorite mouseberries.*

Dragon steak loaf could be fun, I replied. *Topped with potato frites?*

Are those like french fries?

What are french fries? I asked, frowning at him.

Fried potatoes.

I blinked. *Purple ones? Or green ones?*

He glanced at me, his green eyes sparkling. *We are definitely not talking about the same food.*

Probably not, I decided. I almost opened my mouth to detail the flaming mush, but a disturbance within the paradigm had my focus shifting to the Academy.

Shade had shadowed us most of the way back, saving us time and energy from having to walk. We were near the main gates now, and I could see the group of Quandary Bloods lurking beyond it.

The gargoyles were all agitated, as were the snake-vines, but a breath of calmness from me settled them all as we approached.

Other Midnight Fae watched from the sidelines, their expressions grim. "Go back to your dorms," I said to them, my tone holding a command to it. It was the middle of the day. They should all be asleep despite the ever-present moon on this side of the paradigm.

Several bowed and scampered back into their buildings, giving me slight pause.

Hot, Zeph praised. *So fucking hot.*

All I did was tell them to go inside.

In a regal-as-fuck queenly tone, he said. *I want you to use that on Kols later.*

I almost rolled my eyes. *Do you ever not think about sex?*

A chorus of "*No*" sounded in my head, all my mates apparently having heard my question. Probably because it had the word *sex* involved.

Zakkai's fingers locked with mine, his palm heating my senses as his power rolled through me to flirt with the embers created by the staff in my other hand.

Zeph stood on my opposite side with Kols and Shade behind us.

A united front, just like Zakkai had said.

The gates opened for me as I approached, Laki standing on the other side. He had his hands tucked into the pockets of his charcoal-colored dress pants, his white button-down shirt unclamped at the top with the sleeves rolled to the elbows on each arm.

He looked a lot like Zakkai—same color eyes, similar shade of hair, tall, lean, muscular. Their Midnight Fae genetics gave them a brotherly appearance more than a father-son one, similar to how Zen resembled Shade's older sister, not his grandmother.

But ages for fae were in the eyes.

And I could tell as I met Laki's gaze that he had at least a millennium on Zakkai.

Which made sense with Midnight Fae royalty ascending once every one thousand years.

"Father," Zakkai greeted.

"Son," Laki returned. "I see you're still mated and that you've acquired some new bonds."

"Only one," he replied, glancing back at Kols before redirecting his focus back to his dad. The challenge in his stance dared his father to comment or issue a command, but rather than acknowledge whom Zakkai had bonded to, Laki's attention shifted to me.

"Aflora." He uttered my name with a softness that surprised me. "You've certainly blossomed into something unexpected." His silver-blue irises admired the staff and then my cloak. "Midnight Fae royalty looks good on you."

"She does wear it rather nicely," Zakkai agreed, squeezing my hand.

I smiled and stepped deliberately to the side. "Let's do this inside the gates. While the exterior of the paradigm is well protected, the creatures would feel more comfortable with us inside the walls." My words were instinctual and caused by the agitated hissing of the snake-vines. They weren't upset by the arrival of the Quandary Bloods so much as their location.

Laki's ash-blond eyebrow cocked upward in surprise, then he nodded in agreement and led the others with him inside.

There were fifteen Midnight Fae in total, including Laki, making up only a fraction of the ones I'd seen back at Zakkai's paradigm. "Where are the others?"

"Waiting for the outcome of this discussion," he said.

"I see." I considered where to take them. We needed a place big enough for everyone to speak.

The history library, Shade suggested softly. *It has a big table at the center that will seat us all, and it'll be abandoned at this time of day.*

Where is it? I asked.

Rather than reply, he stepped up to Zakkai's side and gave him a look. The Quandary Blood nodded, releasing my hand.

Laki watched the exchange with a curious expression, his surprise palpable as Zakkai stepped behind me to walk beside Kols.

This way, Shade said to me, taking over the group and leading us to a building toward the center of the Academy.

"I miss this place," Laki said conversationally as we walked. He'd taken up a position beside Zakkai, placing him near Shade's back.

But the lack of aggression in the air told me no one was

in the mood to fight. Laki and his followers had arrived to talk, just like he'd said.

That probably had a little bit to do with Lucifer as well. No one would want to tempt the Hell Fae King into coming down to dole out justice for breaking whatever rules he'd set for this paradigm.

I'd heard whispers and stories about Lucifer, enough to know that, depending on his mood, he might actually enjoy watching a battle unfold here.

Fortunately, no one seemed to be in the mood to tempt fate and invite him out to play.

Shade guided us toward a set of large double doors outside a particularly beautiful building with stone walls and tinted glass windows.

Inside, the ceiling appeared to be at least twelve stories over our heads despite the exterior being no more than two floors tall, and all the interior walls were covered in books and windows. *Oh,* I thought, admiring the beauty of the shelves and the winding staircases leading up to each area individually. *Why haven't you shown me this place?*

We've been a little busy mastering physical arts, he replied. *And no, that's not a euphemism for sex.*

Any other time, I would have laughed.

But we had a horde of very serious fae behind us.

Shade squeezed my hand, then started toward the center of the space where a table with four chairs sat conspicuously in the middle of an ornate blue-and-white rug fringed with gold.

He placed his foot on loose strings, then stepped back as the table and chairs began to rattle.

"Oh, hello, hello!" a feminine voice called from above. "Well, well, what do we have here?"

"A party of twenty, please," Shade said.

"Yes, yes, of course!" Wind whipped through the air as an invisible figure began pulling the table apart.

A figment? I guessed. *Like at Acaward?*

Figments, Shade replied. *And yes.*

I almost asked why it was plural, when another female called, "No, no, over here."

"Yes, just like that," added a third.

"Drinks? Snacks? Blood?" a fourth offered.

"Blood coffees," Zakkai said. "And scones."

"Oh, he's fancy. Fancy, fancy, fancy. I like fancy." His white strands blew around his face as the figment did something to his cheek.

Did she just kiss you?

Unfortunately, he muttered, glaring at the space.

"Grumpy, too!" The figment giggled and repeated the action against his face.

"Careful," Zeph drawled. "He belongs to the Midnight Fae Queen."

"Oh, I don't mind," I said, absolutely amused by Zakkai's expression right now.

His silver-blue eyes slid toward me. *You're going to regret that later, little star.*

Am I? I gave him an innocent look. *How terrible for me.*

Brat, he accused, grunting as the figment placed a third kiss against his face with a loud smack before tittering off into the distance. *Pretty sure she just grabbed my groin.*

I'm sure it impressed her, I replied. *She'll probably kiss you again now.*

Laki cleared his throat, I thought perhaps to grab my attention, until I realized it was to smother a chuckle. "Figments are always attracted to power," he said, his tone not matching the humor in his gaze.

"Then, by that account, it's Aflora they should be hitting on," Zeph drawled.

The figments all giggled again, chairs and table pieces appearing out of thin air as they reassembled the center of the room. I stepped back as the rug began to grow to accommodate us, the area transforming in a wild show of moving furniture and chittering figments.

When they finished, one of them kissed me on the forehead, and another whispered, "Lucky, lucky queen," in my ear. I suspected that comment was from the figment who had fondled Zakkai.

After a whirlwind of activity, the air began to calm, coffee cups and carafes manifested along a white cloth down the center of the table, and plates of scones appeared at every place setting in front of twenty chairs.

"Enjoy!" the figments cheered, disappearing up into the rafters above, likely to watch and wait for further desires.

Well, that... I swallowed. *That was something else entirely.*

Welcome to the library, Shade replied, then pulled out a chair at the center of the table. Somehow he knew I wouldn't want to sit at the head position, but among the others to better hear them all.

He took the position on the other side of me, then Zakkai held out a chair next to me and looked pointedly at Kols.

The Elite Blood stared at him for a beat before taking the offering.

Zakkai settled in the seat beside him, stretching out his arm along the back in a show of clear protection of Kols, and placed his palm on my shoulder.

The Quandary Bloods in attendance watched the interaction with rapt attention.

Laki might be their leader, but Zakkai was their king.

And he'd just demonstrated through action that he considered Kols to be under his protection. More than that, he'd treated him as royalty by pulling out his chair like one would for a better.

Zeph sat down next to Shade, his expression giving nothing away. But I heard the wonder in his mind, his surprise over Zakkai's actions evident. I think we were all feeling that way.

Having a link to my Quandary Blood mate allowed me to understand why he'd done it. He was demonstrating his affiliation with our circle, claiming us as his.

Which meant his people should treat us with respect.

"Be seated," he told them.

Laki smirked but did as his son had demanded, taking the position across from us. Then the others began to find their locations as well.

I turned to lean my staff against my chair, not wanting to hold it through the meal, and rotated back around to find the entire table staring at my magical conduit. Frowning, I glanced back at it, then at them, and then back at my staff again. *What?* I asked my mates. *What's wrong?*

It disappeared again, Zakkai explained, his focus on the others. *And going by the expression on my father's face, he knows why.*

"Zen gave you the staff," Laki said, admiration in his tone. "Which, I gather, means that you now speak for her and those under this dome. I suppose we should begin, then."

Symbolism, I realized. That was the meaning for Zenaida giving Aflora the staff today.

Oh, I had no doubt it was also because of the cape and the source showing its favor by kissing Aflora with magic, but Zenaida had strategically chosen that moment to present the staff, knowing my father would see it for what it meant —*Aflora is our queen.*

Clever, Zenaida, I mused, relaying my knowledge to Aflora in a brief synopsis of the thoughts in my head.

Does that mean she agrees with my path forward? Aflora wondered.

Undoubtedly, I said. But I could have told her that without the staff. Hell, I hadn't even known the thing existed until today, but clearly, my father had recognized it.

"You never mentioned the staff to me before," I said to him. "Why?"

"Because it was never relevant. Zen was the Midnight Fae Queen, the staff a gift presented to her by the source over a thousand years ago. She rarely used it, and I never expected her to give it to another fae." His focus went to Aflora. "But I'll admit, it suits you."

"Yes," I agreed. "It does."

A few others murmured positive remarks as well, the respect at the table seeming to increase with each passing second.

Finally, the other Quandary Bloods sat, their gazes reverently downcast rather than staring at Aflora head-on.

Zephyrus broke the silence by reaching for one of the carafes first, filling Shade's mug and then his own. My lips twitched in memory of the breakfast where I'd done the same to Shade, treating him as the Omega of our circle.

His icy gaze slid to mine now, his lack of humor evident.

I made a show of distributing coffee on my side as well. First to Aflora, then to Kolstov, and eventually to myself before passing the ceramic carafe to my father.

Everyone else began pouring their own, some of them taking eager sips after tasting the blood lacing the warm liquid.

Aflora only gingerly tasted hers before focusing on my father once more.

He relaxed into his chair, eyeing her with a mixture of admiration and wariness. "So I assume you've chosen the side of reformation, then?" he guessed. It wasn't a question for me, or he would have spoken in a harsher tone. This one was for Aflora, and I was genuinely curious to hear how she would reply.

"No." She leaned forward, clasping her hands on the

table beside her untouched pastry plate. "I've not chosen reformation or retribution. Because you're both wrong."

A few of the Quandary Bloods glanced at each other. My father merely lifted an eyebrow. "I see." He studied her for a moment. "Then tell me what you believe is right. Detail your plan."

She shook her head. "No," she repeated. "First, I need you to understand why retribution isn't the correct path." Her gaze flickered to Kolstov apologetically, causing my brow to furrow.

Then I felt the energy shifting in the room as she brought up a memory spell to showcase what she'd observed in the village earlier.

I wasn't even aware she knew this charm, but before I could ask how she'd learned it, the memory began to play before my eyes like a vivid picture.

I could not only see everything, but I could also feel the warmth of the crowd, hear their laughs and cheers, and sense the urgency coming from the dark source, just as Aflora had earlier.

Emelyn was already dead.

Then Dakota appeared, dragging an unwilling Ella onto the stage.

Constantine read out her conviction.

Ella screamed.

And Aflora focused on Trayton.

Which was where she froze the memory, her voice entering all our minds as she said, *Do you see it? The compulsion wrapping around him like a thick rope, strangling the male beneath?* She increased the clarity, ensuring we all could see and feel the malevolent energy.

Then she slowly pulled the memory from our minds, returning us all to the room on a shiver of cold air.

She picked up her coffee to take a sip, her stance perfectly composed, but I felt her aching for Trayton as well as for Kolstov.

A hum of static opened between them as he spoke to her, and her to him.

Then he reached beneath the table to press his palm to her thigh, squeezing it gently.

She set down the ceramic mug, the sound echoing in the stillness of the room. "Well," she prompted, meeting my father's impassive gaze. "Did you see it?"

"Yes."

"You're aware of what it means?"

"Yes," he repeated.

She nodded. "For the others, in case you couldn't sense the compulsion charm around him, Tray is a prisoner in his own body. The spell isn't visible to others. He acts and appears completely normal to them. But the dark source showed me the truth. And it showed me that truth because it aches for those who are being manipulated by this magic, which tells me Tray is not the only one compromised by this spell."

A fair deduction.

And a reasonable explanation.

"Constantine is clearly the orchestrator of this magic," she continued. "So he needs to be removed."

My eyes narrowed slightly at her word choice—a word that reverberated through her mind, telling me she'd chosen it with purpose. But she didn't allow me to follow it to completion, her strategy already moving ahead to the next phase of her decision.

"Once he's removed, we will need to try those who have been involved in the extermination of Midnight Fae and test them for this spell." She clasped her hands once more on the table, leaning forward ever so slightly. "Those found to be complicit by choice will be dealt with accordingly. Others will be freed from their confinement."

I took a sip of my coffee, considering her words along with the others. Not once did she mention death. Just *removed*, which was a very carefully selected word.

Because my mate was all about life.

And that told me whatever she truly intended to do would be about creation, not destruction.

"It's not a fully contrived plan, but it's a fair one," she concluded. "It marries retribution to reformation. Because we will punish those who have wronged the Midnight Fae, and we will reform this realm."

"And you expect us to just join you in this effort? To trust you to see it through?" my father asked, a hint of censure in his tone.

"Yes," she replied.

Both his eyebrows shot up. "Just like that?"

Now it was her turn to repeat the word. "Yes."

He huffed a laugh. "I had no idea you were so naïve, Aflora."

She responded with a laugh of her own, but it lacked humor. "Why do all Midnight Fae mistake my sincerity for naïveté?" She voiced it as a rhetorical question, her expression sobering after a beat. "I'm not naïve, Laki. I'm the Earth Fae Queen, a mantle I took on at the young age of seven after the Midnight Fae Elders killed my parents for consorting with Quandary Bloods."

She pressed her palm on the table, a tree beginning to take root over her fingers, growing while she pressed on.

"I'm not naïve. I'm a survivor. A survivor who stood up to a crazy abomination not once but twice, and lived. A survivor who was bitten against her will and taken to a kingdom starkly different from her own, yet learned how to not only use their magic but embrace it as well."

The tree sprouted upward, igniting in a flurry of branches as she stood, her hand functioning as a root beneath the creation as she continued to speak.

"A survivor who nearly destroyed a roomful of Elite Bloods in fury after the Midnight Fae Council killed her mate. A survivor who then helped bring that mate back from the dead, only to be rewarded with an ascension she never wanted, thereby marking her as an abomination for life."

Magic swirled through the limbs, the tree itself only about a foot tall but boasting a hell of a lot of power.

"A survivor who has mated *four* different Midnight Fae lines," she said, the smoky tendrils of energy taking on the various hues of all her mates. *Cerulean. Red. Purple. Green.* "A survivor who has passed three ascension trials in less than two months, earning favor with the dark source and finding a way to successfully combine it with the earth source."

The tree began to grow upward, the movements measured and controlled by Aflora's power.

"I'm not *naïve*. I'm energy redefined. A queen of two worlds. An abomination. And a royal who craves creation and life over death. Midnight Fae have been taught to adore violence for too long. It's time for an outsider to show them how to *live* again. I'm that outsider, the survivor who knows how to fight without bloodshed. The survivor who knows how to *win* without killing those she's up against."

Multicolored leaves sprouted from the branches as she sent the tree sprawling across the table like vines, the organism morphing before our eyes.

"The Midnight Fae have forgotten how to love and respect one another," she concluded softly, her focus falling to her invention as the roots and branches began to twine together to form beautiful arrays of color as their pieces blended and matured as one. "Together, we can unite the Midnight Fae." The branches went up in flames in her next breath, her stunning tree disintegrating to ash. "Or together, we can watch them all burn."

She took her seat once more, clasped her hands before her, and said, "The choice is yours."

Sweet Fae.

Aflora's display of power, coupled with her words, had me wanting to push back from the table and bow at her feet.

She'd burned down her tree. Destroyed it. And then she'd accompanied it with a statement that had floored me.

I had no idea what to say to her. Hell, I'd forgotten how to fucking breathe.

From the expressions of others at the table, I wasn't the only one wanting to worship the goddess among them.

But it was Laki everyone waited for.

He studied the ash on the table, his expression giving nothing away. Then he stood, causing Zakkai to straighten in his chair beside me, immediately on guard.

Aflora didn't move, her eyes holding the former Source Architect's gaze.

He walked around the table, all of us observing his every move.

"Stand," he told Aflora as he moved into position behind her.

Zakkai appeared ready to tell his father what he thought of that demand, but Aflora shadowed to a standing position beside him, her show of power not lost on the others in the room or the male now standing before her.

They locked gazes for another long moment.

And he knelt at her feet. "I choose to unite the fae." A softly spoken, powerful announcement that sent a rush of energy through the room.

It's done, I realized. *She just bloody passed her fourth trial.*

This amazing, beautiful female had achieved what I had not.

She'd just united the fae in her own way, proving her worthiness to the dark source and ascending to the fifth level.

Rather than rejoice or celebrate, she went to her knees in front of Laki as well and drew his gaze to hers. "Then we unite as equals," she told him. "I don't want a constituency that bows. I want one that stands proudly together, rejoicing in life and our prolonged existences. I desire equality among the Midnight Fae factions. No more superiority."

Laki gave her a soft smile. "Then you truly are our queen," he told her. "Because only a queen could deny her obvious superiority in favor of unity." He leaned in to kiss her forehead. "Your parents would be proud. Just as I'm proud of my son, too." He looked at Zakkai. "He's a survivor, too. And with all he's endured, he never truly lost his heart."

He stood then and held out his hand for Aflora. She

accepted the offering, more as a symbolic gesture than anything, and allowed him to pull her to her feet.

The Quandary Bloods at the table all seemed to relax, their stances suddenly tired, and I realized how on edge they had been for this meeting.

They want revenge for what happened to them, Aflora whispered. *But that doesn't necessarily mean they crave death.*

Only she would be able to see that. In a realm riddled with darkness, it was hard to find the light. Especially when everyone was drowning in the need for blood.

She took her place beside me once more, the figments reappearing to fill our mugs and plates again.

The conversation flowed from Aflora's plans to a discussion on what the future world might look like. Laki offered some suggestions for council development, as did Zeph and Zakkai. Aflora listened without commenting, taking in all the ideas and hearing from several of the Quandary Bloods as well.

Shade and I remained quiet as former members of the Midnight Fae Council. While we had our own suggestions and opinions to share, we were more interested in listening to the others.

Aflora must have known this because she didn't ask us to speak. Instead, she sat between us, holding both our hands in each of hers while absorbing the comments from the others.

When they concluded their discussions, Zen arrived in a flourish, saying she'd finished preparing their accommodations. They might not be staying indefinitely—something Laki made clear when he said they would be leaving after they rested—but at least they would be comfortable.

"You're welcome back anytime," Zen informed Laki. "Or at least until Lucifer says otherwise."

Laki snorted. "I will never understand this arrangement you have with him."

She merely smiled.

I would like to understand it, too, I thought at Shade.

Understanding my grandmother is an impossible task, he replied dryly. *But I know their arrangement involves him being allowed to send a set number of Hell Fae to study here annually. They're too powerful for his Hellhounds to guard and train, so he lets her do it.*

Intriguing, I admitted. *Have you met him?*

Yes, Shade replied, his tone telling me he didn't want to elaborate on it.

As our mate appeared ready to pass out, I decided not to press him and caught her by the waist instead. She'd just finished saying goodbye to the last of the Quandary Bloods and looked ready to sleep on her feet.

Zakkai was in front of us in an instant, his mouth finding Aflora's as I held her steady with her back to my chest. The metallic scent of blood taunted my senses, telling me he was feeding her his essence to help bolster her strength again.

I frowned and engaged my link with Zeph. *She just fed from us earlier.*

Yes, he replied, watching the exchange. *The dark source seems to be taking a lot from her. Is that normal?*

I don't think so, I replied. *My father never required this much blood.*

Is it because she's mostly taking from other Midnight Fae and not the human vein?

Perhaps, I replied. *But the blood coffee contained more than enough mortal essence to replenish her today.*

I considered her as she moaned against Zakkai's mouth, her body hungry for more of his blood. He didn't hesitate in offering more, but my lips curled further downward at the display.

I think the source is preparing her for the next trial, I said slowly to Zeph. *It must sense something big coming.*

Sacrifice, he replied. *Yes?*

It doesn't necessarily have to come in that order, but yes, that would be the typical path. And it could require so many things of her.

With my grandfather leading the way, who knew what he would do?

Then let's take her back to the suite and properly nourish her, Zeph suggested.

Yes, I agreed.

We'd bathe her in blood if that was what she needed.

And then we'd hold our breaths and hope that we'd given her enough.

MY STOMACH CRAMPED, stirring me from my sleep.

Hungry, I thought. *So hungry.*

But I'd fed from all my mates before falling into bed. Then Zeph and Kols had invited me to play sex gymnastics with them… and they'd fed me again before I'd passed out.

Yet I was *starved*, and it wasn't food that I desired, but blood. *Ugh*, I groaned to myself. Zeph slept soundly beside me, his palm on my hip.

Kols was at my back with his arm wrapped around my waist, holding me to him.

Both of them were sound asleep, content, and well sated.

Disturbing them felt wrong. *I'll just, uh, shadow to the kitchen, and pop back after I have a bag of blood.*

I'd never actually indulged straight from the plastic

before because Zeph had been adding it creatively to my meals. But I knew there were bags in the fridge for that purpose.

Twisting my lips to the side, I engaged in Shade's ability to teleport by shadow and magicked myself a pair of pajama pants with a tank top as I materialized in the kitchen.

Zakkai stood next to the fridge with his shoulder braced against the wall and a bag of blood already in his hand. "It's warm," he said softly.

"How did you…?"

"You were dreaming of blood," Shade murmured from behind me.

I looked over my shoulder to find him sitting at the table with a book and a glass of red juice beside him.

"Made this in case you prefer it over the bag," he said, gesturing to the drink. "Or in case you need both."

I swallowed, my mouth watering.

Zakkai handed me the bag, the top uncapped and releasing a metallic aroma.

I wrapped my lips around it and sucked, groaning as the liquid hit my tongue. Zakkai remained against the wall as he watched, his irises flaring with power. He was dressed in a pair of sleep pants and nothing else. Just like Shade.

When I finished the bag—in what had to only be a minute—Shade stood and handed me the juice.

I put the straw between my lips and began to suck while Zakkai disposed of the bag and pulled another from some sort of warming unit next to the refrigerator. It appeared to be uniquely crafted for the purpose of heating blood.

It wasn't until I finished the juice and the second bag that I finally felt like I could breathe again, the ache in my stomach subsiding.

But somehow I knew it would only be a temporary reprieve.

"Is this normal?" I asked. Because Kols had never needed blood like this. Or, if he had, I hadn't noticed.

"No," Zakkai replied, not bothering to sugarcoat it. "We suspect the dark source is preparing you for the next trial."

"Or that perhaps it's already started." Shade resumed his seat at the table, sliding his book to the side. "Constantine won't like that you not only circumvented his trap but also passed another trial soon after. So it's likely he's already initiated the next one in hopes of catching you off guard while you're exhausted."

Zakkai dipped his chin in agreement. "Yes, and if that's the case, then the dark source is aware of what's coming and wants you prepared, which is why you're craving an abundance of blood."

"I see." I shivered, both explanations unnerving. "And you didn't crave blood like this before any of your trials?"

He shook his head. "No. Just the normal amount."

"Oh." I bit my cheek. I'd have to ask Kols about this as well, but I suspected his answer would be the same as Zakkai's. "Um..." I trailed off to clear my throat, my mouth suddenly dry despite all the blood I'd just imbibed. "What...? What was your fifth trial?"

"My sacrifice trial?" he clarified.

I nodded. Kols had told me all about his own trials in an effort to prepare me for mine, but he'd never moved beyond the unity test.

"Yours will be different from mine," he warned.

"I know. I'm just curious about what you had to sacrifice." Maybe it would give me an idea of what I'd have to sacrifice in mine.

He fell quiet for a moment, his gaze flicking to Shade before returning to me. "I had to sacrifice memories of my mom," he admitted. "But in doing so, the source strengthened me by helping me to heal wounds I hadn't realized were left open from her passing."

I considered that for a moment, my lips tugging downward. "But how do you know that if you can't remember those moments?"

"Because the source returned my memories upon my ascension," he explained. "After I'd healed."

"So the source… helped you?"

"In a way," he replied. "The trials are about preparing a leader—testing their boundaries and helping to strengthen their weaknesses. In forgetting my mother… I was able to better focus. And then I was able to better appreciate her memory when I ascended, too."

That made sense in a way. "Do you think the source will take the memories of my parents?"

He studied me for a moment, his expression giving nothing away.

"Tell her," Shade said. "Tell her your theory."

I glanced at him and then back at Zakkai. "You have a theory?"

He threw a glare at Shade. "I do."

"She needs to know," my Death Blood mate insisted. "It'll help her prepare."

"Or freak her the fuck out for no reason."

"You're the one who keeps lecturing Zeph about her training," Shade retorted. "Go eat your own words, *Kai*."

Zakkai clenched his teeth together, his irritation and discomfort palpable.

"He's right," I told him softly, my palm lifting to rest over his heart. "Tell me your theory."

He remained silent for a moment, breathing expertly even as he released some of the tension in his shoulders and jaw.

His lashes fell as he blinked.

Then his expression mellowed.

"Given your increasing thirst, I think the dark source might require you to make a choice—between Midnight Fae and Elemental Fae. It might make you sacrifice your connection to the earth."

My heart dropped to my stomach.

Oh.

Now I understood his hesitation.

"That's an impossible choice," I whispered.

"Which makes it a likely trial," he replied. "Especially with Constantine holding the reins."

I reached for the counter, needing to steady myself. "I really hope you're wrong," I admitted.

"I hope I am, too."

Silence fell between us.

Then my stomach growled again.

Zakkai said nothing, just went to the fridge and began warming another packet of blood.

It only took a few minutes. By the time he handed it to me, I was already salivating again, confirming his theory that this was somehow related to my pending trial.

I sucked it down while considering everything he'd said.

It was an intelligent prediction on his part, one I really hoped didn't come true.

He took the bag from me as I finished, and tossed it away. Then he returned and tucked a strand of my hair behind my ear before tracing the pointed tip. His ears were rounded like those of the other Midnight Fae. The touch almost made me want to jokingly ask if my points would disappear as a result of choosing his kind over my own.

But I wasn't ready to joke yet.

Instead, I focused on his eyes and the tenderness radiating from their depths.

"Thank you," I said, expressing my gratitude to him for

telling me about his suspicion. Then I met Shade's pretty eyes and repeated the words, making sure they knew I was thankful to both of them for taking care of me.

We'd all come quite a long way in our relationships. It was night and day compared to my first days at Midnight Fae Academy.

The forbidden bite.

My enrollment.

Being trapped in a suite with Kols.

The rivalries.

Looking between Shade and Zakkai now, I couldn't help my smile. They appeared so relaxed and content in the kitchen, something I doubted would have happened two months ago.

"What put that grin on your face?" Zakkai asked, his silver-blue eyes gleaming in the moonlight streaming in through the glass doors of the dining area.

"Just thinking about how much I love you all."

His eyebrow lifted. "Even me?"

"Even you," I replied, going to my toes to brush a kiss against his lips.

"Shade?" he said against my mouth. "Be sure to take notes. Blood is how we provoke emotion from Aflora."

"That's definitely not the only way," my Death Blood mate drawled as he slid up behind me to gently nibble the back of my neck.

I shivered, their touch doing things to me that it probably shouldn't after spending so many hours playing with Kols and Zeph.

But these men made me insatiable.

For both sex and blood.

Zakkai hummed in approval against my mouth, his tongue tracing the seam before sliding inside to engage me in a deep, sensual embrace underlined in passion and adoration. I moaned, curling into him and losing myself to his touch as Shade drew his teeth to my pulse. Rather than bite down, he sucked on my skin until my knees threatened to give out beneath me.

My palms went to Zakkai's shoulders, my nails digging into his muscles as I fought to remain standing.

He growled, the sound hypnotic and taking away my breath.

I expected him to grab me, hoist me up onto the counter, and rip the clothes off me.

But he pulled his mouth away from me instead and stared down at the wolf standing just inside the door. "What?" he demanded.

I realized then that his growl hadn't been meant for me… but for Zimney.

Zakkai studied the creature, then released me to walk over and kneel before him. "What's wrong?" he asked, his voice gentler as he reached for the arctic-white beast. "What's in your mouth, Zimney?"

The wolf grumbled in reply.

Then it whined as its black eyes met mine.

Zakkai glanced back over his broad shoulder, my nail prints still embedded in his skin. "He's saying it's for you."

I swallowed. "Do I want to know what it is?" Because the blood pooling from the beast's mouth suggested I didn't.

He made a noncommittal noise before studying his familiar's jaw again, the low lighting of the moon painting dark shadows on the wolf's muzzle. "Looks like…" He tilted his head, glancing at the other side. "A stonepecker." He frowned. "Why are you bringing Aflora a stonepecker?"

"Didn't Clove bring you a stonepecker after the attack on the Academy?" Shade asked.

"Yeah," I whispered. "Right before the Warrior Bloods showed up to search Kols's quarters."

Was Zimney trying to give us a warning? To tell us that Midnight Fae were coming?

"We never did find out who sent that stonepecker," Zakkai said slowly. He reached for Zimney's mouth, only for the wolf to back away, his eyes still on me. "He really wants you to take it, Aflora."

"What's going on?" Zeph's low voice came from the kitchen entryway, his dark hair mussed with sleep as he walked in wearing a pair of pajama bottoms like the others. Kols followed close behind, his palm hiding his yawn.

"Zimney brought us a dead stonepecker." Zakkai straightened, his brow furrowed. "You're the one who disposed of the last one, right?"

"Want me to do it again?" Zeph guessed.

"No, I was wondering if you'd noticed any magic on the other one. I was just saying to Aflora that we never found out who'd sent it. I thought it might have been Zimney playing with Clove, but after she told me the purpose of it, I know it wasn't him. He would never put her in danger like that." He folded his arms over his bare chest, his legs bracing like he expected an argument.

But Zeph just shook his head. "I destroyed it in a hurry because Shade showed up to say the Warrior Bloods were coming."

Zakkai glanced at Shade.

"Don't look at me," my Death Blood mate replied. "I was just trying to protect Kols. And I definitely wouldn't give Aflora a dead stonepecker as a gift."

"Tadmir?" Zakkai guessed.

"Why would Tadmir give her a stonepecker?" Kols interjected.

"Because he's Zakkai's uncle and he's the one who left me the rock," I replied, trying to avoid a snarky reply from the Quandary Blood.

The twitch of his lips told me he knew exactly why I'd been the one to respond.

"We never found out why he'd done that, either," I added, thinking back to the day I'd cast that object history enchantment. "You were talking to me…" I frowned. "Except, no, it wasn't your voice." It was deeper. Different. "Was it Tadmir talking to me? He said he was coming for me. That I knew him. That I would become him. Why would he say that?"

"To move fate along," Shade replied. "He was probably pretending to be Zakkai in order to prepare you." He shook his head. "It's hard to say exactly what he intended, but I know it wasn't nefarious."

Zakkai nodded. "I agree. He's been working through time for too long to be trying to hurt you or any of us."

"Hold on." Kols held up his hand, his expression one of stark confusion. "*Tadmir.* As in, Malefic Councilman *Tadmir?* He's your uncle?"

"Half uncle," Zakkai explained. "He's a Paradox Fae Quandary Blood masquerading as a Malefic Blood."

Kols just gaped at him.

Zeph, too.

"And he's been on our side the whole time," Shade finished for him. "He helped create a diversion after your, uh, excommunication."

I cleared my throat. "He also left the rock, so I'm wondering if the stonepecker is from him. Like a message, maybe? Or a warning? Did he send me the stonepecker and rock before as a warning?"

No, that didn't seem right either.

I'd never met Tadmir, so I had no way of knowing if it'd been his voice in my head or not.

My nose scrunched.

Then I shook my head.

"There's really only one way to find out," I continued. "We'll just take the stonepecker and, uh, run some spells to find out who sent it." I grimaced with the words, not liking the idea of playing with a dead animal. But I didn't see another option, and the looks coming from my mates said they didn't either.

"You're the commander of the creatures now," Kols said. "That makes you closest to them."

"And you can use my magic to see if there are any messages left within its death," Shade added.

I nodded. "Great. Okay. I just need to get it from Zimney."

Take the dead stonepecker out of the beast's mouth. Right. Easy. Everyday task. Yep.

I shivered as I stepped toward him, the metallic scent all wrong. It made my nose scrunch, unlike the pouches I'd drunk from a bit ago. Probably because this blood came from a corpse.

"Aflora?" Zeph said. "Do you want…?" Zimney growled as he took a step toward the wolf. "Or maybe not."

"He won't give it to me, either," Zakkai muttered. "And he's *my* familiar."

"It's fine," I said, stealing a deep breath and kneeling before the beast. I held out my hand. "I'll do"—Zimney dropped the stonepecker into my palm—"it."

Energy hummed through the air, causing the hairs along my arms to dance.

My forehead crinkled, the sensation leaving me queasy.

"Uh, guys?" I asked. "Do you all feel that, or…?" I started to turn as I spoke, only to realize the room no longer existed around me.

My mates were gone.

Zimney had disappeared, too.

Just the stonepecker remained.

Aflora! Zakkai's voice echoed through my mind, his presence oddly distant.

Kai?

The stonepecker began to writhe on my palm, causing me to drop it in alarm. Roots shot up out of it as it spun across the dark space at my feet.

"I'd grab those if I were you," a deep voice said from the shadows.

"What?" I spun around, searching for the source.

Then the stonepecker began to whine, and my mates all yelled in my head.

I looked down to see the creature twisting into smoke, the roots the only part left behind.

Except, no... those weren't roots. *They're souls,* I realized, recognizing the essence from Shade's Death Blood magic courses.

The beings twisted in agony, their hums of magic familiar.

I reached for them on instinct—all four strands—then jolted as they shot out in all different directions, their ends securing themselves to the inky walls around me.

What....?

The beings began to stretch, causing me to cry out as they dug their opposite ends into my palms, their roots deep and solid and joining with my being. *Again.* Like they had always been a part of me and it was the atmosphere around us that had forced me to release them.

What's happening?

"Poor Aflora," the deep voice murmured, Constantine's tones familiar and recognizable. "Always choosing her mates over herself."

I couldn't see him, but I felt him all around me, his power pulsing against mine, demanding I stay put until he finished toying with his prey. My mind stroked through his spell, trying to learn the nuances of it and how to counteract it, but the yanking on my strands had me focusing on the here and now and my innate need to *hold on*. They rooted deeper, securing themselves to my soul… their voices beginning to return…

"Did you know that stonepecker is how I first confirmed your connection to my grandson?" Constantine asked conversationally, like I wasn't being ripped apart by the vines digging into my hands. "I originally sent it with the expectation of it being found among his things during the search. But a falcon disrupted my spell. A familiar. *Your* familiar. Which I found deeply fascinating at the time. Until I realized *why* that familiar had interfered."

Aflora? Kols's voice trickled through my mind in a whisper, the soul in my palm vibrating.

I'm here, I told him. *I'm—*

"You mated my grandson, the heir to the Midnight Fae kingdom. No doubt because you bewitched him with your abomination magic. I'd hoped he'd be stronger. I had also hoped the Death Blood had been lying. Alas, here we are. And it seems Shadow was attempting to outmaneuver me, too. But I'm the one holding the final play in this game." He paused. "Actually, no, that's not quite right. *You* are holding it."

The souls writhed against my palms, their agony touching my soul as the space began to move, stretching them… taking them from my *heart*.

"Who will you sacrifice?" Constantine asked, his voice low and menacing. "Which soul will you release to survive?" His energy kissed my skin. "Let the trial begin."

AFLORA'S AGONY shredded my heart into a thousand pieces. I hit her with another defensive spell, trying in vain to pull her from this magical coma.

She didn't move. Didn't respond. Barely breathed.

Zakkai had caught her when she'd fainted, the stonepecker disappearing into black mist. His familiar had howled and cowered in a corner, his tail firmly between his legs. He was still there now, shaking with fright as Zakkai ran a spell over him.

Kols and I had moved Aflora to the couch, where Shade paced frantically back and forth. He kept fisting his hair and cursing himself for not seeing this sooner. "Your grandfather did this," he said, looking at Kols. "He used to send me messages via Draco all the time, always in the form of dead crows. He thought it was symbolic."

"Of Night," Kols inferred darkly. "That piece of information would have been useful ten minutes ago."

"He's never used Zimney for that purpose before," Zakkai interjected. "*I* should have sensed what was wrong. He tried to tell me by disobeying my word and looking to Aflora for direction. But I deduced incorrectly that he was deferring to her as the queen." He ran his hand over his face, his frustration palpable. "That fucking grandfather of yours needs to die."

"Indeed," Kols agreed.

Aflora's shriek inside my head sent me to my knees beside her, along with the others. "What is he doing?" I demanded, my chest aching as though I'd just finished an intense battle session with a fellow Warrior Blood.

I felt drained.

Ruined.

Exhausted.

"Is she pulling energy from us to survive?" I wondered out loud as I massaged my agonized ribs.

"It's all the blood." Zakkai's voice was as strained as mine. "The source was preparing her... to hold it together."

"What?" I didn't understand what that meant.

"I can feel it fracturing. The trial Constantine has set is requiring too much. The dark source is in agony. That's what we're feeling—Aflora's reaction to the source being split into pieces."

"How is that even possible?" Kols demanded. "Constantine isn't stronger than the source."

"No. He's just the acting conduit. And he's commanding a hell of a lot of power right now—more than any monarch should. Which means *all Midnight Fae* can feel this right now.

Just as they can sense Aflora's anguish over having to keep it all together."

"Do you think he realizes that?" Shade asked.

"I think he's too arrogant to see beyond this trial," Zakkai gritted out. "I'm trying to help her, but it's too… too chaotic. And it's draining too much."

Kols collapsed against Aflora's abdomen, his breath leaving on a wheeze. "It… it's like…" A subtle hum came from his mind, causing Shade's eyes to widen.

"Oh, fuck," the Death Blood whispered. "No."

"Yes," Kols hissed.

"What?" I demanded. "What is it like?"

"When I died," Kols breathed, his forehead touching Aflora's flat abdomen.

A burst of energy sent me forward, my hands roaming over her, checking her vitals and evaluating her still form. She felt okay, like she was sleeping.

Then Kols released a wheezing cough, and my gaze went to Zakkai. "You said it's like the source is breaking and protesting the trial. Because it doesn't agree with the sacrifice?" It came out as a question, but as I voiced it, I could sense the answer. "She's being forced to choose." Something I vowed only this week would never happen. "Fuck."

"She's holding our life strands," Shade said, his pupils flaring. "Just like I did with Kols."

My Elite Blood mate nodded wobbly, his skin exceptionally pale. "Feels… like… that."

"And Kolstov is slipping fastest because he's the clear choice for death," Zakkai said solemnly. "He cheated it once already. The source is demanding its due… by forcing Aflora's choice. That's why it's breaking."

"It feels the wrongness of the trial," I realized in a

breath. "We have to do something to help her. There has to be a way."

But Zakkai's expression said otherwise.

As did the grim line of Shade's mouth. "There's nothing we can do. This is her path to walk… and her path alone."

I SCREAMED, my arms stretched impossibly wide as I refused to release any of my mates.

Constantine's cruel laughter circled me in an invisible rope of sound, slithering across my skin and taunting my ears.

I hated him.

Hated *this*.

"I refuse to choose!" I yelled.

Which only made him laugh harder.

"Oh, Aflora. You act as though that's an option." His voice came from right in front of me, his body encased in shadows, leaving me in the perpetual dark with the ropes of magic tearing from my palms. "You must sacrifice one."

"No." I wouldn't do it. I could never sacrifice any of my

mates. I'd rather die. I'd rather lose. I'd rather not ascend. "Take it all back. Take the power. Take the source. Take it all back!"

His amusement blackened my soul, telling me there was no reasoning with him.

He's insane. Mad. Completely lost to this idea of genocide.

I could feel his hatred whipping around me, his need to destroy all those he considered to be *other*. Abominations. Vile beings with too much power.

Except *he* was the one abusing the dark source now, forcing me into a wicked web of death and despair.

This isn't the way, I thought. *This isn't how the dark source wishes for someone to ascend.*

I could feel it weeping, begging the ruler—*Constantine*—to stop. To take it all back. To redirect the trial to something of growth and potential, to have me prove my worth in a more appropriate manner.

But Constantine ignored the plea, his mind made up.

This was the path he'd chosen, this cruel game of "sacrifice a mate."

I shivered, my heart fracturing into a million pieces. I could feel Kols's strand weakening, his ties to death too tender and fresh. The dark source was absorbing him, the lesser of all evils.

He'd almost died once.

It made logical sense to take him again and finish his path.

No, I thought, shooting energy down that strand and emboldening it with my earth source. I was a being of life and creation, and I used that gift to root Kols to me now.

Aflora? he whispered, his voice a beautiful caress to my mind.

Kols, I breathed, sending more vitality to him and renewing his strength.

What are you doing?

Holding on to you, I replied, strained as the source rippled around me in a demand for me to release a mate.

I cried out as it pulsed, stretching me wider, thinning the souls of those I loved most. *No!* I screamed, slamming the vines with another bout of inner strength, drawing my own version of vines around them to reduce their strain.

But to the detriment of my own soul.

It burned.

Ached.

Left me breathless in this mass of black magic.

You can let me go, Kols said, his voice soft and understanding. *It's okay, sweetheart. I've already been gifted with more time, a chance to say goodbye to you all. To love you, even in my short weeks left. It's enough for me to dream of you for eternity while I rest, Aflora. It's enough for me to have lived a full life.*

No! I snapped. *Stop telling me this.* I wouldn't let him go. I wouldn't choose. I wouldn't allow him to be the sacrifice Constantine demanded.

There had to be another way.

There had to be—

"This is pathetic," Constantine said. "And it's exactly why a female can never rule. You're thinking with emotion and not practicality. Kolstov is the obvious sacrifice as the closest to death. But rather than choose the weak link, you're making them all suffer. What a pitiful queen you would be."

I growled. "You know nothing of the queen I will be."

Because he underestimated the powers of the bonds, the strength of mating, the bolstering of the heart. This Midnight Fae Elder only thought in terms of practical recourse, making decisions about life and death on a whim.

No ounce of remorse.

No concern for others.

Just a need to be in charge, to lead by his own example,

and to never accept anyone outside his skewed view of superiority.

He was the reason abominations were shunned, the reason Lucifer had had to reopen the gates to the Hell Fae realm a thousand years ago, and why Zen had had to craft the paradigm to protect the exiled Midnight Fae.

That wasn't the mark of a worthy king, but of a dictator who led the people by his own instincts alone. Never listening to his fellow fae for guidance or requesting their opinions. He merely told them what to do and expected them to bow.

He'd tricked the Quandary Bloods into his ascension, rewriting the power away from the Morte line to bolster his own, because he had a vision for his people.

A vision that cast out women.

Cast out those he believed were stronger.

Cast out those with the ability to stop him.

Then he'd forced the ascension onto me as some sort of trick of fate, to paint me as a monster to his people. When, in fact, he was the evildoer in this scenario, the villain who craved a worthy opponent.

And he'd chosen *me*.

The dark source had accepted *me*.

My mates had claimed *me*.

"I won't choose," I said again, my voice stronger now. "They're my *mates*. My heart. My soul. Without them, I'm not worthy enough to be queen. They're my rocks, my foundation, my roots. I won't destroy them. I won't release them. I won't sacrifice those who make me who I am, because otherwise I'll lose myself."

"Then they'll all die," Constantine whispered, his words cruel. He kissed me with his power once more, the pulsing walls yanking on me with a vengeance, the dark source bellowing in agony at being forced to abuse the one it had chosen to ascend.

I screamed with it, my soul in tatters, my mates yelling inside my mind and heart to stop this madness, to embrace the choice.

They all told me to pick them, to sever them, to live, to survive.

But this world wouldn't work without all four of them together.

My mates represented four branches of Midnight Fae kind, their bloodlines invaluable, their power insurmountable.

Yet I felt them all dwindling, their energy waning, their lights blinking in and out as the trial raged around me, Constantine demanding my sacrifice.

I couldn't just forfeit or walk away.

He'd ensured that I either picked one mate… or I lost them all.

Either way, I'd lose my heart in the process.

Aflora! Kols called to me again. *Please, sweetheart. Listen to me. I can't let you do this. Pick me. Sacrifice me. I can't live in a world where Shade and Zeph are gone. They're dying, love. They're… we're all… I'm ready… I swear to you that I'm ready, that I can do this. Just let me go, sweetheart. I'll be with you always. You know that. I'll be part of the source for—*

Don't you dare listen to him, Zeph interrupted. *I can feel his energy waning, Aflora. Don't listen to him. Don't let Kols do this!*

Aflora, Shade whispered. *Just take me… I've already lived seven lives with you. Eight including this one. It's enough… it's enough for me to know… that you've chosen this path, that you're—*

Zakkai's growl infiltrated my mind as I released a pained gasp, the darkness roaring around me. *I'm trying, but I can't… I can't hold on much longer… Aflora… Aflora, you have to…*

No! I shouted to them all. *I won't choose!*

This wicked game had to end.

I wouldn't sacrifice them.

I couldn't.

And I told them that with a blast of power that left me breathless… yet bolstered their strands. Similar to what I'd done to Kols, my vines thriving around him, solidifying my grip.

I did it again.

They all pulsed back to life, their voices clearing more in my head.

Aflora, Zakkai warned.

I ignored him, shoving more vitality and power into their cords as the darkness around me began to shiver and retreat.

When I stopped, it crept forward again, yanking on my mates and weakening their bonds.

But when I pulsed outward once more… it stilled.

Constantine's presence seemed to pause around me, his confusion a tangible brush to my senses.

And I smiled.

"I will not choose," I said for a third time.

Then I released all my power and vitality into my mates, blasting them with every ounce of my strength and life, giving them my entire heart… and soul.

They shouted in my mind, demanding I stop.

But I couldn't. I wouldn't.

This was my sacrifice.

Wind whipped around me, the dark source accepting my path.

My veins began to throb, the energy spilling from me through four strands, invigorating my mates as my own soul began to weep.

They begged me to stop.

Kols demanded I listen.

Zakkai's power wrapped around me as he tried to control my efforts, but I snapped his spell with one of my own, my heart breaking a little in the process at his resounding agony. *I love you,* I breathed to him.

I love you all, I said, whispering through their minds with my final words as I fell to my knees on an exhausted wheeze.

I was wrong before. Constantine wanted me to choose. I refused. Until now.

"I choose to sacrifice myself."

My palms met the black floor.

And I unleashed every last drop of my being into their vines, their cries of pain at my loss… following me down… down… down…

Eight lifetimes.

Seven of which I'd watched her nearly die. I'd always changed time. I'd always brought her back. I'd always started over. I'd always *fixed* her.

But there was no coming back this time.

I had no Paradox Fae. I had no sword. I had no power to stop this.

"Aflora," I whispered, looking down at her bluing skin. The obsidian power lining her veins was gone. No more dark source. No more ascension. No more… *life*. Just like Kols. Only worse.

Because it matched a fate I thought I'd altered.

I'd done everything right this time, had finally taken us down the path meant for eternity.

And now… My heart cracked. *Little rose…*

"Please don't do this." It came out in a whisper, my voice failing me.

So many lifetimes. So much sacrifice. So much pain.

But nothing amounted to this, to watching her skin change… hearing her breath rattle… seeing her soul wither…

My pulse refused to beat. "No." It left my lips on a choked sound. "No, Aflora. *No.*" I whispered a spell, my mind latching onto her final strands, my soul refusing to release her. "*No!*"

I yanked her back, my magical hold slipping as she fought me, her spirit moving on without my permission.

"No!" I shouted again, desperate now.

Too many lifetimes.

This couldn't be the end.

This couldn't be it.

I'd loved her for what felt like eons of an existence, our souls tied in a way few others would ever understand. I'd bitten her. She was mine. I would keep her. She couldn't leave me. That wasn't how this worked.

"This isn't supposed to happen!" I raged at her. "I gave up everything for you! Why wouldn't you let me give you this?" I would have been her sacrifice. I would have died at her feet if it meant hearing her breathe once more.

My grasp on her soul slipped again, and I grabbed at the air, my fingers going through her. My spell was waning. Dying. Just like her. Just like my heart. Just like my own fucking soul.

Zakkai whispered some sort of incantation next to me, his attempt to bring her back bolstering my hope for a split second of time.

Until her final gasp graced my ears.

A sound I would never forget.

A sound that would follow me to my grave.

A sound that told me I'd failed.

"Eight lifetimes," I whispered, my head falling to her chest as her pulse slowed to a silent beat.

I love you. Her words blew across my mind, her soul kissing my cheek as she escaped my last attempt to hold on to her.

I'll always be with you, Shade. Watching from above. I will forever love you. Something soft and feathery fell across my hand.

A rose petal.

Graced by her magic, her Earth Fae touch… her final goodbye.

My little rose. My sweet, beautiful Aflora. Taken by this world. This unfair, cruel, wretched existence.

There was no coming back from this.

No more tricks of time.

No more plays up my sleeve.

This was it.

Just me… my Aflora… and her final kiss of a rose petal on my wrist.

He's won, I realized. *Constantine… has won.*

I was always meant to love her and lose her. *Because death will always find a way.*

AFLORA'S LIFE strands circled my wrists, the invisible power one I could feel more than see. "She's here," I said, talking to no one and everyone.

But no one replied.

Shade had his forehead pressed to her chest, his shoulders hunched in agony at her loss.

Kolstov and Zephyrus were behind him, watching with expressions of horror mingled with pain.

They were in shock.

"She's here!" I repeated, my voice strained as I tried futilely to grab their focus. But they were lost to their grief, seeing her body frozen and not breathing, her heart no longer beating.

I growled in annoyance, not ready to give up.

But I felt Aflora pulsing through the dark source web, the last vestiges of her strength urging me to release it.

It's my choice, she seemed to be saying. *Let me go, Zakkai. Please... let me go.*

My chest ached, my mind unwilling to comprehend what had just happened, how quickly I'd lost my mate.

Sacrifice wasn't supposed to be like this.

Sacrifice was about growth, perseverance, *power.*

It wasn't about death. It wasn't about giving up the cords of life to the dark source. But Constantine had forced that trial upon her, making her choose.

And she'd chosen herself.

Like a true queen, putting everyone else before herself.

All of the Midnight Fae knew. They'd all felt her decision, her sacrifice, her putting our love and lives over her own.

I felt them weeping, sensed the dark source breaking from the loss of a powerful royal, an ideal candidate to rule.

And I sensed Constantine's victory over it all, his malicious laughter as he watched her perish inside that dark void... alone... without her mates.

Aflora, I breathed, her soul slipping through my fingers, the spell Shade had uttered disappearing into the wind.

She'd kissed his hand with a rose petal.

Just as she whispered her love into my mind.

I'm okay, she told me. *It's okay... to let me go... to let me be free, to lead the fae to life. I'll watch you all from above. I'll see you from the stars.*

My knees gave out, tears blurring my vision as a bright light blinked above her, twinkling like a little sun.

My star.

My little star.

My sweet, beautiful star.

Aflora… She'd been my other half for so long that I wasn't sure how I'd survive without her.

This was so much worse than cutting off our bond all those years ago. So much worse than all the pain Constantine and the Elders had inflicted on my life and being. So much worse than my own ascension and the pain of taking on the Source Architect role.

This was like having a million stars combust inside me, leaving only one above to guide me and watch over me for an eternity of solitude.

Because there would be no other Aflora.

No other queen.

No other star.

She was my one and only… and I'd failed her.

I'd failed… my sweet… beautiful… star…

My head fell to my hands, my world breaking as the dark source wept with me, the pain echoing through all vestiges of my being and spirit.

The Midnight Fae knew.

Their queen had just died… because she'd sacrificed for them all. Not just for her mates, but for all of Midnight Fae kind.

A demonstration of what power should be, how it should be used, how a true queen should lead.

The dark source blinked with the rightness of her choice, praising her for her leadership and grace. It was a beautiful goodbye.

And a stunning… *hello.*

I blinked, feeling the paths and magic whirling and shifting and embracing the sacrifice she'd given… by regenerating with life.

My hands fell from my face as I stared up at that blinking light, the star in the room that only I seemed able to see.

Her light in the dark.

Her life at the center of the dark source.

A royal… ascending to her desired throne.

Sacrifice and respect, I realized. *She just passed two trials at once.*

Because she'd sacrificed herself for those she loved, and all of the Midnight Fae had felt it… and respected her choice.

Which left only one trial for her to pass—her ascension.

Energy shot through me, the dark source calling for my focus once more as it revitalized our bonds, reigniting Aflora's veins, and shoving power back into her heart.

I felt her moving, her soul venturing *through* the dark source and back into the light.

Her light.

Her radiant star.

Her earth.

Her life.

Her vitality.

Soaring through the Midnight Fae web of power with a finality befitting a queen.

And landing in the still-warm body before me.

Her eyes opened, stars painting her pupils in blinding lights. And she took a renewed breath.

Our queen has officially risen.

I could feel it in my bones, in my soul, in my every breath. The dark source had accepted her sacrifice. And allowed her soul to pass through the heart of Midnight Fae power before returning to her corporeal state.

She passed her trial.

Not just the sacrifice test, but the respect one as well. The knowledge echoed around us, the whole of Midnight Fae kind bowing to their chosen queen. It was the sort of respect that didn't need to be seen, but felt. And it sent me to my knees.

"My queen," I breathed, tears pooling in my eyes, battling the moisture that already existed from my earlier sadness. These new tears were ones of profound happiness and pride. "You did it."

Zeph stilled beside me, so lost in his grief that he hadn't noticed her return. Then he fell to his knees beside me for an entirely different reason, emotion ripping from his chest on an anguished cry he'd held within himself for too long, his pain overwhelming our bond.

I reached for him, steadying him and allowing him his moment. He'd been so shocked, and then stricken, that he hadn't been able to react. And now that Aflora was awake, he'd released a wave of anguish he could no longer contain.

Anguish that quickly turned to exuberance as he crawled toward her, his hand seeking hers.

It was probably the one and only time I would ever see him bend in such a way.

Shade? I whispered, noting his hunched shoulders and broken form. His forehead rested against Aflora's chest, his body unmoving.

He didn't reply.

Zeph kissed Aflora, a possessive growl going through him. "Don't you ever do that again."

Shade? I repeated, trying to find his mind in our connection. But all I heard was silence.

"Are you all right, little star?" Zakkai asked, kneeling beside the arm of the couch, close to her head and near Zeph.

Shade still didn't move, even as Zeph's body nudged him from the side.

Aflora nodded slowly, her blue eyes blinking up at Zakkai and Zeph. She glanced at me next, then down to Shade's bowed head.

She lifted her hand to run her fingers through his hair, saying nothing out loud. But I felt the hum of energy that suggested she spoke into his mind.

He didn't react.

I frowned.

"Shade." Aflora's voice was soft with sleep, like this had all been a strange nightmare, not a heartbreaking experience. "You've given us everything, Shade. It was my turn to sacrifice something for you."

Her fingers continued to comb through his hair, her motions tender and rhythmic.

"It's still the right path," she continued. "And you're the reason we're here." She looked at each of us. "You all are my purpose for being here." Her attention returned to the broken man against her chest. "And you made that possible, Shade."

She drew her touch down to his nape, his dark hair a stunning contrast to her pale skin.

"Life cannot exist without death," she whispered. "I understand that now. Because of you, Shade. Because of all of you."

She smiled, her expression breathtakingly real, and yet she glimmered like an intangible goddess.

You wear power beautifully, I said into her mind. *You're stunning.*

Electricity kissed my skin as she responded with magic instead of words, her control over the dark source nearly resolute.

"You're mine to protect now, too," she murmured to Shade. "We will all make sacrifices for each other. It's what makes us stronger. And we all know we have you to thank for paving the way for us. You gave us a gift that will never be repaid. But I will spend my eternity with you, trying to repay it."

"I don't want to be repaid," he muttered against her chest. "I just want you."

"You have me," she vowed. "You have me entirely."

His head slowly rose from her chest, his shoulders still rounded in pain. "It's my path in life to take risks for you. Not the other way around."

I had never heard him speak so gravely. He always boasted a worry-free air about him, like nothing ever disturbed him. But he acted with the utmost seriousness now.

"And it's my path in life to love you all," she whispered. "To never have to choose."

She pulled him to her, his body moving beneath her physical command.

"I would give anything and everything for all of you. Including myself. Because you demonstrated the importance of sacrifice, Shade. You showed me how to live. You taught me how to hate and how to love. You helped me learn how to fly free without restraints. And you're the reason I'm here today. Right now. Right here. With all of you."

She kissed him, her devotion branding our bonds as she committed herself to us all on a level that defied existence.

We were hers.

She was ours.

And together, we would persevere.

Together… we would fly.

We surrounded her, each taking turns to worship our goddess with our mouths, to express our gratitude and love and absolute reverence.

I was last, my lips tasting hers and all her other mates. A perfect union. A joyous occasion. A tender embrace.

She whispered my name, her fingers in my hair as I indulged in another kiss. Languid strokes. Heat. Beauty. Love.

I pressed my forehead to hers, sensing the budding urgency inside her.

It wasn't sexual, but arduous. Our embrace one underlined in the future, and a destiny calling her name.

Queen Aflora.

"It's time," she breathed, her power wrapping around all of us as she engaged Shade's shadow and took us to the LethaForest outside the main Academy, to the place where Midnight Fae life originally began.

It was a sacred platform surrounded by creatures and night and the hum of approval in the air. *Pure magic.*

Midnight Fae only congregated here once every one thousand years, the grounds a known place for dark source ascension.

That was what made the LethaForest so dangerous—the plant life, animals, and air were haunted by ancient magic. It made events unpredictable.

But today, the LethaForest was quiet. Hopeful. Waiting.

Aflora stood in the middle of it all with her enchanted cloak and staff, her blue-black hair blowing in an intangible breeze created by power and not the elements around her.

A circle of ancient trees surrounded us, their black branches flickering to life with fire to illuminate the night.

Magic brushed my skin as my cloak appeared at my shoulders, my bare chest suddenly covered by a button-down shirt, and my pajama pants replaced by black trousers.

Zeph, Zakkai, and Shade were all adorned in similar attire.

But the clasps of our cloaks were ruby roses with glistening stars at the center. The edges flared with defensive energy borrowed from Zeph, and the clasps connected themselves to the fabric with a series of multicolored roots.

One for each mate.

My heart warmed at the clear claim, our queen having gifted us all with her own token of favor.

And they shimmered in the moonlight, the red petals bleeding with renewed colors to match the roots.

A truly magical series of charms.

I stroked it with my thumb, sensing Aflora's touch, and smiled. *Thank you, love.*

She blew a kiss into my mind, then finished her own wardrobe with a flowing black dress that glimmered like a diamond, showcasing all the colors of the Midnight Fae.

Her gaze went to the tree line, her stance powerful as the branches began to rustle.

Then a wave of spells flew at her from the forest's edge—each one bouncing off a shield I hadn't felt her create.

Magnificent.

Our cloaks were the shield, her clasp the bearer of the protective spell. That was why I'd sensed Zeph within the magic. He'd taken up a guarded stance next to her with Zakkai on her opposite side, their positions ready for a fight.

But Aflora was clearly done with this battle.

She didn't cast any enchantments back at the approaching Warrior Bloods. She merely absorbed their charms and turned them to rose petals on the ground.

Shade took up a position behind her, so I stepped in front of her, the four of us creating a clear mate-circle around her.

That didn't stop the Warrior Bloods or the Elders behind them.

However, every offensive spell disintegrated into flowers, Aflora's power resolute.

Her hand settled on my shoulder, her petite frame hidden by my much taller one. I shifted as she stepped to my side, Zeph coming up next to me, with Zakkai and Shade completing the line on Aflora's left.

My grandfather appeared with my father and brother beside him, their collective fury stealing the breath from my lungs.

"Abomination!" they shouted.

"This cannot stand," my grandfather concluded.

"Yet you ensured my ascension yourself," Aflora replied

calmly, a memory charm appearing as she blasted the event to all Midnight Fae.

"Soon they'll see you for what you are, Queen Aflora," my grandfather's voice reverberated through the LethaForest and all our minds. *"An abomination in the truest form. A monster. A being consumed by power, both Elemental Fae and Midnight Fae in nature. And I can't wait to watch you burn."*

"An abomination, yes," she agreed. "But I'm not the monster, Constantine. I'm not the being consumed by power. However, they all witnessed me burn, just like you'd said. And now they know my true nature, too."

Aflora's pity poured through our bond, her heart breaking for the man before her.

Not my father.

Not my brother.

But my grandfather.

"You want to control them all," she whispered. "Because you fear what you do not understand. You refuse to listen, to observe, to *learn*. You crave power as a protection, and it's consumed you entirely. Because you never learned balance."

Energy flowed through our connections as Aflora grounded herself by pushing the dark source to her mates, demonstrating her version of balance.

"You never learned how to love," she continued sadly. "And for that, I'm sorry for you. Emotions are what root us to life. Without them, we soar too high and forget how to feel. My mates—the ones you tried to force me to choose between—are my rocks. My foundation. The reasons I'm able to absorb and maintain connections to two sources."

She reached for my hand and Zakkai's, squeezing our palms.

"These Midnight Fae represent my balance. They're my kings. My equals. My own personal council. They're the reasons for my ascension today. Because they taught me how to live and love."

Silence fell, my grandfather's eyes narrowing.

However, all around the tree line... the Midnight Fae began to kneel.

Not to the Nacht line.

But to Aflora, Queen of the Midnight Fae.

A sliver of power slipped from beneath our shields, Aflora's energy wrapping around my father and brother as she untangled some invisible web from their auras. I couldn't see it, but I felt it.

Zakkai reached out as well, emboldening her work.

"What are you doing?" Constantine asked, sensing it as well. His eyes began to widen. "Don't you feel this witchery?" He looked to the Elders and the kneeling Warrior Bloods. "She's enchanted you all. Don't you sense it?"

"I'm not the one weaving enchantments, Elder Constantine," she replied. "I'm merely... undoing them."

My father gasped as he collapsed to one knee, his hand at his neck.

His golden irises found mine, abject horror radiating in his depths. "Kols..." Then he looked down at his own hands in shame as memories of what he'd done rolled through his features. "Dear Fae..." His attention turned upward to the man beside him. "My own son. You made me kill *my own son.*"

"For the betterment of Midnight Fae kind," my grandfather growled. "Which, clearly, you've all forgotten because *that thing* has bewitched you." He pointed to Aflora, his ire mounting by the second.

Zakkai's stance straightened, his gaze narrowing, his reaction telling me that my grandfather had accessed the dark source.

But a wave from Aflora's hand dismantled it all and caused flower petals to rain down from the clear sky.

My grandfather cursed.

And Tray clocked him with a fist to the side of the face. "Where the fuck is Ella?" he demanded, taking the old man by the collar and strangling him with his grip. "Where is she?"

"She's coming." Aflora's reply was carried on the wind, her power so resolute that even I wanted to kneel. I'd never felt anything like it. My father had always boasted an energy that took my breath away, but Aflora… she was like holding on to the source itself. "She's safe, Tray."

My brother crumpled then, his agony shattering my heart.

I wanted to go to him, to hold him, to promise him that Ella would forgive him.

But a stroke from Shade's mind kept me steady.

Because my mate needed me more right now, my position beside her symbolic in so many ways. And she'd meant what she'd said—we were her anchors, the ones who kept her grounded.

If I left our cocoon of protection, my grandfather would use me against her. I couldn't allow that to happen.

My grandfather blasted Tray with a spell that put him on his ass, then lifted his hand with a lethal ball of WarFire meant to destroy. "You're all useless," he hissed, taking aim.

A jolt hit my heart, the fear on my twin's face causing me to take a step forward.

Don't, Shade demanded, his word freezing me in place.

The WarFire left my grandfather's palm, angling downward toward my brother's chest.

Tray! I tried to move, to go to him, to save him from his fate, but Zeph caught my shoulder, holding me in place.

My brother cried out as the spell hit him, only to freeze

half a breath later as stone engulfed his form. I blinked, shocked by the instant marbleized state of death.

My father bellowed in fury, the dark source responding to his call and wrapping my grandfather in a sea of darkness.

But the man just laughed, dissolving the spell with a flick of his wand and shooting a volt into my father's abdomen, sending him to his knees beside Tray's still form.

"Magic is fascinating," a new voice said, deep and carrying and familiar. "It can be manipulated in so many ways." Tadmir stepped through the trees with several Councilmen at his back.

Gone were his usual black robes, replaced by a cloak edged in cerulean, his long white hair flickering with bluish-green flames.

"Sorry I'm late," he said. "I had some spells to unwind." He directed his wand at my brother, the stones fracturing around Tray's skin to reveal my irate twin beneath.

I blinked, confused by the sight of him squirming out from the marble encasement.

My grandfather appeared equally as enthralled and partially dumbfounded. He gaped at the approaching Councilmen, his gaze settling on the white-haired one at the front.

"Oh, yes, you don't recall this from our history together," Tadmir drawled. "Well, in a previous timeline, you knew my true nature. You killed my Quandary Blood mate. Tried to take my son, too."

A dark-haired male with tattoos swirling up his arm appeared in the next instant to lean against a tree. My eyebrows lifted in recognition. *Kyros. Paradox Fae.* He'd been the one helping Shade manipulate time.

The male winked at me as though he'd heard my thoughts, then kicked up his foot behind him to rest against the trunk of the tree.

"Unfortunately, time did not allow me to save my mate. But it did allow me to properly prepare for you and your destructive plans for the Midnight Fae." He waved a hand over himself. "You wanted an all-male council, so I became a Malefic Blood and took a new mate—a female who was best friends with my previous one. It's a long, drawn-out story that ends in a myriad of timelines, this one being the preferred avenue, of course."

His eyes lifted to Aflora.

"The timeline where she becomes queen," he concluded with a smile. "I told you that you knew me. And now you see why. We're alike, you and I. Abominations who use our power for the betterment of the world, not to destroy it."

"The message on the rock," she breathed, her lips curling faintly. "I remember, and now I see."

"You do," he agreed, bowing his head in subtle reverence. "My queen."

"This is what I've warned everyone about," my grandfather said, his fear palpable. "That abominations live among us and will take our kingdoms. You're proof. This is proof. The fae kingdoms need to see!" He sent up a spark of power that blew in a sudden gust of wind, dissolving in fire a beat later.

He gaped at it, then his gaze flew to the tree line as an abundance of power rocked the earth.

A familiar presence touched my senses as the trees parted in reverence, allowing the Elemental Fae Queen to enter with her Spirit Fae King and Water Fae King mates on either side of her.

And a very irritated-looking Earth Fae behind them.

I swallowed.

The last time I saw that giant rock of a man, he'd introduced his fist to my face. And I really wasn't in the mood for a repeat performance.

A Fire Fae and an Air Fae appeared next, the queen's entire circle surrounding her in obvious protection.

Then her gaze locked on Aflora.

Everyone stilled.

Until my grandfather smiled. "I told you she was an abomination. Just like Elana. I think you know what has to be done."

Oh, fuck.

I squeezed Kols's hand, sensing his tension.

We both knew what Constantine's words implied and how they might be perceived, but I felt the earth source shining down upon me. Which meant Sol could sense it, too.

His green-brown irises met mine over Claire's head, his concern evident in his features. But one look and his lips curled at the edges.

He knew I was still me. Just a new and improved version.

An enhanced one.

More powerful.

But still an Earth Fae at heart.

I curtsied to my Elemental Fae Queen, showing my respect. "Queen Claire," I greeted softly. A few months ago, I would have run up and begged her to take me home. But seeing her now, surrounded by her mates, I realized that they no longer represented my preferred haven.

The Midnight Fae realm was my home now, my roots having grown deep into the soil of this world and claimed it as my own.

Because of my mates.

And the dark source.

These fae needed me more, too. They required my light and life to guide them into a phase of regrowth and prosperity.

Which required me to do something destructive first.

Something I would never have considered doing just weeks ago.

But I'd learned through my trials that sometimes we must destroy to pave the way for re-creation. For life could not exist without death.

Constantine was a bad seed, his mentality so warped by wrongness that he could no longer see the light. Being a queen required tough choices, and this would be my burden to bear.

My final ascension trial.

Returning the bad seed to the earth, where it could eventually be reborn and blossom into something good.

Claire studied me, her blue irises intense and guarded as memories flashed through her eyes. I recognized the haunted gleam in her features because I often felt it myself when I thought about Elana. She'd destroyed nearly all the Spirit Fae with a plague that she'd later turned on the Earth Fae.

I'd felt that dark magic, had absorbed and dismantled it before it could reach the heart of my source. I hadn't understood it at the time, my mind working on protective instinct alone, but now I knew that gift had come from Zakkai.

As his Quandary Blood mate, I'd been able to save my

fellow Earth Fae by reconfiguring Elana's spell and pushing it away from my kingdom.

Which meant I'd been an abomination all along, since the young age of seven.

Yet I lived in peace with my fellow Elemental Fae. And now I would share that peace with the Midnight Fae.

"I'm not a threat," I told her softly. "It's not how much power we have that matters; it's how we use it." And if anyone would understand that, it would be Claire. As an Elemental Fae with access to all five elements, she knew better than anyone what power could do to a fae.

"Being connected to two sources makes you beyond powerful," Constantine seethed. "It makes you wicked and deceitful, and I'll ensure that everyone sees through this charade you've created." Inky wisps of energy seeped from his fingertips while he spoke, but no one else seemed to notice.

The dark source protested in my heart, telling me this wasn't the way, begging me to fix it.

This was the magic he'd used to manipulate and control others, the wicked spell that had consumed two Elite Bloods and likely several others.

Tadmir's obsidian gaze met mine, knowledge sprouting from his depths.

He can't see it, but he can feel it, Zakkai explained. *Just like me. Although, I can sense it more clearly through your mind.*

It's like black tendrils of smoke, I told him. *Pouring out of him in waves.*

This is his final stand, Zakkai whispered as the power strengthened, sending electric sparks across my psyche.

Yes.

But I wasn't going to fight Constantine.

Enough fae had been injured and hurt by his games and antics. I wanted to blossom on a platform of regrowth and life. Not stand on the skulls of those who had wronged fae kind.

This kingdom had been ruled by death for far too long.

It was time to demonstrate what vitality and light could do.

Constantine sent his power outward on a rush of air, touching the souls of everyone nearby, even Claire. But I caught the roots before they could connect to the cores of their beings.

And I gently pulled it back, refusing to allow their spirits to be tarnished by his darkness anymore.

"Constantine Nacht," I said, my voice carrying through the LethaForest and beyond. "You rule from a throne of destruction and hate. It's time for a new era of re-creation and love."

I pulled his spell into my staff while I spoke, the black ribbons easily responding to my call.

"Abominations are not who should be feared. They're beings of love, created by fae who choose to mate outside their kingdoms to other beings of similar but different heritages. That's something to be celebrated, not destroyed." I looked at the Elemental Fae Monarch. "Wouldn't you agree, Queen Claire?"

She was a Halfling, a being born of an Elemental Fae and a human. But because of her mortal half, no one seriously referred to her as an abomination—just a few used it as an insult when feeling cruel. However, was it really so different?

"I would," she replied, her tone regal, her head high. "Love is the most powerful element of all."

"Emotions are powerful tools," I agreed, returning my attention to Constantine. He'd created more of that smoke, his expression impassive in his attempt not to give anything away. Because he had no idea I could see him for who he really was—a broken soul trapped in the body of a powerful Elite Blood Elder.

Destroying his shell wouldn't fix the darkness inside him.

He needed to live. To see. To *witness*.

His fate appeared to me in the blink of an eye, the dark source agreeing with my decision in my next breath as I began to spin those obsidian fibers into vine-like roots near his feet.

He didn't notice, too focused on creating more… and more… his desire to manipulate and control consuming him from the inside out and blackening his ability to decipher his destiny.

He was a being of his own creation.

Dark ire.

Obsidian flames.

Obsessive soul.

Tadmir gave a brief nod, having either seen my intent or felt it, I didn't know. But Zakkai's palm squeezing mine suggested the latter. Because he could see the enchantment forming now, weaving around and through Constantine's legs as the Elder continued to exude power.

He didn't seem to understand why it wasn't working, his frustration beginning to mar his brow as he issued a demand through the dark source.

But the dark source no longer responded to him.

It was mine to command.

I couldn't say when I'd ascended, but I felt it thriving through my veins, the energy calling me queen as I stood upon the ancient breeding ground of Midnight Fae power.

I'd had no idea why I'd run here all those months ago to expel the abundance of vitality swimming through my being. But I understood now. The LethaForest had called to me for a purpose, demanding I revitalize the land here in preparation for my eventual ascension.

I'd been the chosen queen all along.

Kols had been the Midnight Fae Prince meant to guide me through his trial… and then sacrifice his throne to me, the rightful royal.

An Earth Fae Queen connected to two regal Midnight Fae bloodlines, the mate of the Source Architect, and the chosen ward of a strong Warrior Blood.

This is the path we were always meant to walk, I whispered to Shade.

Yes, he agreed. *It just took eight tries to get it right.*

I merely smiled. *I have some stubborn mates.*

He snorted. *Understatement.*

I heard that, Zeph replied dryly.

I think we all did, Kols replied.

Our minds were connecting in a strange way, almost as though I'd crossed all our wires to ensure we could have one open link. I still had my links to each of them as well, but this new open forum… was the result of my Earth Fae magic.

I glanced at Claire in surprise, noting her smile.

Earth Fae bonds, I realized. *The fourth level.*

It always required a ceremony, a ritual of magic and words, but somehow Claire had urged us all along, creating a divine mating unlike any I'd ever heard of existing.

Her access to the elements had grown. I could feel that now as she lurked on the edge of the earth source, her roots stroking the energy without anchoring.

Because she respected me as the Earth Fae Queen.

And this gift of intensifying my mating to Kols, Zeph, Shade, and Zakkai was her way of demonstrating that it was indeed not about how much power we possessed, but how we used it.

Thank you, I thought, conveying the message with my eyes.

She smiled slightly and curtsied, her head bowing in deference, just as I'd done when she'd arrived.

Two queens acknowledging the rule of the other.

Respecting boundaries.

And celebrating each other's monarchy.

Which meant she knew I wasn't Elana, that despite my abomination status, she trusted me in a way. And from the looks of her mates, they did, too.

Constantine growled then, drawing my focus back to him, his fury a sharp spike in the air as he tried one last time to issue an enchantment. But it was already too late for him. The roots were well dug into the soil below him, the smoky embers of his earlier spells solidifying to obsidian rock around him as the trunk of a new tree sprouted upward in a series of lethal vines.

His eyes widened. "Don't just stand there!" His shout was directed at the still-kneeling Warrior Bloods. Or maybe at the other Elders and Councilmen. "Do something!"

"We are," Tadmir replied flatly. "We're watching and admiring our Midnight Fae Queen's choice of punishment." His black orbs sparkled at me, his lips curling in faint amusement. "Which I must say is quite fitting."

Indeed, Zakkai agreed in my mind. *You're trapping him in a tree.*

I'm creating a symbol of our future, I corrected. *By... wrapping a tree around him.* Which would trap him for eternity, but that wasn't the point.

His hand squeezed mine, his entertainment palpable.

I ignored the urge to smile and focused on the life growing against the earth below. "Destruction is sometimes required to renew life. But it's how we administer that destruction, and the lessons that are born with it, that matters most," I told Constantine softly. "You'll forever serve as a reminder of that, as your soul will reside within the tree of your own magical creation… for eternity."

He opened his mouth to reply, his gold irises flaring with magic, but the trunk of the tree silenced him as the dark, tendril-like vines slid over his mouth and wrapped around the back of his head.

Blissful silence fell as the life continued to sprout upward, the trunk sturdy and wide and wrapped in all the dark sins of the man beneath. I'd taken his dark magic and made it corporeal, each pulsing vein a spell I'd retracted from the Midnight Fae of this realm.

Because now that I knew what enchantment he favored for his manipulation, I could sense them all over the kingdom.

I pulled them back through my connection to the dark source.

And wrapped the power around the base, watching as it curled higher and higher until the tree was several stories in the air, its branches dusted with burning flames that would always burn as a reminder to the Midnight Fae of how far we'd come.

"A show of rebirth," I sighed, content with the design. "A tree of retribution, meant to inspire reformation."

A show of light came from the forest, little dots flickering in the air as hundreds of Midnight Fae approached, their wands held like torches.

Zenaida led one side.

Laki led the other.

Midnight Fae of all types followed behind them, entering the clearing of the trees, filling up as much space as the ground would allow.

They lifted the wands toward the sky.

And bowed their heads.

"Our queen has ascended," Zen proclaimed.

"Our queen has ascended," several repeated.

And then they began to chant an ancient hymn, the words lyrical to my ears.

It's a song of the Midnight Fae, praising the dark source for its choice, Kols explained softly, his lips ghosting over my temple. *They're singing about you, Aflora. About our new Queen of the Midnight Fae.*

"Your ascensions are a lot more exciting than ours," Cyrus murmured as he sipped from a glass of fiery lemonade. His water magic kept cooling the liquid before it reached his tongue, thereby defeating the entire purpose of the spell. But I wasn't about to correct the Water Fae King.

"You turn former kings into trees, nearly burn down a forest with a bunch of flickering wands, and then throw one hell of a party," he continued. "I mean, seriously, I'm impressed, and a little miffed that this only happens once every thousand years."

I snorted. "I assure you, they are not all like this." At least, none that I knew about, which was arguably only one.

And actually, that'd been a rather deadly ascension

considering the Quandary Blood extermination that had followed.

I frowned.

Maybe Cyrus had a point.

"I know a way to make this all even more exciting," a deep voice said behind me, the tone reminding me of grating rocks.

I shivered as the giant boulder of an Earth Fae placed his palm on my shoulder and gave it a good, not-so-tender squeeze.

"Kolstov," he said.

"Sol," I replied. *Shade? I might need you to shadow me in a moment.*

His amusement came back through the bond. *And miss watching that Earth Fae knock you in the face with his fist? Nah, I'm good right here.*

I narrowed my gaze at him. *Shall I tell him how you bit Aflora against her will? Then insist upon an introduction afterward?*

"Cyrus," Zeph's voice interjected, his presence at my side reassuring and protective as he looked at the hand on my shoulder and followed it up to the owner. "Sol."

"Zephyrus," the Earth Fae replied coolly.

"Well, this ought to be fun," someone said from behind us, causing Cyrus to roll his eyes.

"You just want to watch them fight," the Water Fae King said.

"Correction"—Titus, who I assumed was the one to speak previously, joined our little circle and bumped shoulders with Zeph—"I want to see this one fight."

My Guardian snorted. "You couldn't handle me in a fight."

"Is that a threat?" Sol demanded.

I sighed. *Aflora?*

She shadowed over to us in a blink, her blue eyes blazing

with power. The second she appeared, Sol released me and engulfed her much smaller frame in a hug that had Zeph growling beside me. She squealed as the larger Earth Fae picked her up and whirled her around, then she laughed as he set her down, their friendship clearly born of brotherly and sisterly love.

But I also knew she used to harbor a crush on the brute.

So that soured some of my amusement.

As did the look he gave me as he put his arm around her.

Protective didn't even begin to describe that look. It was more of an expression that said, *If you hurt her again, I will rip you apart and enjoy it.*

Claire joined us then, her indulgent gaze going to Cyrus and Titus before Sol. "No, you can't turn them into rocks. Aflora wouldn't approve."

He grunted. "Soiling my fun."

Soil, I thought, snorting. *Earth Fae puns?*

I suddenly see where Aflora's vocabulary comes from, Zeph returned.

"Stop being such a boulder, Sol," Aflora murmured, kissing him on the cheek and earning another low growl from Zeph.

"I think you need more lemonade," I suggested lightly, glancing up at my Guardian.

He didn't move.

"Right," I murmured. "Well. Thank you all for coming."

I wasn't sure what else to say, so I kept to the formalities of thanking the royals for attending the ascension. I'd learned from Cyrus that Constantine had reached out to the other realms to tell them about Aflora and had requested assistance. Claire had been the only one to respond, the other fae kingdoms telling him to handle his own mess.

I suspected the Hell Fae King had something to do with

those refusals. I couldn't say why; it was more of an instinct that I'd inherited from Shade.

Keep rummaging in my head and you'll lose yourself, he warned now, picking up on my thoughts.

Shouldn't have mated me, then, I tossed back.

Wouldn't change it for the world, he admitted, flashing me a quick grin before refocusing on Tadmir. He'd been in the middle of providing an update on Ajax, something about him taking a new position with Zen. I hadn't quite followed but intended to ask about it after the ceremony.

Especially since whatever Tadmir was saying about Ajax seemed to have Kyros's full interest as well, something I gathered might not be common for the Paradox Fae.

Aflora stepped out of Sol's embrace and squeezed in between me and Zeph, her arm going around his waist as her head rested on my shoulder.

Where's Zakkai? I asked her.

With Zen and Laki, she replied on a sigh. *They're talking with your dad about how to move forward.*

Is that where you were? I wondered, feeling bad for interrupting such an important discussion.

Yes.

Do you need to go back?

No, I'm tired of discussing politics, she replied. *I would much rather act as a barrier between you and Sol's fist.*

I snorted. *I can handle myself.*

You can. But I want to be the only one who draws blood from you. She shifted to kiss my jaw while the Earth Fae watched.

He clearly didn't approve, but a nudge from his queen had him relaxing marginally.

Titus had taken Cyrus's drink from him, his fascination over the flames evident as he created several of his own to dance with the embers. Meanwhile, Cyrus had lowered his focus to the neckline of Claire's dress, which he clearly found more intriguing than the lemonade in Titus's hand.

What an odd little circle we all made.

Exos and Vox were off talking philosophy with Chern, who Aflora stated wasn't under a spell at all. The Sangré Blood Councilman had never outwardly displayed emotion or preference, marking him as a Midnight Fae to watch. However, I suspected he approved of Aflora's ascension because he'd told her sincerely that it was a logical choice.

Tray and Ella were nowhere to be seen, having run into each other's arms shortly after the wand ceremony. I had a pretty good idea of what they were up to, but didn't want to go searching to find out. I would share a private moment with my twin later. For now, I was satisfied knowing my twin was healthy and alive.

Everyone else seemed to be tentatively conversing, several fae having not seen old friends for over a thousand years, and younger Midnight Fae softly asking Quandary Bloods questions about their paradigms and how they'd been hiding.

The sky above was bleeding with color, the sun rising to overtake the moon.

Our evening ascension was slowly coming to an end, the LethaForest preparing itself to return to its usual protective antics.

With Constantine's tree lingering at the center of it all, the twisted black branches littered with flames.

It was a sight to behold, one I could never have imagined.

So many lives had been lost. Friends, family, innocent fae.

But as Aflora had said, where there was life, there was death.

Fortunately, my mother was not among those souls. She'd been locked up by my grandfather and now stood in the clearing near Shade's mom.

Aswad lurked nearby, his expression one of confusion and loss. He'd been a victim of my grandfather, as had several other Councilmen, including Emelyn's father, Lima, who had broken down into hysterics shortly after being freed from the spell. At least, that had been Tadmir's report and explanation as to why Lima had not attended the ceremony.

I felt for the Elite Blood on some levels but blamed him on others. Lima had always craved power, hence his arranging a marriage between me and his daughter. So while he might have been more recently under my grandfather's spell, he hadn't always been that way.

As far as Aswad was concerned, I wasn't sure how I felt. I could sense Shade's disbelief surrounding his father's sincerity and his questions around whether or not he had truly been under a spell. However, Tadmir did confirm that he'd unwound the manipulation charm himself prior to the ceremony. And he also sensed that it had been there for quite some time.

Exos had overheard our brief conversation and mentioned something about a Spirit Fae named Mortus undergoing a similar experience with Elana. Shade had asked if he trusted the Spirit Fae, and Exos had frowned, saying, "Not quite."

A sentiment Shade and I shared not just about Aswad but about the other Councilmen and Elders as well.

We'd be watching and ready to deal with those threats as they arose, because no one would be touching our queen.

Zeph hummed in agreement in my head, our connections wide open, thanks to the Earth Fae bonds that had settled between us all.

Although, Aflora mentioned it wasn't normal for the link to be so vast, saying that she was fairly certain Claire and her mates couldn't speak this way. Of course, she'd never sought definitive proof of that belief because it really wasn't anyone's business whether or not Claire's mates could speak to one another.

Regardless, I suspected our ability to converse was due to the mingling of dark source and earth source together, and perhaps the result of several of us sharing our own bonds with each other, too.

Aflora sighed contentedly against me, her body seeming to sway.

I think our star is ready to go home, Zakkai said to us all. *The question is, which home?*

I know a place, Shade replied.

Of course you do, Zeph drawled. *Another paradigm?*

A final secret feels like a right of passage, Shade said, ignoring the question. *Shall we?*

Aflora hummed, saying she needed to wish a few fae goodbye, which included Claire and all her mates. They were heading back to their kingdom rather than staying, Exos stating that the Death magic was irritating his ties to the Spirit Kingdom—a fact Shade found amusing.

Eventually, the formalities were done. I didn't hug my father but told him we would talk. His expression said he understood, our last meeting not having been a favorable one. And if I was honest, his inability to stand up to my grandfather bothered me a bit. As the Midnight Fae King, he should have been stronger.

But that was a conversation and concern for another day.

Shade didn't approach his own father but did hug his mother.

When I couldn't find Tray or Ella, I decided to give them their peace and returned to my mate. *They're okay,* she whispered to me, taking my hand. *I can sense their content.*

Thank you, I replied, reaching for Shade as he wrapped us all up in a cloak of shadows.

He grabbed my hip, pulling me toward him and stirring a growl from Zeph.

I just shook my head and smiled. Because possessive Zeph was my favorite kind.

Which meant we were in for a whole day of wicked fun.

MY HEART SKIPPED a beat as we materialized in the middle of a rose garden—one I had created a month before I'd bitten Aflora.

I'd promised myself then that I wouldn't come back here until she was ready.

And I hoped now that I'd made the right choice. Because I couldn't imagine a better time.

Zakkai frowned as he wandered to the edge of the garden to look over the cliff into the ocean, his white brow arching upward as he glanced back at me. "California?" he guessed.

I nodded.

"Why California?" Kols asked, his eyes on the bright blue sky overhead. "This isn't Death Blood territory."

"No. But the future Fortune Fae Alpha of this region is a friend." Assuming he got his shit in order and followed his right path. Unfortunately, his mother's death might alter it. In addition to a dozen other obstacles. But I had faith he'd work it out. In time.

"Seif?" Kols guessed, aware of my friendship with the Death Blood who had recently turned into a Fortune Fae Alpha.

"Yes."

He stared at me for a moment, a question lingering in his mind about how I knew this would eventually be Seif's territory. But rather than voice it, he just went back to admiring the sky. *Does he know about Anrika yet?* he asked softly.

Grandfather Kodiak said he was handling it. I would have done it myself, but with everything else going on, there hadn't been time. *He's making sure Seif receives Anrika's death message, too.* Because she'd cast a charm above her body, the message of it meant for Seif. I didn't know what it said, nor did I want to know. Some things weren't my story to tell.

"This is beautiful," Aflora whispered, her fingers traveling over the rosebushes and causing the flowers to bloom. She knelt to touch the soil, excitement radiating off her as she began studying all the life around her.

This was why I'd chosen this home.

It went on for acres along the cliffs, the expensive property front private and stunning and perfect for a little garden nymph to run around and play.

She seemed to sense that purpose now as she giggled and began to frolic through the garden to the copse of trees beyond. There was a pool somewhere, too. But I doubted that was her intended destination.

Zeph followed her with a predatory grin, something I felt Kols responding physically to through our bond.

Zakkai seemed content to admire the sea, his nostrils flaring as the ocean breeze tousled his thick white hair.

"My mother used to love the ocean," he told me as Kols followed Zeph in pursuit of Aflora. "I remember her always wanting to make sandcastles with me as a child." His lips curled with the memories. "Aflora and I used to make them, too. But out of dirt in the Elemental Fae realm. I wonder if she remembers."

"I'm sure she does," I said quietly.

He dipped his chin, then sighed. "This is a beautiful home, Shadow. I suppose all those trips through time allowed you to gamble a little with human currency?"

I merely stared at him, not inclined to give anything away.

"Don't suppose you stopped by a casino in the region? Perhaps one in the Vegas area?"

"Why would I do that?" I countered, neither confirming nor denying the obvious guess.

"Why indeed?" He slid his hands into his black slacks and looked out at the ocean again. "How many times do you think Tadmir has taken all of us back in total?"

"Too many to count," I answered honestly.

He nodded. "My thoughts exactly." Then he smiled, the sight a rare expression of enjoyment in his features. Because it lacked mockery. This was just Zakkai… grinning in content. "We owe you both a great deal of gratitude."

"You more than them," I half joked.

"Yes, I imagine I was quite difficult."

"Because you knew." Not a question, but a statement.

"Because I knew," he admitted. "Just not the extent or particulars of what you were doing, but I could feel it as a result of my ascension."

Yeah, I suspected as much. "Why did you go along with it this time?" In previous timelines, he'd always fought me or found a loophole. But in this one... he was almost acquiescent.

"Maybe I was tired."

"Or maybe you fell in love," I suggested.

"I absolutely fell in love," he agreed, his irises flaring as he looked in the direction Kols and Zeph had gone. "We should go after them before they have all the fun."

"Yes, I imagine Aflora is already naked." Because I could feel Kols's amusement and intrigue in the bond.

"She is," Zakkai replied, grinning. "She's gone full garden nymph, just like you desired."

"Poking around in my head?"

"Always." He glanced at me with an unrepentant look. "Your mind is fascinating, Shadow. So many secrets and hidden agendas. Which reminds me, that meeting with Lucifer that you scheduled on my behalf for next week? You're coming with me."

I sighed. "Of course I am."

Wickedness darkened his features. "It'll be fun, Shadow."

"Deals always are," I muttered, walking with him to find our Aflora.

She was indeed naked.

And dancing through a bed of flowers that definitely hadn't been there when we'd arrived.

Zeph had taken up a position by a tree, his shoulder braced against the bark. Kols stood with him, both of them aroused and entertained by the sight of our mate spinning with glee.

"Don't we need to fuck to finish the Earth Fae mating?" Zakkai called to her, his direct manner causing her to stumble and nearly fall.

I shadowed to her side, catching her on instinct. And she giggled against my chest. Her blue eyes met mine, the little nymph drunk on her earth source. "Sex sounds nice," she said on a sigh. "Shade goes first."

Then she pulled me down to the flowers and covered us in a canopy of petals.

Zeph and Zakkai both protested, while Kols merely laughed.

My clothes disappeared beneath her power, leaving me as naked as her and on my back in the soil. I arched a brow. "No foreplay?" I teased, already rock hard from her show of strength alone.

"Mmm." She straddled my hips, her expression radiating pure, unadulterated joy. "We've been playing for months." She seated herself to the hilt, her body moving sensuously against mine. "Now I just want you, Shadow. My Death Blood Prince. And your very impressive *cock*."

I chuckled, grabbing her hips to flip her to her back. I settled between her thighs and drove into her again, my lips going to her ear. "You've been talking to Zeph too much. He's dirtied your mouth."

"Do you prefer *willow stump*?" she asked on a breath as her hips rose eagerly to meet mine.

"Do I feel like a *willow stump* to you?"

"I don't know," she moaned. "Fuck me harder and I'll report back later."

I chuckled against her neck. "You really are a nymph, little rose."

"Yes," she agreed. "Now stop talking and take me to oblivion."

"Anything for you," I whispered, loving her with my body, my mouth, and my hands. Our Earth Fae bond was very much alive and fully in place, but sex was how Elemental Fae culminated the act.

And I felt it now, that warm energy of her sunbathing me

in rightness, claiming me as Aflora's mate, and ensuring my roots forever twined with hers.

"I love you," she told me softly, her arms around my neck as our bodies joined together as one.

"I love you, too, little rose." I kissed her then, unleashing all my gratitude and longing and appreciation into her mouth. All those years of dancing with fate. All those timelines. All those mistakes. All those near ends. I'd almost lost her so many times. But here she was, my sweet, beautiful Aflora, in a bed of her own creation, blossoming with life and happiness.

Finally, I thought, reveling in the dream of the moment. *It's finally... done.*

She cupped my cheek, her legs encircling my waist as I slid deeper into her. *You can rest now, Shade,* she murmured. *You can finally enjoy the moment without worrying about what comes next. You can finally... exist.*

With you, I replied, my pace increasing. *I can finally exist... with you.*

Yes. Her teeth skimmed my lower lip. "Bite me," she breathed. "Bite me like it's the first time. Claim me as yours the right way."

I shivered, then did exactly as she'd asked, my teeth sinking into her throat as I pulled her powerful blood into my mouth on a groan that traveled miles and miles.

She moaned in response, her tight sheath squeezing me as she came undone, her orgasm yanking me down with her, our shared pleasure burning through my veins and touching my very soul.

Her blunt teeth caught my pulse and she bit down, drinking from me as I'd done from her.

Our connection only strengthened, our souls already married as one.

But some part of me felt even more complete, even more owned, even more accepted.

I pressed my head to her shoulder, panting from the exertion of our connection.

Then I closed my eyes and did exactly what she'd said.

I existed and didn't worry about the next moment.

Because, for the first time in my life, I didn't have to.

I could just… be.

I WATCHED Aflora take Kols deep into her mouth, my little garden siren coming alive as she drank down his climax and urged him to give her more with her tongue.

She was stunning.

Perfect.

Alluring as fuck.

I was so damn hard, my balls aching in protest at wanting to be inside her. But this was about bonding. She'd already taken Shade… *twice*. Now she'd finished with Kols, leaving me and Zakkai naked on either side of her.

We'd never all played at once, but something about the uniting of earth had required it.

Aflora had beckoned us into her garden, her canopy of

flowers growing to create a pretty little shelter to hide our afternoon fuck fest.

Shade was off to the side, watching from beneath heavy lids.

Kols crawled over to him, and they started making out, which only seemed to make my cock harder and Aflora needier.

She was three orgasms in, two from Shade and one from my mouth.

But the Earth Fae bonds required more.

Elemental Fae were famous for their insatiable need, particularly with their mates. And we were all fourth-level bonded now, which explained her growing desire for *more*.

She wrapped her palm around my neck, pulling me to her as she went to her knees, and forced me to accept her kiss. Gone was my obedient little Earth Fae, and in her place, a hungry vixen who took what she wanted. I knelt with her, aligning our thighs and pressing my cock into her lower abdomen.

Zakkai moved in behind her, his tongue traveling down her spine as his hand disappeared between her spread legs.

I knew what he intended because I felt it through the roots in my mind—he wanted to take her from behind while I went in the front.

I hadn't planned to make sharing Aflora with him a regular occurrence, but I wasn't going to complain. The man packed a hell of a lot of power. If he wanted to fuck her with me, then I'd be a fool to say no.

She moaned against my tongue, liking what he did below.

I reached up to palm her breast, her nipple tight and needy against my skin. She threaded her fingers through my hair to guide me down, needing my lips against her tender skin.

Fuck, Kols whispered in my head, drawing my attention to him.

Shade had kissed a path down the other man's body to suck him in the same way Aflora had only moments ago, and from the pleasure in her features now, she very much approved of the show.

I distracted her by skimming my teeth against her tit and capturing her rosy peak. She shuddered, then moaned as Zakkai entered her pussy, filling her to the hilt without warning. Then she groaned in annoyance when he pulled out.

I met his gaze, saw the certainty in his features that she was ready for us both, and watched as he slid into her ass.

She grabbed my shoulders to steady herself for his intrusion, her eyes flaring wide with lust and excitement.

It was the look of a woman ready to be shared.

I caught her mouth and grinned as Kols cursed again, Shade proving to be quite skilled with his tongue.

Something I might have to indulge in someday.

But for now, I wanted Aflora's slick heat and tight channel.

I moved into her, securing her between me and Zakkai. Then I lifted her leg up to wrap around my hips, leaving her to balance on one knee. She didn't protest, her body already angling toward me in preparation for my entry.

Rather than deny her, I slid home in a single thrust, filling her to completion and feeling Zakkai's throbbing shaft through the thin wall inside her.

So hot, I thought, groaning into her mind. *You're so fucking hot.*

Fuck me, she replied, using my favorite command. *Fuck me hard. Don't hold back. Please don't hold back.*

I don't think I could if I tried, I admitted, setting a pace that Zakkai met in equal measure.

He had one palm on her hip, his other around her throat as he guided her back to kiss him. I held on to her leg, my other hand sliding between us to better access her clit.

She moaned, her nipples sharp little points against my chest as we drove into her.

Kols and Shade had stopped their playing to enjoy the show, their intrigue only heightening the moment. Then they both moved forward to worship Aflora with their mouths, kissing her shoulders, her arms, licking her fingers, and ensuring she felt them with her as Zakkai and I took her body.

It was sinful decadence and depraved indulgence, and I loved every fucking second of it.

My teeth sank into Kols's throat, needing his essence. He groaned in response, then pulled Aflora's mouth away from Zakkai to kiss her.

Zakkai went to her throat, biting her deep and eliciting a tender sound from her lips.

Our fucking turned animalistic, blood-sharing happening between all of us as Aflora bit our tongues while kissing and we bit each other to fulfill our darker cravings.

Aflora's hands left my shoulders, her palms wrapping around Shade and Kols on either side of her as she strove to provide them with as much pleasure as we were giving her.

Her power pulsed around us, her inner vixen demanding we unwind and come as one.

"Fuck," I breathed. "*Fuck*, Aflora."

Zakkai echoed my sentiment, his muscles strained as he teetered on the edge of climax.

"*Now*," Aflora screamed, energy shooting out of her through our bonds and taking us beneath a cloud of ecstasy that blanketed my mind in dizzying passion.

My stomach clenched, my cock throbbing as I unloaded inside her, filling her with my seed as Kols and Shade came undone on either side of us, their cum painting Aflora's skin.

Zakkai was last, his orgasm whipping through us all, his power making me explode again, right on the heels of my first climax.

So damn intense.

So fucking amazing.

So incredibly *us*.

I caught Aflora's mouth, feeling her tight sheath pulse around me with the residuals of her own pleasure, and told her how much I loved her, how perfect she was, and praised her for accepting us all.

She kissed me back, then Shade, then Kols, and finally Zakkai, her heart wide open and ours.

And we gave our love and adoration back to her in kind.

Then I scooped her up and carried her inside the large home Shade clearly owned, and asked, "Where's the bedroom?"

We'd spent most of our weeks here in Shade's home on the cliffs, indulging in our bonds and enjoying a much-needed break from Midnight Fae life.

However, Shade and Zakkai had left a few times to "tie up loose ends." Which I translated to mean meeting with Lucifer, meeting with Zen, and generally supervising the former Councilmen.

They'd also tracked down Dakota, as she'd been missing from the ascension ritual. I wasn't sure what they'd done to her, but I'd felt her life strand sever from the source. Which told me she was dead. I just didn't ask how, because I preferred not to know.

And Kols had gone back home twice to see Tray and his parents. He and his father were still on uncomfortable terms, but at least they were talking. Tray had also moved out with Ella, and they were residing in Massachusetts right now at the Nacht Estates.

I intended to go visit them next week, as I missed them.

But for now, I was content to just be here. Relaxing. Living. And preparing for our next steps.

Which was pretty straightforward—we needed a new Midnight Fae Council.

While most of the Councilmen had been under Constantine's control, it remained to be seen how long they'd been suffering from his power trip. They'd also lost the faith of Midnight Fae kind. As had the Elders. Even those like Kols's great-grandfather, who had been put into a magically induced coma by Constantine, were no longer trusted.

Therefore, we were proposing a new Council and allocating advisory positions to take over for the former Elders.

"Have you spoken to Tadmir about Stiggis and Cordelia?" I asked Shade.

He finished swallowing his bite of food and nodded.

"Yeah, he's still talking to them about the Council. I think he wants them to shadow him for a bit first since neither of them was ever really prepared to take over. Well, Stiggis was to an extent, but not Cordelia. And I think she might be the better option."

"She's certainly more even-keeled than her brother," Zeph agreed. "Minus losing her shit over your infidelity."

Shade snorted. "It was an arranged marriage front that gave me access to Tadmir."

"I don't think the poor girl saw it that way," Zeph drawled. "Hence my questioning her ability to be on the Council. Anyone who loses their mind over you is clearly not stable."

"Don't mind him," Kols said, setting down his fork and reaching for his beer. "He's just sour that you won't suck his cock."

"And he wonders why I won't," Shade muttered.

My Warrior Blood mate glowered while Zakkai grinned, entertained by their bickering. "Well, I think Cordelia has potential," Zeph said. "But I'm disappointed that Tray won't join."

"He doesn't want to have anything to do with Midnight Fae politics right now after they almost killed his mate," Kols replied, glancing at me. "I can't say I blame him."

"We'll give him time." Which was what I'd said earlier this week when Kols had delivered the news about his twin turning down the Council position. "Change doesn't happen overnight, which is why we have a mix of ages and expertise on the Council."

Shade's mom had agreed to join, so long as Shade sat with her. She was a timid woman after being kept in the dark for a thousand years. But we would be patient and work with her on reform.

Zen had also turned down a position, stating she had

other obligations to the Hell Fae King to fulfill first. But she'd agreed to act as an advisor so long as we ventured to the Hell Fae realm to visit her.

Kols's father would serve as an Elder, but a well-watched one.

And Vadim had agreed to an Elder position as well.

"What are we going to do about Svart and Chern?" I asked, referring to the Warrior Blood and Sangré Blood Councilmen.

Zakkai was the clear choice for the Quandary Blood position, with Laki as his Second. Kols had taken the Elite Blood leadership role—where he would wait until Tray either agreed to take over or perhaps join as his Second-in-Command. And Shade had agreed to the Death Blood mantle, with his mother serving as his Second.

All of us looked expectantly at Zeph.

Who proceeded to say, "No," for the thousandth time.

I sighed. "You're a clear choice for the Warrior Blood Councilman position, and you know it."

"I have a duty to guard my queen, not play politician. So no."

My lips pinched to the side as I glanced at Kols. *So stubborn.*

Tell me about it, he replied. *We might need Shade to suck his cock after all.*

I laughed out loud, causing them all to look at me.

Kols merely smirked.

I cleared my throat and acted as though I hadn't just snorted a laugh in front of all of them, and refocused on the Councilmen discussion.

But Zeph was adamantly against joining.

So we started going through other names and making a list of whom to visit. Chern was on our *potentially trust* list. He hadn't been consumed by Constantine's power, but he also hadn't been for his plans at all. He'd apparently voted down several of the Council decisions but had been ignored in favor of the majority.

What concerned me was that they claimed those decisions had been unanimous.

So either he was lying—huge possibility—or Constantine had lied—also a huge possibility.

Regardless, we were watching him. And he couldn't remain on the Council.

"We don't have to figure it out today," Zeph said, sliding a plate of orc steak with a side of berries my way. "That's the beauty of time."

"At least in this path," Shade interjected.

A few of us smiled at him, then silence filled the dining area as we all ate our respective meals. Zeph had apparently made beef steaks for himself and Zakkai, which, gross. Their penchant for eating animals in this realm was seriously unnerving.

I'd sooner try a stonepecker.

Shuddering, I cut off a piece of orc and brought it to my lips as a commotion sounded outside near the in-ground pool.

Zakkai groaned as Zimney howled. "Your fucking snake is going to drown one of these days," he said, looking at Zeph.

"He sees your beast as an equal and just wants to play," Zeph returned. "I'm not going to stop him."

More splashing sounded, followed by Clove chittering as she chastised the animals for roughhousing.

Draco swooped in through a window to huddle on Shade's shoulder, his bat wings vibrating with irritation.

Then Kols's crow landed on the windowsill with an expectant look.

I studied them all and shook my head.

This was my life now, filled with crazy familiars, stubborn alpha mates, and a future with no end date.

Zeph's irises smoldered as he caught my gaze, his mind prodding mine and hearing my thoughts.

Which meant I could hear his and the plans he had for me later in the garden.

He kept making all these jokes about seeds and growth.

Each time, I rolled my eyes, but inside, his puns spoke to my Earth Fae heart.

Yeah, this wasn't a bad life at all.

Actually, it was a pretty amazing one. Surrounded by beautiful men. Protective familiars. Magical spells. And bonds built to withstand eternity.

My heart blossomed with joy as my thighs clenched with anticipation.

Earth Fae were all about creating and joy.

And I couldn't think of anything or anyone who brought me more joy than my four handsome mates.

You have five minutes to finish that, Zeph told me. *Then I want to play a game of "hide the snake in the garden."*

I looked at him. *Well, good. Because I could use a little seed.*

He smiled. *I'll give you more than a little, pixie flower.*

I can't wait, I whispered back to him.

And I meant it willingly.

Who needed orc steak when I had four ready and willing mates to fill me up?

I stood up and waved a spell that disintegrated my clothes. "Come and get me," I said, taking off for the garden with a chorus of growls in my wake.

Definitely an amazing life, I thought, grinning when the first of them caught me just as I reached the flower bed. *One I wouldn't trade for anything in the world.*

Now I knew what it was like to wake from a nightmare and be fully immersed in a dream.

A dream built to last for an eternity.

With four sexy Midnight Fae mates.

And a future that was entirely our own.

No more meddling. No more games. Just me and my mates. For the rest of time.

Thank you for reading Midnight Fae Academy. This story and world captured a piece of my heart. The voices were so powerful, and the world captivated me in a way few others have. And now Aflora has finally received the happily-ever-after she deserved. I couldn't be more thrilled for her and her mates, and I hope you loved them as much as I do. <3

You might be wondering what's next in the fae universe... The epilogue that follows will answer this and much more. Enjoy.

Epilogue

Several Years Later

"You realize you don't have to accompany me every time I go to visit my grandmother, right?" I asked as a presence materialized behind me—an action that made me strongly regret bonding Zakkai because now he could shadow anywhere he wanted at will.

Which was great for protecting Aflora.

And horrible for my privacy.

"I'm aware," he replied. "Just as I'm also aware that Lucifer will be there today, and I'm eager to check in on my pet project. You know, the one from that meeting? The power exchange that I didn't want to do but had no choice to do because you had already agreed to it on my behalf?"

I snorted, this incident one he loved to bring up despite it being several years old. "You would agree to anything where Aflora is concerned."

"Yes, but that's not the point, is it?"

I sighed. "I'll never apologize."

"I know."

"And you'll forever bring it up anyway."

"I will."

"Excellent," I deadpanned, shadowing to my grandmother's front door.

Zakkai appeared beside me, humored by my annoyance. Because he was a dick who enjoyed provoking me.

Pretty sure that was why we'd bonded, too—just so he could have more thorough access to my thoughts and ample opportunity to piss me the fuck off.

Aflora also likes watching us together, he added via our link. *And I like making her happy.*

Couldn't fault him for that logic.

I lifted my hand to knock, only for the door to open. My grandmother stood on the other side with cookies, which elicited another sigh from me. *More bad news.*

What food does she make when it's good news? Zakkai wondered.

Not cookies.

Ah. He stepped inside and took a chocolate chip cookie, then proceeded to inspect it for magic with his mind.

If she wanted to poison you, she wouldn't use cookies.

You say that, he drawled. *But Zenaida is quite clever.*

Which means she knows you're inspecting her cookies and would ensure you couldn't feel or find whatever she's hidden, I pointed out, ignoring the platter of treats and hugging her instead. "Hi,

G'ma," I whispered against her ear before kissing her cheek. "I've missed you."

"I know. I've missed you, too," she replied, leading us to the table. "But Ajax keeps me on my toes."

"It's true," the male in question agreed as he appeared in the middle of the living room. He'd been living in the Hell Fae realm with my grandmother, helping her maintain the paradigm. My grandfathers were here, too. But my old friend had become her pupil of sorts, training to become whatever it was Lucifer had in mind.

Ajax wandered over to the table and sat down, his tall, muscular form flexing with the movement. Zakkai studied him, his calculative nature taking over.

"Hmm," he hummed. "Your magic is finally settling."

Ajax grunted. "Just in time, too."

"For what?" Zakkai pressed.

Ajax merely smiled. "You would like to know, wouldn't you?"

"Yes, I would," Zakkai admitted. "Particularly as it's my ability that has morphed your power."

That had been his part of the deal with Lucifer—the Hell Fae King had asked him to rewrite Ajax's magic and align him to the Hell Fae source.

Zakkai had refused at first.

However, then he'd realized Ajax wasn't just a willing subject but an eager one as well, and he'd complied, after penning a whole bunch of loopholes into the agreement with Lucifer, of course.

It'd been a fascinating debate to observe between Zakkai and Lucifer, both of them evenly matched in power, and neither afraid of the other.

Zakkai had essentially made it so Lucifer could never ask Aflora for a single favor or demand anything from her or her mates.

In exchange, he'd help him as required with Ajax's development only.

And anything with my grandmother was up for negotiation, meaning Zakkai would step in to help her if he wanted to. And I knew he would under the right circumstances.

"It's the opening ceremony of the bride trials." The deep tone belonged to a dark presence lurking in the shadows of the room.

Zakkai didn't react, clearly having sensed Lucifer's arrival before me. "That sounds vile," Zakkai murmured. "Tell me more."

Lucifer chuckled as he stepped into the room through some sort of invisible door. My grandmother didn't react, just set a cup of coffee at the head of the table and took a seat beside me.

The Hell Fae King took the chair like one would a throne. The white streaks in his black hair glimmered beneath the low lighting, his piercing blue eyes flashing with amusement as he nudged the mug aside. "Nice try," he told my grandmother.

She shrugged.

And Zakkai snorted. *See?*

So maybe she did attempt to bespell drinks or whatever.

She wasn't a typical Fortune Fae Omega by any stretch of the imagination, her magic having been altered by Grandfather Kodiak a thousand years ago.

"I'm organizing a bride trial to satisfy the Hell Fae males of my world," Lucifer said conversationally. "As you know, the source rarely accepts females. Which means I'm governing a bunch of bloodthirsty men. The best way to tame them is to mate them. So. Bride trials." He spread his hands like that explained everything.

"And where are you acquiring these females?" Zakkai asked, his tone just as casual and calm.

Lucifer's lips twisted into a feral grin. "From other fae realms, of course."

"Through deals." Zakkai didn't voice it as a question but as a statement.

Lucifer merely waved his hand again as though to say, *Obviously.*

Zakkai studied him for a long moment before focusing on my grandmother. "And you knew this was going to happen. That's been your agreement all along, hasn't it? That you could protect the Quandary Bloods in this paradigm and build a magical school to train them. All the while preparing for the inevitability of Lucifer turning this into a training camp for potential Hell Fae brides."

My blood ran cold at his suggestion.

But the look in my grandmother's eyes told me he was right.

"There's always a price for leadership, Zakkai. I did the best I could with what I had on offer. And now I'm fulfilling my part of the obligation."

"By acting as Headmaster to these brides," he completed for her.

"Not entirely accurate." She looked at Ajax. "He's the chosen Warden. I'm merely here to keep the paradigm safe and alive while Lucifer organizes his trial."

Zakkai whistled. "That's one hell of a price." Then he looked at Lucifer. "Aflora has no part in this."

"We've already negotiated our deal, Source Architect. I'm merely here for amusement purposes today." He smiled and cocked his head. "But how is your beautiful mate? Pregnant yet?"

"Is this the part where you demand our firstborn?" Zakkai tossed back.

He looked affronted. "I would never do such a thing."

Zakkai grunted, his disbelief palpable.

"You're right. I absolutely would and have, but your pretty mate is free from my negotiations."

"Good," Zakkai and I said at the same time.

Lucifer met my gaze, his amusement carrying a lethal edge that made me uneasy. "I've always liked you, time meddler. You're... exceedingly resourceful." He smiled before focusing on Ajax. "Are you ready to begin welcoming the bridal candidates?"

"I am, sir," Ajax replied, his serious tone nothing like my easygoing friend from our Academy days. This new version was hard around the edges, strong, and held a sorrow in his dark gaze that never seemed to abate.

He'd taken Emelyn's death hard, having wanted to lash out with revenge.

But with Aflora taking over and reforming the full Council, there hadn't been anyone for Ajax to hurt.

So Tadmir had brought him here... where Lucifer had recruited him.

He'd seen a broken soul, and he'd offered him something he couldn't refuse—a chance for retribution.

Which was the whole point of this project.

Lucifer would take female fae from all the realms and force them to fight. Those who won would be rewarded with a forced marriage to a group of his men. Those who lost would die.

Either way, it served as a wicked form of justice against those who had ostracized abominations for over a thousand years.

It made me wonder what trick my grandmother had up her sleeve. She would never agree to such a ploy without some sort of secret path.

As I glanced at her now, I caught the knowing twinkle in her gaze.

It was similar to the one she'd given me years ago when I'd told her about Aflora.

A plot was unfolding.

And it seemed Ajax and Lucifer were at the heart of it.

I would have laughed, but something told me this would be a dark tale lacking in humor.

Fae were going to die.

But in the end, perhaps the deadly Hell Fae King would find something he never knew he needed. *Love.*

HALL FAE CAPTIVE

Welcome to the Hell Fae realm, a place where only the strong survive.

My parents made a deal with the devil, and now I'm a Hell Fae captive.

Enslaved. Owned. Thrown to the Hellhounds and expected to survive.
Because only survivors earn their mates.

It doesn't matter that I don't want to be a bride.
I'm a Halfling. Part Hell Fae and part girl-who-doesn't-give-a-shit.
But because of a bargain, *he* owns me.

Lucifer. The Hell Fae King who created this godforsaken realm.
Also known as the orchestrator of these deadly bride-trial games.

Okay, Luci, I'll play.
By burning this whole kingdom to the ground.

Assuming I don't get caught in the hot Midnight Fae Warden's web first.
Or ensnared by the brooding Hell Fae Commander lurking outside the gates.
And don't even get me started on the Hell Fae King's favored prince. That sexy lunatic won't stop sending me gifts.

No amount of hotness or sensual persuasion will keep me here.
I'm not bride material.
I'm a menace.

You made a deal for the wrong girl, Lucifer.
Prepare for the fight of your life.

Authors' Note: *Hell Fae Captive* is a dark kidnap paranormal romance with four tormented mates and no choosing required. If you like your anti-heroes dominant and sexy, you've come to the right realm—the Hell Realm where the romance is hot and no forgiveness is required.

USA Today Bestselling Author Lexi C. Foss loves to play in dark worlds, especially the ones that bite. She lives in Chapel Hill, North Carolina with her husband and their furry children. When not writing, she's busy crossing items off her travel bucket list, or chasing eclipses around the globe. She's quirky, consumes way too much coffee, and loves to swim.

Want access to the most up-to-date information for all of Lexi's books? Sign-up for her newsletter here.

Lexi also likes to hang out with readers on Facebook in her exclusive readers group - Join Here.

Where To Find Lexi:
www.LexiCFoss.com

ALSO BY LEXI C. FOSS

Blood Alliance Series - Dystopian Paranormal

Chastely Bitten

Royally Bitten

Regally Bitten

Rebel Bitten

Kingly Bitten

Dark Provenance Series - Paranormal Romance

Heiress of Bael (FREE!)

Daughter of Death

Son of Chaos

Paramour of Sin

Princess of Bael

Elemental Fae Academy - Reverse Harem

Book One

Book Two

Book Three

Elemental Fae Holiday

Winter Fae Holiday

Hell Fae - Reverse Harem

Hell Fae Captive

Immortal Curse Series - Paranormal Romance

Book One: Blood Laws

Book Two: Forbidden Bonds

Book Three: Blood Heart

Book Four: Blood Bonds

Book Five: Angel Bonds

Book Six: Blood Seeker

Book Seven: Wicked Bonds

Immortal Curse World - Short Stories & Bonus Fun

Elder Bonds

Blood Burden

Mershano Empire Series - Contemporary Romance

Book One: The Prince's Game

Book Two: The Charmer's Gambit

Book Three: The Rebel's Redemption

Midnight Fae Academy - Reverse Harem

Ella's Masquerade

Book One

Book Two

Book Three

Book Four

Noir Reformatory - Ménage Paranormal Romance

The Beginning

First Offense

Second Offense

Underworld Royals Series - Dark Paranormal Romance

Happily Ever Crowned

Happily Ever Bitten

X-Clan Series - Dystopian Paranormal

Andorra Sector

X-Clan: The Experiment

Winter's Arrow

Bariloche Sector

Vampire Dynasty - Dark Paranormal

Violet Slays

Sapphire Slays

Crossed Fates

First Bite of Revenge

Other Books

Scarlet Mark - Standalone Romantic Suspense

Carnage Island - Standalone Reverse Harem Romance